和老外聊中國

U0070460

外國人不懂的中華文化，
用他們能懂的英語來解釋！

在西方人眼裡，中國始終蒙著一層神祕面紗，
面紗下究竟隱藏了什麼？令人好奇又猶豫……
就讓我們在這裡輕輕掀起，細細端看它完整的面貌！

楊天慶 編著

目錄

第二章
中國烹調
Chinese Cuisine

第三章
中國酒
Alcoholic Drinks in China

第四章
漢字與書法
Chinese Characters and Calligraphy

第五章
中國繪畫
Chinese Painting

第六章
中國傳統棋牌
Traditional Chinese Chess Games

第七章
中國武術
Chinese Martial Arts

第八章
中國絲綢
Chinese Silk

第九章
中國陶瓷
Chinese Pottery and Porcelain

第十章
中國醫藥學
Traditional Chinese Medicine

第十一章
中國古書
Ancient Chinese Books

第十二章
中國古代神話
Ancient Chinese Mythology

第十三章
中國戲劇藝術
Chinese Opera Arts

第十四章
中國古代建築
Ancient Chinese Architecture

第十五章
儒學
Confucianism

第十六章
道教
Daoism

第十七章
佛教
Buddhism

第十八章
民間信仰
Chinese Folk Belief

第十九章
日常禮儀
Daily ceremony

第二十章
婚姻禮俗
Marriage Etiquette and Customs

第二十一章
中國民間傳統節日
Traditional Chinese Festivals

前言

　　全書分為若干專題，每個專題都有一段中文概述。接著分為中英文提問、英文簡述、單詞簡表三個部分。採用鮮活的筆調，融知識性、趣味性、可讀性為一體，由點及面，鋪敘出意趣盎然的中國文化。除了適用旅遊相關科系的學生和英語導遊，還可以成為外商員工、外派人員和大學學生的工具書，讀者可以此書來學習如何用英語講解中國文化，用中國文化的內容來練習英語口語。

　　願本書能夠為讀者帶來收穫。文化內容十分豐富，限於水準及視野，書中的疏漏、缺點乃至錯誤在所難免，敬請專家和讀者批評指正。

楊天慶

前言

第一章
茶與飲茶
Tea and Tea Drinking

　　人類發現和利用茶已有幾千年的歷史,「茶之為飲,發乎神農」。中國是茶的原產地,也是茶文化的故鄉,茶的芳香讓人清心雅志,品茶的情趣讓人和敬廉美,茶的減肥、防癌功能讓人健康長壽。本篇將介紹茶學的特點以及有關飲茶的基本知識。

關於中國茶的由來有哪些傳說？
What are the legendary origins of tea in China?

According to legends, over 5,000 years ago in China, there was a divine farmer named Shen Nong (神農), one of the noble figures of Chinese mythology. He taught people agricultural and medicinal practices. One day when he sat beneath a tree and was ready to taste herbs, and at the same time his servant began to boil drinking water. By chance, some dry leaves dropped from a tree into the water. As usual, Shen Nong drank the boiled water. It tasted a little bitter, and the water looked slightly yellowish, but it refreshed him. The tree turned out to be a wild tea tree.

Buddhist legends have another story. Once Bodhidharma (菩提達摩) stayed in a cave-temple outside Nanjing, where he practiced meditation. One day as he meditated, he felt sleepy. He cut off his eyelids in an attempt to keep himself awake; and to his surprise, tea plants sprang up from the ground where he had tossed the severed eyelids. Later, he used these leaves to brew tea to help him stay awake for meditation.

Notes
yellowish 淡黃色的；refresh 使清新；eyelid 眼瞼；toss 扔；
sever 切斷

茶最初的功能是什麼？

What was the function of tea when it was first used?

In ancient China, tea was regarded as one of seven daily necessities, along with firewood, rice, oil, salt, soy sauce and vinegar. But from the very beginning, tea was used as medicine. At initial stage, the ancient men drank it to relieve poison. The ancient medical book, Shen Nong Bencao Classics (《神農本草經》) says that tealeaves taste bitter and so can make people spirited and think clearly. In Eating Classics (《食經》), Hua Tuo (華佗) says that the continuous drinking of bitter tea is good for thinking.

> **Notes**
> necessity 必要性；vinegar 醋；tealeaf 茶葉；continuous 連續的

飲茶的習慣源於什麼地方？

Historically, where did the habit of tea drinking come from?

It is commonly believed that the habit of tea drinking originated in Sichuan Province about 3,000 years ago. There is evidence that people there began to drink tea early in the Spring and Autumn Period. In the Qin Dynasty, tea drinking spread to other areas of China; and according to The History of Sichuan (《四川志》), local people began to plant tea during the Western Han Dynasty. Zhang Jingyang (張景陽) of the Western Jin Dynasty spoke highly of tea produced on Mt. Qingcheng (青城山) near Chengdu. In a poem entitled "Climbing Chengdu's Bai Tu Tower" (《登成都白菟樓》). Zhang says, "Fragrant tea is superior to the sixth quiet story of Daoism; and its pleasant taste spreads to all the states

(芳茶冠六清，溢味播九區)."

The custom of tea drinking gradually spread out from Sichuan; and towards the end of the Western Han Dynasty, tea was regarded as the drink of imperial and noble families. Later, from the Jin to the Sui dynasties, tea drinking became popular among the common people.

Notes
fragrant 芳香的；superior 有優越感的

唐朝飲茶有些什麼習慣？
What was the fashion of tea drinking in the Tang Dynasty?

Tea drinking prospered in the Tang Dynasty. As it became more and more popular, the way of the drinking varied. Before that time, people were not particular about their tea drinking. They drank tea to quench their thirsty or for medical purposes. Beginning with the Tang Dynasty, however, people tended to have more delicate tea tastes and went through a rather complicated process in tea drinking. Usually one went through several stages before drinking. The first stage was to select tea; the second was to choose excellent tea cups and cooking utensils; the third was to prepare charcoal; the fourth was to get water; the fifth was to bake the chosen tea; the sixth was to grind it; the seventh was to boil the tea; and the final stage was to drink the tea. People thought that the taste would be better by going through the above procedures. They also took great care about water. The best water was from the mountain, the worst from the well.

At that time, Lu Yu (陸羽) published The Book of Tea (《茶經》), the first book about tea in China. There also appeared anther book Supplement to the History of the Tang Dynasty (《唐國史補》), which talked about tea from Mt. Mengding (蒙頂山) in Sichuan. This book says, "the local people have a custom of entertaining their guests with good tea. High quality tea falls into several different types, ranked first by taste and scent."

> **Notes**
> prosperous 繁榮的;utensil 器皿;charcoal 木炭;grind 磨（碎）;
> procedure 步驟;supplement 增補

你對唐代以後茶的生產和飲茶習慣了解多少？
What is the history of tea production and tea drinking after the Tang Dynasty?

In 907, the Tang Dynasty fell and China split into a number of independent states. The south split into separate kingdoms, which remained peaceful. Trade and commerce developed rapidly, and tea production in Jiangsu and Zhejiang provinces developed so quickly that these areas gradually became the center of tea art and culture.

People in the Song Dynasty came to drink tea even more delicately than in Tang times. In the Tang, tea drinking was popular mainly among noble families, but in some cities during the Song Dynasty, teahouses sprang up where common people could go and have tea. In Chengdu, tea service centers were set up to offer "official tea" for passers-by free of charge.

In the Ming and Qing dynasties, tea drinking differed from that of previous dynasties. In those times, people drank piece-tea (散型茶) instead of solid-tea (餅茶) and tea makers stir-fried tea in an attempt to strengthen tealeaves' flavor.

In the Ming Dynasty, green tea was the most common tea drink, but flower tea also came into being. Down to the Qing Dynasty, jasmine tea was produced in Suzhou. In the Qing Dynasty, Oolong and black tea appeared.

Notes

passers-by 過路客；piece-tea 散型茶；solid-tea 餅茶；stir-fry 炒

英文單詞「tea」是如何出現的？
What is the derivation of English word "tea"?

The word "tea" is one of the few English words of Chinese origin. It is derived from the plant's name as it is pronounced in South China. In standard Chinese, it is pronounced "cha（茶）." In South China, it is pronounced "te" or "tay" the vowel sound being "e."

There are two versions concerning the early spread of tea outside China.

In the 17th century, tea was introduced into Indo-nesia where local people in Java picked up the sound of "te" or "tay" from South China. Later, Dutch arrived there and soon learned how to drink tea. They brought tea back to Europe, where "te" began to be known both on the continent and in Britain.

The other saying is that the Portuguese opened up sea routes to China. Some says that the opening-up was as early as

1515, Jesuit priests, including Father Jasper de Cruz, were on the Portuguese ships; and they brought the tea drinking habit and tea word "te" or "tay" to Portugal. By 1610, tea was shipped, on a regular basis, to ports in France, Holland and the Baltic coast.

紅茶與綠茶的主要區別是什麼？

What are the main differences between black tea and green tea?

Black tea appeared in the Qing Dynasty. Incidentally "black tea" was translated into Chinese as "red tea" (紅茶), which is perhaps a more accurate description of the color in liquid and gradually people have accepted the translation. This tea, being made from leaves more heavily oxidized than the green variety, is generally more flavorful.

What is green tea? Green tea is tea that has undergone minimal oxidation during processing. This type of tea is popular in China and Japan, and recently has become popular in the West, where people formally drink only black tea. The main difference between green tea and black tea is that green tea keeps the original color of the tea leaves without fermentation during processing, whereas black tea is fermented before baking.

什麼是烏龍茶？
What is Oolong tea?

Oolong tea is a traditional Chinese tea. It is semi-fermented, with its oxidation time somewhat between that of green and black tea. The term "Oolong" (烏龍) means "black dragon"; and various legends describe the origin of this curious name. According to one legend, the owner of a tea plantation was scared away by drying tea leaves that appeared like a black snake. But several days later when the owner cautiously returned, he realized that the leaves had been oxidized by the sun. Besides, it gave a delightful brew. Oolong tea leaves are bruised to oxidize under the sun after their picking though not as long as leaves intended for black tea. Tieguanyin (鐵觀音) from Fujian Province is considered the excellent grade of Oolong tea.

> **Notes**
> semi-ferment 半發酵；curious 好奇的

什麼是團餅茶？
What is tuanbing tea?

Tuanbing tea is a kind of compressed tea in the shape of a round cake. Traditionally a tuanbing tea producer uses wooden pestle to pound fresh tealeaves into a cake shape. The production usually goes through several following steps:

➤ Steam and wash tea leaves.

➤ Repeatedly squeeze the tea leaves in order to eliminate any bitter juices.

➤ Grind squeezed tea leaves with spring water.

➤ Put ground tea into a molding presser to compress and shape.

➤ Bake the shaped tea cakes over a low fire temperature until it became completely dry.

When drinking, a tuanbing tea drinker pounds a tea cake to pieces first, puts them into a kettle, and then fills the kettle with hot boiled water. In addition, the drinker may add spring onions, ginger, and oranges to improve the taste.

In ancient times between the Song and Yuan dynasties, the tribute tea was categorized as tuanbing tea. In addition, tribute tuanbing tea cakes appeared with dragon and phoenix patterns on the surface, and thus named as "Dragon and Phoenix Tuanbing Tea Cakes (龍團鳳餅)."

Notes
squeeze 榨，擠；eliminate 排除；ginger 薑，薑黃色；categorize 將……分類

什麼是功夫茶？
What is Kungfu tea?

Kungfu literally means "learnt skilled" and is a philosophy applied to any time-honored pursuit of excellence. This style of tea-drinking is common in Fujian and other areas in southern coastal China. Local people prefer Oolong Tea when they brew "Kungfu tea." The gongfu teapot appears as small as a fist in size, and a tiny cup only as large as a table-tennis ball in half size. Each cup is just large enough to hold about two small servings of tea.

Usually the server first puts Oolong Tea leaves in a teapot and then fills the teapot with hot boiled water. The server drains the water immediately, leaving the tea leaves behind. The draining is repeated one or two times for the practical purpose of washing the leaves. Then the server pours the tea into the tiny cups one after another continuously. Each cup of tea is expected to have the same flavor. After the procedure is completed, people start to savor the tea while exchanging local gossip.

<u>Notes</u>
philosophy 哲學；time-honored 確立已久的；pursuit 追求；serving 一份；continuously 連續不斷地；procedure 工序；gossip 小道傳聞

你知道如何選茶葉嗎？
What is the way to select tea?

Selecting best tea always challenges tea drinkers. Customers usually buy jasmine tea（茉莉花茶）according to its quality grades, which may come in as many as ten or more grades, with grade one being regarded as the best. Jasmine buds are intentionally put into the tea to produce an agreeable scent; but tea connoisseurs classify the tea by the shape of the leaf, the color of the liquid, and the aroma, taste and appearance of the infused leaf.

The following are some simple ways that may help tea drinkers select tea:

a. Tea leaves should always be kept dry. Customers can use their fingers to press tea leaves to see if they are dry. Slight finger press easily breaks dry tea leaves into small pieces.

b. Aroma is the most important factor. Good tea always smells good.

c. The color of the tea liquid and the shape of tea leaves vary with different types of tea. Generally, the tea liquid should remain clear and free of impurity, and the shape of good tea leaves in the liquid should be whole and even.

> **Notes**
>
> customer 顧客；jasmine 茉莉花；agreeable 令人愉快的；connoisseur 鑑賞家；aroma 香味；impurity 不純

有需要準備茶的特別場合嗎？
Are there special circumstances in which tea is prepared?

There are some popular sayings like "Tea comes first when entertaining guests (待客茶為先)", " There is no ritual without tea (無茶不成儀)" or " The friendship between gentlemen appears indifferent but is pure like water; the friendship between tea drinkers appears mildly intoxicated but is flavorful like tea (君子之交淡如水，茶人之交醇如茶)."

People usually host guests with tea at home or at work. At a special tea party serving a cup of tea is more than a matter of mere politeness. It is a show of respect to guests. Before brewing tea for guests, the host should wash hands, clean cups or teacups. A ceramic tea set is preferred. The host should ask guests what kind of tea they prefer:green tea, black tea, jasmine tea, or another. Each cup is 70% full with boiled water, and the tea water tastes neither too strong nor too light.

Generally the host places the teacups on the saucer before he presents them to guests. In addition, the host often uses his two hands to present the teacups to guests. As he uses his two hands to present the teacups to guests, guests should rise to their feet and take over them also with both hands. At the same time, guests should express their appreciation by saying "thank you."

Following are special circumstances in which tea is prepared and consumed.

In China, the younger generation commonly show respect to the older generation. One traditional holiday activity is to offer a cup of tea to one's elders at a family dinner gatherings.

In the past, people of lower ranks served tea to those of higher ranks. Today, however, parents may sometimes pour a cup of tea for their children when at home, and a boss may even pour tea for subordinates at restaurants. However, the lower ranking person should not expect the higher rank person to serve him or her tea on a formal occasion.

In Chinese culture, people make serious apologies to others by pouring them tea as a sign of regret or submission.

In the traditional Chinese marriage ceremony, the bride and groom kneel before their parents and serve them tea to express their gratitude. The parents usually drink a small portion of the tea and then give them a red envelope, which symbolizes good luck.

Notes

indifferent 不關心的；intoxicated 使陶醉；appreciation 感謝；cir-cum-stance 儀式；subordinate 下級的；ranking 等級；apology 道歉；submission 歸順；bride 新娘；groom 新郎；gratitude 感激之情

中國茶道有什麼特點？

What is the feature of the Chinese tea ceremony?

As for the tea ceremony, different areas may have different ways to display their unique ceremony. Unlike the Japanese tea ceremony, the Chinese tea ceremony emphasizes the tea rather than the ceremony. During a Chinese tea ceremony, participants are most concerned with the tea taste and smell, as well as the difference between different tea.

The tea ceremony doesn't mean that each server will perform the ritual in the same way, nor is there a relationship to religion. This style of tea-drinking uses small cups to match the small, unglazed clay teapots; each cup is just large enough to hold about two small servings of tea.

The teas used in tea ceremonies are particularly refined. The server passes the dry and unbroken tealeaves around for everyone to see and smell. Then he displays a tiny teapot made from zisha clay. After heating water to boiling, the teapot is first rinsed with hot boiled water. The server uses pointed chopsticks to put the tea into the teapot and pours hot boiled water into it. The server rinses the tealeaves by filling the pot half full with hot boiled water and draining the water out immediately, leaving only the soaked tea leaves.

The server then fills the pot to the top with more hot boiled water. As he does this, he holds the pot over a large bowl, allowing the bubble water to run into the bowl. The first infusion should be steeped for only 30 seconds before he pours the tea into the tiny cups. Instead of pouring one cup at a time, the server moves the teapot around in a continual motion over the cups so they are all filled.

As the server empties the pot, he passes out the tiny cups, telling drinkers to smell the tea first. When they drink the tea, the tea tastes much different than it smells. It has a bitter, green-twig taste, very satisfying.

The server refills the teapot with hot water. He refills the cups as the drinker hands back them for the next round. Each pot of tea serves three to four rounds and up to five or six, depending on the tea and the server with the goal that each round tastes the same as the first.

Notes

ceremony 儀式；emphasize 強調；unbroken 完整的；rinse 沖洗；
bubble 水泡；twig 嫩枝

成都有許多茶館嗎？
Are there many teahouses in Chengdu?

There is a saying, "China has the best teahouses in the world, and Chengdu has the best teahouses in China." When you are in Chengdu, you will see teahouses everywhere, sprawling over the sidewalks, in back-alleys and in the suburbs. They offer hot boiled water and tea snacks, and provide a comfortable setting with bamboo armchairs, low tables and sooty kettles. Some teahouses present performances, or local operas. Jasmine tea is especially popular but people who go to the teahouses are not really thirsty. They usually go there just to sip tea and chat. Elderly persons may pass their whole day there, playing games or cards.

Recently some changes have taken place in downtown Chengdu teahouses. There have sprung a sort of pub-type teahouses with a pleasant interior decor. These are usually busy in the afternoon and evening, and mainly cater to young people, who come to chat or talk business. However, traditional family-type teahouses are still popular in the suburbs. On weekends, friends and families from all the walks of life go to tcahouses in the beautiful countryside where they enjoy drinking tea, chatting, playing cards or dozing off in their armchairs. Many pleasant weekends can be spent here over a bottomless cup of flower tea at a low cost.

> **Notes**
> sprawl 蔓延；sidewalk 人行道；sooty 炭黑色的；interior 內部的；
> doze 打瞌睡

茶館裡主要使用的是什麼茶具？
What utensils are mainly used for tea drinking in teahouses?

The use of tea wares has a long tradition in China. In Chengdu, tea-drinking utensils are made of bronze or ceramics; and consist of mainly teapots, cups, tea bowls and trays, etc. Some first-class teahouses are equipped with high quality utensils. Unglazed earthenware like that used in ancient China is still used in Sichuan for brewing tea today. In the Tang Dynasty, metal wares were used to serve the noble families; porcelain earthenware for ordinary citizens. In the Song Dynasty, tea bowls became common. They were glazed of black, dark-brown, gray, gray-white or white colors. Gray-white porcelain ware was predominant in the Yuan Dynasty, whereas white tea ware became popular in the Ming Dynasty. Later during the middle of the Ming Dynasty, teapots made of porcelain and purple clay were in fashion. Porcelain wares made in Jingdezhen (景德鎮), Jiangxi Province, and purple clay wares made in Yixing (宜興), Jiangsu Province, occupied the top places among various kinds of tea wares.

為什麼宜興紫砂壺非常有名？
Why is the Yixing ceramic teapot so well-known?

Chinese people in different regions often use different teapots for tea drinking, but Yixing ceramic teapots are widely regarded as the best.

Yixing ceramic teapots are produced in Yixing (宜興) of Jiangsu Province. The basic material is the zisha clay, or "purple sand," found in the hilly areas around Yixing. Yixing clay deposit has three colours: light-buff, cinnabar-red and purplish-brown. Teapot makers create teapots in an array of colours simply by adding to paste mineral pigments, or mixing clay of the light-buff, cinnabar-red or purplish-brown.

Yixing ceramic teapots are unglazed pottery. Some additional features of the teapot include:

➤ The teapots are uniquely non-toxic.

➤ The teapots have an exceptional ability to retain heat due to the firing process. Unlike porcelain wares, the paste for a Yixing ceramic teapot is fired at somewhat lower heat. After heating, the teapot becomes solid and smooth in texture, and it has an appropriate absorption rate and a low thermal conductivity.

➤ Although the teapots are porous, they do not seep. In addition, this porous nature gives another outstanding attribute to Yixing ceramic teapots. When tea is brewed in a Yixing ceramic teapot, a tiny amount of tea is absorbed into the pot. So after a period of daily use, the pot will develop a patina coating that retains some of the taste, scent and colour of tea. Because of its absorbency, many households in China have several teapots, each teapot being used for one type of tea.

➤ Yixing ceramic teapots offer a rustic but elegant beauty. Many tea drinkers are attracted to these teapots solely for their appearance. Their designs portray natural themes that incorporate flowers or animals.

In addition, Yixing ceramic teapots each has its "chop" marks. A potter usually places his/her personal mark or seal on the bottom of each piece. It serves to identify its creator and reflects the potter's pride of workmanship. Sometimes modern potters who work in teapot factories offer their photos or an authenticity certificate to be with their teapot products at the teapot market.

It is said that the first ceramic teapot was created in the Ming Dynasty. In the years that followed, the Yixing reddish stoneware teapots became so popular and considered to be the "best" by Chinese tea lovers. In the late 17th century, Yixing ceramic teapots were introduced to Europe along with tea shipments, and these products became the models for the earliest teapots made in Holland, Germany and Britain.

In 1954, the Chinese government established communes to gather master-level potters in order to train a new generation of potters and ensure the perpetuation of the local tradition. Today contemporary Yixing potters continue their traditional pursuit, and their artistic potential has blossomed into a variety of beautiful teapots.

> **Notes**
>
> teapot 茶壺；ceramic 陶器的；buff 暗黃色的；cinnabar-red 朱紅的；purplish-brown 略帶紫棕色的；non-toxic 無毒的；absorption 吸收；attribute 屬性；absorbency 吸收力；incorporate 合併，混合；authenticity 真實性；shipment 裝運；裝船；commune 社區，社區居民；contemporary 當代的；potential 潛能的

什麼是茶博士？
What is the Tea Service Master?

A servant who offers customers tea in teahouses is respectfully called the Tea Service Master (茶博士). They provide good service and skillfully brew tea for tea customers. Tea Service Masters wear a traditional costume and prepare tea water in the traditional way. They have a good knowledge of tea and skillfully mix tealeaves. In fact, tea servants normally have to go through intensive years of painstaking and vigorous training before they are able to obtain the title of Tea Service Master.

Once visitors enter a teahouse, Tea Service Masters will greet them with a smile, holding in their hands teapots and cups. After the visitors are seated, the masters will set the cups on the table and pour the water from behind the guests or from above their heads. When the cups are almost full, the masters will raise their hands high suddenly, but not a drop of water is spilt.

Notes

respectfully 恭敬地；normally 正常地；pain-staking 勤勉的；vig-
orous 精力充沛的

第二章
中國烹調
Chinese Cuisine

　　烹調是傳統文化中的瑰寶，在世界上享有盛譽。本篇簡要介紹烹調的歷史、菜餚的基本特點、菜系以及飲食習俗。

你對中國烹調了解多少？
How do you think of Chinese cuisine?

Chinese cuisine is one of the delights of the world. There are few people who have not tried Chinese dishes of some sort at one of the many Chinese restaurants that exist in their own country. Most visitors appreciate the fact that Chinese cooking has traditions, which go further back in history than those of French cuisine. They understand that Chinese cuisine is an art, which grew out of a highly developed civilization. The infinite numbers of Chinese dishes, flavors, textures, and methods of cooking, make eating Chinese food exciting.

Another fact is that Chinese cuisine can be conveniently prepared in home kitchens. Chinese people value their way of dining very much. There is an old saying that says, "Food is the first necessity of the people (民以食為天)." Delicious and nutritious food has been regarded as the basis of life. Chinese cooking uses almost all the meat, poultry, fish, and vegetables known to the Western palate, but also embrace other foodstuff which, to Western taste, appear exotic. Compared with the food served at many of the Chinese restaurants abroad, visitors will almost certainly find a difference in quality, substance, and style in the food prepared in China itself.

Notes
cuisine 烹飪；civilization 文明；texture 質地；conveniently 方便地；
delicious 美味的；nutritious 有營養的；poultry 家禽；palate 味覺；
exotic 奇特的；substance 物質

辣椒是中國自古就有的嗎？

Was red pepper a local product in ancient China?

Sichuan cuisine has enjoyed a worldwide reputation, and people immediately associate it with hot or spicy food. Actually, however, these flavors were introduced only in last 200 years. Before that time, there were no hot dishes in Sichuan, and few were cooked with pungent and hot flavorings. Originally, the flavor of Sichuan cuisine was quite mild.

Research shows, red pepper is, in fact, native to Mexico, Central America, the West Indies, and parts of South America. It is called capsicum pepper. The Spanish discovered it in the New World and brought it back to Europe. Before the arrival of Spaniards, Indians in Peru and Guatemala used capsicum pepper to treat stomach and other ailments.

Before the Ming Dynasty, there was no red pepper in China. It was introduced into China only around the end of the 17th century. Local people in Chaozhou area, Guangdong Province call red pepper fanjiao (番椒), which means "foreign pepper." At the beginning, it was used for medical or ornamental purposes. Only later did it appear in Southwest China where the local people treasure its taste. Sichuan has humid climate which encourages people to eat strongly spiced foods, and the red pepper may help reduce internal dampness ailment.

Notes
reputation 名聲；spicy 辛辣的；flavoring 調味料；capsicum 辣椒（的種子）；Peru 祕魯；Guatemala 瓜地馬拉；stomach 腹部；ornamental 裝飾的；humid 潮溼的；internal 體內的

中國烹調注重菜的「型」和「味道」嗎？
Does Chinese cuisine pay attention to the appearance and taste of dishes?

Chinese food appeals to the senses through color, shape, aroma and taste. Shape mainly depends on methods of cutting. Cooks cut raw materials to be sliced, diced, shredded, or minced, based on the requirements of the dish and the character of the raw food. Improper cutting makes food unattractive and causes unevenness in color and taste. In stir-frying, improper cutting will result in the small pieces being overcooked and big pieces remaining raw.

Taste mainly depends on the seasonings. There are many tastes-salty, sweet, sour, pungent, fragrant, bitter and so forth. The proper use of seasonings will produce a variety of dishes to suit a variety of appetites. A good Chinese cook knows what to add, how much to add and when to add. Chinese cooks even now have created new tastes, including mala (麻辣 , numbing spicy sauce), yuxiang (魚香 , tasty fish-flavored sauce), guaiwei (怪味 , strange salty, spicy, and sesame sauce) and so on.

Notes
slice 切成薄片；dice 將（蔬菜等）切成小方塊；shred 切成條狀；mince 切碎；requirement 要求；unattractive 無吸引力的；uneven 不平坦的；overcook 使煮過頭；seasoning 調味料；appetite 食慾；sesame 芝麻

中國烹調注重「火候」嗎？

Does Chinese cuisine pay attention to the fire temperature?

Chinese cooks pay particular attention to fire temperature to bring out certain flavors. They have known the importance of this ever since ancient times. The eight delicacies (八珍) of Ritual of Zhou call for stewing, braising or simmering over a slow, small fire for a long time. A proper fire means a delicious dish. Generally speaking, raw food should be cooked over a small fire for a long time as it is cut in large pieces. On the other hand, raw food cut in small pieces is cooked over a high flame on a form of frying or stir-frying. There are several other cooking methods to use, depending on the dishes to be prepared. Instead of the common everyday pot, a special pot is sometimes used. It is sealed before being placed over the fire. Usually its cooking period lasts for a fairly long time, and the ingredients smell good and make eating exciting.

> **Notes**
> stew 燉 ; braise 以文火燉煮 ; simmer 煨

如何劃分中國主要地域菜系？

What are the main regional cuisine in China?

Since ingredients are not the same everywhere, Chinese food began to take in a local character by virtue of the ingredients. Chinese regional cuisine have evolved over the course of the centuries, and the precise number is disputed. Generally speaking, there are four basic gastronomic areas: Shandong, Cantonese, Sichuan and Yangzhou; but these designations have no specific geographical boundaries. Beijing cooking, for instance, falls within the realm of Shandong cuisine and includes some Sichuan dishes and Mongolian-influenced specialties. The cuisine in the Changjiang River delta area, including Huaiyin, Suzhou, Shanghai and Hangzhou dishes, falls under the category of Yangzhou cuisine.

The four regional cuisine have influenced each other, and their cooking methods are shared among themselves. Nevertheless, each regional cuisine has its own history, unique techniques, distinguished dishes and prevailing tastes.

Notes

gastronomic 烹飪的；designation 名稱；boundary 界限；realm 領域；specialty 特產；delta 三角洲；pre-vailing 主要的

你對山東菜系了解多少？
How much do you know about Shandong cuisine?

Shandong Province was the birthplace of Confucius, who, twenty-five centuries ago, presided over a rich mixture of philosophy and gastronomy. Shandong cuisine belongs to the Northern cooking style and should be more correctly described as the cooking tradition in kitchen in the North China Plain. Within this realm of northern provinces, Beijing, Hebei, Shanxi, Shaanxi and other northern areas all have their own unique cooking styles. Wheat buns and pancakes, not rice, are the staff of life here. Shandong cuisine includes the menus of the emperors of the Yuan (1206-1368), Ming (1368-1644) and Qing (1616-1911) dynasties, when the imperial capital was located in Beijing. Popular dishes are noted throughout China, such as Dezhou braised chicken, roast pork and fried pig stomach.

Located on China's eastern seaboard, one would expect that Shandong cuisine might include many seafood dishes, including shark's fin, sea cucumbers (not a local product), and scallops. All of them are available in dried form. The coastal areas are also home to such dishes as Swallow's Nests in Consomme, Fried Oysters, Steamed Porgy, and Conch in Brown Sauce.

> **Notes**
> birthplace 出生地；preside 管轄；gastronomy 烹飪法；plain 平原；
> bun 包子；pancakes 薄餅；scallop 扇貝；consomme 清燉肉湯；
> oyster 牡蠣；porgy 鯛；conch 海螺

你對粵菜系了解多少？
How much do you know about Cantonese cuisine?

The Guangdong style of cooking is probably the most familiar to the Western palate, for many Chinese restaurants established outside China are of this type. The name for this cuisine comes from the old name for the southern city now known as Guangzhou. Features of this style are the great variety of dishes and the beauty of their presentation. The abundant fresh vegetables in the area are cooked for the shortest time possible to maintain their natural crispness. The dishes have a slight tendency to be sweet, and spices are used with moderation. Cantonese cuisine draws on an extraordinary range of ingredients, including some dogs, cats, rats, ants, snakes and snails.

Cantonese cuisine covers the southeastern corner of the country. Within the Cantonese cuisine family, there is an enormous range of various local cuisine in Chaozhou, Shantou, Dongjiang, Daliang, as well as the cuisine of the Hakka people.

Some of the flavorings used in Cantonese cuisine are oyster sauce, shrimp paste, plum sauce, and fish extract. Some of the best-known dishes are Roast Suckling Pig, Battle Between the Dragon and the Tiger (a stew of snake and cat), Fried Milk, Salt-Baked Chicken, Dog Meat Casserole, along with roast duck, chicken, goose and pork.

Teahouses in Guangzhou and Hong Kong serve as places for breakfast. Customers drink tea accompanied by the consumption of light food. A variety of boiled, baked, fried and steamed delicacies are offered for customers' convenience.

Notes

presentation 呈現；crispness 酥脆；tendency 趨勢；moderation 適度；extraordinary 特別的；snail 蝸牛；enormous 巨大的；suckling 哺乳的；casserole 砂鍋；consumption 吃，喝，飲用

你對揚州菜系了解多少？
How much do you know about Yangzhou cuisine?

Yangzhou is located in China's agriculturally rich Changjiang River valley. The cuisine of Yangzhou is a true melting pot, and it would be more accurate to label this heritage as the Lower Changjiang Valley cuisine.

The Yangzhou cuisine has a great variety of dishes, borrowed widely from the surrounding delta, notably from the provincial kitchens of Jiangsu and Zhejiang province, where cities such as Suzhou, Hangzhou, Shanghai and Nanjing are located. The rich variety of vegetables available in the region ensure their widespread use in many of the dishes. Shanghai's position on the coast ensures the area of a rich variety of seafood. Yangzhou cuisine usually takes slightly longer time to prepare so that vegetables and meats can absorb more of the sauces. Much of the food is fried, and there is greater use of sesame oil and vinegar. Spices like garlic, ginger, and small (but very hot) red peppers are used; the seasonings tend to be sweeter with more sugar and dark soy used in their preparation.

Yangzhou cuisine is famous for both exquisitely crafted snacks and main dishes. Famous dishes include Steamed Mandarin Fish in Vinegar Sauce, Lion's Head meatballs, French-fried White Bait and Boiled Shreds of Pressed Tofu.

> **Notes**
> agriculturally 農用地；melting pot 大熔爐；label 把……稱為；
> heritage 傳統；widespread 普遍的；absorb 吸收；ginger 生薑；
> crafted 精巧地製作的；bait 食物

你對川菜系了解多少？
How much do you know about Sichuan cuisine?

In Sichuan Province, some dishes are highly spiced and peppery, so it is often said that numbing, hot spices are the main characteristics of Sichuan cuisine. Nonetheless, popular belief, Sichuan dishes have many other flavors. A popular saying says that, "China has food, and Sichuan has flavor (食在中國，味在四川). " The flavors of Sichuan cuisine can be rather complex. Chefs blend many spices together to create various flavors, including suanla wei (酸辣味 , hot and sour sauce), yuxiang wei (魚香味 , tasty fish-flavored sauce), mala wei (麻辣味 , numbingly spicy sauce) and yanxun wei (煙燻味 , smoked flavor sauce).

Sichuan cuisine carefully balances color, odor, flavor, shape and nutrition, so dishes not only look pleasant and appealing, but also are nutritious. There are several hundred indigenous dishes, besides some dishes that are intentionally toned down for tourists. So travelers at home and abroad have no difficulty in getting Sichuan food that suits their tastes at a banquet, dinne, lunch or as snacks. Famous dishes include Spicy Chicken Fried with Peanuts, Fish-flavored Sliced Pork, Mapo Tofu and Twice-cooked Pork.

> ## Notes
> spiced 調過味的；peppery 辛辣的；numbness 麻木；chef 主廚；
> blend 使混合；numbing 使麻木的；nutrition 營養；appealing 動人的；
> nutritious 滋養的；tone down 使柔和

什麼是火鍋？
What is Hotpot?

Hotpot originated in Chongqing and it is noted for its peppery and hot taste. Being a very popular way of restaurant eating, it can be found at every corner of Chongqing and Chengdu, where numerous sidewalk hotpot operations, as well as exquisite hotpot restaurants, have been set up to meet the increasing local demand. Customers gather around a small boiling wok filled with nutritious soup base. Around the wok are placed numerous plates of paper-thin slices of raw meat and other ingredients. Customers select the raw ingredients and boil them in the soup. They then take them out of the wok and dip them in a small special-sauce-filled bowl sauce before eating them.

Restaurants offer various kinds of hotpot to suit customers'tastes so that friends or families with different tastes can huddle around and enjoy the feast. One of the most popular variety is yuanyang hotpot (鴛鴦火鍋), in which the wok is partitioned into two parts, with a thin wall. One part is filled with a hot, spicy soup base, and the other with a mild spicy broth. This kind of hotpot suits many customers both at home and abroad.

> **Notes**
> wok 鐵鍋（帶把的中國炒菜鍋）; huddle 聚在一起

什麼是傳統形式的飯和菜？
What are traditional forms of the fan and cai?

In China, the food stuffs are commonly classified as along tracks of fan (飯), staple foods and cai (菜), prepared dishes. The former refers to grains and other staple starch grains; the latter to supplementary vegetable or meat dishes. Fan is the more fundamental. Chinese have the habit of eating more of this food and less of non-staple dishes. Grains make up most of one's caloric intake, and an adult may consume two or three bowls of rice or a large bowl of noodles. At the daily dining table, everyone has his or her own bowl of fan; but when there are a lot of cai dishes, some may prefer not to have any fan.

In the preparation of cai, the rule is to use multiple ingredients and several flavors. These dishes are usually placed at the center of the table to be shared by all. This is conducive to family togetherness and friendship. In restaurants, "public" chopsticks or spoons are used to take food from the dishes to prevent the spread of disease.

Notes

fundamental 根本的；intake 吸收；caloric 熱量的

傳統的中國主食有哪些特色？
What are the features of traditional Chinese staple food?

China has abundant resources and extensive land where different areas produce different staple food. Generally speaking, the staple food in the North includes wheat, rice, corn, soybeans, millet, beans and peas. And people in the South traditionally take dry cooked rice or rice porridge as their staple food due to the fact that rice mainly grows in the South. One type of rice called glutinous rice (糯米) is usually used to make traditional Chinese rice-pudding (粽子), eight treasures congee (八寶粥) and various types of desserts.

In ancient times wheat flour and rice were mainly supplied to the upper classes of society, and coarse cereals or side crops to ordinary families. Gradually wheat flour and rice were considered as "refined grains (細糧)," and maize, sorghum and millet as "coarse grains (粗糧)." At that time only on the festival days did ordinary families have rice food or meat dumplings made by wheat flour. The "coarse grains" were their daily staple food.

After 1949, China carried the planned economy. In 1955 the food coupons and ration booklets appeared in cities. A grain ration book was issued each month by local government grain stores. For example, in Beijing local citizens got 50％ of their grain ration in wheat flour, 20％ in rice, and 30％ in coupons good for buying bowls of rice or noodles in restaurants. In rural areas, for example in northwestern China, peasants usually had more wheat-flour-made food after a summer wheat harvest; in the second half of a year the other types of autumn grains like maize and soybeans are more consumed in place of wheat.

Such a situation lasted until earlier 1990s after China started carrying out the policies of the domestic reform and market economy, which led to the abundant supply of "refined grains" and "coarse grains" in food markets, supermarkets, and department stores across the country. At present, people either in cities or rural areas have a diverse choice of staple food according to their daily menu.

> **Notes**
> staple 主要部分；soybean 大豆；porridge 粥；glutinous 黏的；
> congee 粥；booklet 小冊子；maize 玉米

什麼是粗茶淡飯？
What is the meaning of cucha danfan?

Cucha danfan means "weak tea and a simple food," or "a simple diet." Traditionally it refers to a lifestyle of living thriftily in daily life.

In ancient times, ordinary families usually arranged their daily meals simply to get stomachs full. This brought out a general custom of trying not to eat dry cooked grains if they had porridge-like food made by boiling the grain in water. In winter slack-season and spring-famine period three meals might be reduced to two per day. In addition, they tended to have few fried dishes. On many occasions fried dishes were substituted by paste-like thick sauce, fermented soybeans, or pickled vegetables. Ordinary families usually made a living this way. Even in normal harvest years, they admonished themselves against any indulgence in extravagant eating. There is a belief, "water flowing out in a trickle takes a long time to exhaust（細水長流）.”　“Being diligent and thrifty（勤儉節約）”is another motto that remains an enduring popularity.

However, the situation would be different when a harvest, festival, or wedding occurred. On that occasion, a rich dinner or meal were provided. For example, in a rush-in-harvest or rush-planting season, peasants usually had four meals a day. In some rural areas there would be five meals offered because of hard labor by peasants working in the fields. By then, their meals usually contained abundant meat and fish.

Notes

economical 節約的；slack-season 淡季；substitute 替換；admonish 訓誡；indulgence 沉溺；extravagant 奢侈的；enduring 持久的

你對豆腐了解多少？
How much do you know about beancurd in China?

Beancurd or tofu（豆腐）is the largest and most important soybean food in China. Generally, beancurd is made by grinding soybeans, filtering the resulting soymilk, adding a coagulant and pressing out the excess water. Northerners traditionally prefer a harder beancurd while southerners prefer a softer, more watery product. A large portion of the beancurd made in China is further processed.

One of the most common processed products is the dried beancurd（豆乾）. This is often smoked or stewed in flavorful sauces and sold on the streets.

Another common processed product is fermented beancurd（豆腐乳）. This is made by taking very hard, small beancurd cubes, inoculating them with bacteria or mold and allowing them to ferment. These are sold in the markets in bottles or earthenware jars.

Beancurd jelly (豆腐腦) is a favorite of street vendors in the south. It is extremely soft. You will see the vendors scooping it out of large pots into bowls, adding sauces according to the customer's specifications.

Bean paste (豆瓣醬) is called miso in Japan. Bean paste is made by combining steamed soybeans with a starch-usually wheat or rice. To purchase bean paste, you bring your own container to one of the state markets and ask them to fill it with the flavor of your choice.

Fermented soybeans (豆豉) are steamed, cooled soybeans. The beans are fermented for three weeks and then mixed with salt, alcohol and water. This mixture is sealed in an earthenware vessel and stored for six months. The final product is fried or braised with meat dishes for a wonderful flavor.

> **Notes**
> grind 磨碎；coagulant 混凝劑；ferment 發酵；inoculate 灌輸；
> bacteria 細菌；mold 霉；黴菌；earthenware jar 陶器罐子；
> specification 規格，明細單

餃子的由來有什麼傳說嗎？
What is the legendary story about dumplings?

Dumplings are very traditional food in China. Northern Chinese people call the dumplings jiao zi (餃子), while Southern Chinese people prefer to call them hun tun or won ton (餛飩). Dumplings may be stuffed with a variety of food, including pork, mutton, beef and fish.

There are several stories concerning the origin of dumplings. According to one version, the dumpling was invented by Zhang Zhongjing (張仲景), a well-known herbal medical doctor of the Eastern Han Dynasty who wrote the book Treatise on Febrile Diseases and Miscellaneous Diseases (《傷寒雜病論》).

Once Zhang retired from his government affairs service and returned to his hometown, he found that in winter many local people had painful chilblains on the ear. Zhang realized that his clinic was so small that it couldn't accommodate the increasing number of chilblain patients, so he asked his brother to put up a tent and place a cauldron in the village square. When the winter solstice arrived, Zhang started to offer medicinal herbs to chilblain patients.

His medicine was called quhan jiao'er tang (祛寒嬌耳湯, herbal soup to dispel the cold and protect the ears). It consisted of mutton, red spicy peppers, and other necessary medicinal herbs. Zhang soaked them completely in water and heated them in the cauldron over a fire until the water boiled. Zhang then took all the things out of the cauldron, mincing them into stuffing. His assistants rolled out dough into each small pancake. They put the stuffing in the centre of the pancakes and wrapped them in the shape of the ear. These tiny things were named jiao'er (嬌耳) or "the ear protection," and were then all dropped into the herb soup to cook. Zhang offered each patient a bowl of the soup and two jiao'er dumplings. The patients drank the soup and ate the dumplings and soon their whole body got so warm, including their ears.

For the following days, they continued eating dumplings and drinking soup, and their ear chilblains gradually disappeared. Zhang kept offering the soup and jiao'er dumplings until New Year's Eve. On the New Year's Day, local people all made dumplings as a symbol to celebrate New Year's Day and to rejoice over their recovery from the chilblains. This event turned into a tradition that has lasted until today.

Notes

dumpling 餃子；a variety of 多種；treatise 專著；febrile 發熱的；miscellaneous 各種各樣的；chilblain 凍瘡；accommodate 給⋯⋯方便；cauldron 大鍋；physically 身體上的；celebrate 慶祝；rejoice 感到高興

你知道窩窩頭的傳說嗎？
Do you know the legendary story about wowotou?

Wowotou（窩窩頭, steamed corn bread) is made with corn flour or corn and bean flour. Steamed corn bread has a solid body and a round, flat base that gradually becomes narrower toward the top. The centre of the base is curved inward, allowing steam to easily heat the bread.

There is an interesting anecdote about steamed corn bread. In 1900, a joint force of eight countries invaded China. Empress Dowager Ci Xi（慈禧太后) fled the capital to Xi'an with her palace attendants and staff before the foreign expeditionary force moved into Beijing.

On the way to Xi'an, the empress felt hungry and extremely fatigue. The eunuchs searched everywhere, hoping to find food for the empress. They found nothing but one cold steamed corn bread from a villager nearby.

The empress quickly devoured the corn and then felt full. When Empress Dowager Ci Xi returned to her palace, she had cooks in the imperial kitchen make the steamed corn bread for her. The cooks made the bread in the same way as the common people made it. However, the bread made in the imperial kitchen was small in size, consisting of refined corn, soybean flour, sugar and sweet osmanthus petals.

The empress enjoyed eating the bread，and so this kind of corn bread was later named xiao wowotou (小窩窩頭 , small steamed corn bread) and became one of the best known snacks from the imperial kitchen of the Qing Dynasty.

Notes

corn flour 玉米粉；curve 曲線；anecdote 軼事；fatigue 疲勞；petal 花瓣；osmanthus 桂花

油條的由來有什麼傳說嗎？
What is the legendary story about Deep-fried dough stick?

Deep-fried dough stick is a traditional snack for breakfast. The origin of this snack is associated with Qin Hui (秦檜) who served as prime minister during the reign of the Southern Song Dynasty Emperor Gao Zong (高宗).

In 1138, Emperor Gao Zong designated Hangzhou as a "temporary capital," and signed a peace agreement with the Jin Kingdom (金國) in 1142. The previous year had seen the death of Yue Fei (岳飛), one of China's most celebrated generals. However, the groundless accusation against Yue Fei was a snare secretly set up by Qin Hui and his wife. After hearing of Yue Fei's death, common people in the capital were furious, and really came to hate Qin Hui and his wife.

At that time, there was an inn near where Yue Fei died that mainly sold oil-fried food. One day the boss of the inn was frying food when he heard of Yue Fei's death. The terrible news caused him to lose control of himself, so he picked up a lump of flour dough from a basin and kneaded it into two small figures-a man and a woman. The boss pasted the two figures together back to back and dropped them into the oil pot while repeatedly shouting, "Come and eat deep-fried oil Qin Hui!"

Upon hearing his shouting, people around understood what he was referring to. Soon people gathered around the pot and ate the figures while shouting and helping the boss knead more figures. Other inns and restaurants in the same city quickly followed suit, frying dough in the "Qin Hui" way. This practice spreaded far and wide across the country and has continued through dynasties until the present time.

Today, people prefer to call this food the Deep-fried twisted dough stick (油條) rather than the oil-fried Qin Hui.

However, in some areas, local people still keep use the old name Deep-fried Hui (油炸燴) or Deep-fried Ghost (油炸鬼).

Notes

temporary 暫時的；celebrate 慶祝；groundless 無根據的；accusation 指控；snare 圈套；lose control of 失去對……的控制；basin 盆；knead 揉成

宴會的一般程序是什麼？
What is the usual process of a banquet?

Banquet menus are quite different in composition from the daily meal at home. A standard banquet consists of four to six cold dishes, eight main dishes, one or two showpieces (such as a whole fish or chicken), along with soup, rice, pastries and fruit.

Cold dishes are normally served before the main dishes. Any number of cold-dish components may be combined into a single elaborate dish, beautifully shaped like a butterfly, phoenix, dragon, or a basket of flowers. The visual appeal is intended, however, to stimulate the appetite.

Each of the main dishes contains a different kind of food, some with meat or fish, some without. Rice or noodles are served last. Even at the end of a banquet, Chinese habitually eat a small bowl of rice or noodles.

在正式的宴會中，來賓和主人的座次應如何安排？
How are the guests and host seated for a formal dinner?

The host and chief guest are usually seated on opposite sides of the table, facing each other. The chief guest is seated at the head of the room, facing the door; the host with his or her back to the door. In most restaurant arrangements, the host is also closest to the door thus in a better position to give orders to the waiters as they come and go.

Other guests are seated to the left and right of the chief guest in descending order of rank or importance. This means that the two lowest ranking members in the party may end up seated to the immediate right and left of the host. This arrangement is just opposite of what Westerners might expect.

The thinking behind the Chinese-style seating arrangement is simple and logical. It assures that the host will have a direct view of the main guests and only slightly oblique views of other guests of importance.

> **Notes**
> logical 合邏輯的；oblique 斜的

如何理解中國人的熱情好客？
How do you understand the characteristics of Chinese hospitality?

When overseas travelers first visit China, they are often surprised to find themselves served what seems a lavish meal consisting of cold dishes, hot dishes, soup and rice. They consider this a lavish spread. However, this Chinese typical meal and especial dinner banquets are social occasions. Moreover, Chinese hosts repeatedly ask their guests to help themselves. They seem to overwhelm guests with food, but they are simply being hospitable. It is not a guest's job to stuff himself to the point of discomfort, but eating too little may dismay the host. If your host serves you something that you don't like, you may simply leave it uneaten on your plate. Traditionally, it is the host's duty to ensure that guests are well served.

> **Notes**
> hospitality 殷勤招待；hospitable 好客的；lavish 非常慷慨的；
> uneaten 未吃的；overwhelm 征服；ensure 保證

筷子有什麼特點？
What are the characteristics of chopsticks?

Chopsticks are made from a variety of materials ranging from plain wood, lacquered wood, bamboo, ebony and ivory, and they have been used in China for thousands of years.

Chopsticks are used to either grasp food or push it from the plate to the mouth and are considered sufficient for all purposes except soups or ice cream, for which spoons are provided. Chopsticks are normally used in China, but you need not hesitate to ask for a knife or fork if you are embarrassed about your ability to use them. However, your hosts will show indefinite patience with your attempts to master their use, and you will be surprised at how quickly you make the progress.

Notes
chopstick 筷子；sufficient 足夠的；purpose 目的；embarrassed 尷尬的；indefinite 不確定的；lacquered 上漆的

第三章
中國酒
Alcoholic Drinks in China

　　1915 年中國人帶著茅臺酒、瀘州老窖酒、紹興黃酒去巴拿馬
參加萬國博覽會，一舉獲得 4 塊金牌。中國酒的主流是糧食酒，
作為一種物質文化，它顯示出中國酒文化的獨特性。本篇介紹的
是中國酒的傳說、歷史、基本特點、各種名酒以及飲酒的習俗。

漢字「酒」在英文中的含義是什麼？
What is the meaning of Chinese character jiu in English?

Wine or liquor has been intimately intertwined with almost every aspect of Chinese culture since earliest times. The Chinese word jiu in Chinese is commonly loosely translated as "wine," but the word actually can refer to any type of alcoholic beverage, from beer pijiu (啤酒) to liquor of any kind including grape wine. Many Chinese "wines" are in fact liquors or spirits, and Tibetans have a brew called qingkejiu (青稞酒), made from barley.

> **Notes**
> liquor 酒；intimately 熟悉地；intertwine 編結； beverage 飲料；
> barley 大麥

中國古代釀酒的由來有哪些傳說？
What are the legends about the origin of alcoholic brewing in ancient China?

China is one of the countries with the longest history of the production of alcoholic beverages. One legend says that at the early stage of the Xia Dynasty, a woman named Yi Di (儀狄) presented to Yu (禹) with a tasty wine that she made by fermenting rice wrapped in mulberry leaves.

Another legend says that people started brewing alcoholic drinks during the era of Huang Di (黃帝). An ancient book entitled The Yellow Emperor's Cannon of Internal Medicine (《黃帝內經》) records a conversation between Huang Di and Qi Bo (岐伯). Huang Di said, "Please tell me how to make a sweet alcoholic drink from rice?" Qi Bo replied, "Rice of fine-quality is required, and rice straw can be used to warm it."

The most popular legend concerns Du Kang (杜康), who is said to have been a shepherd in the Zhou Dynasty. One day when he was herding sheep, he mindlessly dropped a bamboo tube in the pasture. He soon forgot about his loss, and the tube was full of millct. 14 days later when he found the tube, the millet had turned into fragrant wine. This new discovery made him happy. Since then, he never shepherded sheep on the grassland. Instead he brewed the wine. Today his name is still associated with alcohol.

> **Notes**
> alcoholic 含酒精的；brewage 釀製飲料；mulberry 桑科植物的；
> shepherd 羊倌；mindlessly 不小心的；millet 小米

漢代傳說中的故事和「漢磚」講了關於飲酒釀酒的什麼事情？
What is known about the drinking and brewing of alcohols from legendary stories of the Han Dynasty and the Han Bricks?

In the late 1970s, a large amount of ancient bricks and stones dating from the Eastern Han Dynasty were unearthed in the suburbs of Chengdu. On the surface of each stone or brick are figures, animals or houses from ancient local people's daily life, and some patterns in relief display how people brewed or drank wine and managed public wine houses.

A love story between Sima Xiangru (司馬相如) and Zhuo Wenjun (卓文君) that occurred in a small town near Chengdu in the Han Dynasty. One day, a well-learned scholar named Sima Xiangru fell in love with Zhuo Wenjun. However, Zhuo's parents did not approve, so the two secretly ran away. They arrived at the western suburbs of Chengdu, where they managed a public wine house as means of livelihood. Sima Xiangru sold wine, while Zhuo Wenjun cleaned utensils and cups. Before long, Sima Xiangru went to Chang'an, the capital of the Han Empire for an imperial examination. Finally Sima Xiangru returned and picked up Zhuo Wenjun. They two went to the capital because Sima Xiangru had a position in the court government there.

The Han Bricks and the story imply the winemaking industry was well developed in the Han Dynasty.

Notes
secretly 祕密地

果酒和乳酒是古代中國第一代飲料酒嗎？
Was the fruit wine and milk wine the first generationof alcoholic drinks?

During the Old Stone Age Period, wild fruits were a staple food. These contain much natural sugar, and under the action of microorganisms, the sugar easily turns into alcohol when fermented. Animals' milk contains protein and milk sugar that likewise easily turns to alcohol. At the same time, ancient hunters might have chance to get animal milk. The alcoholic drink called lilao (醴酪) recorded in The Yellow Emperor's Cannon of Internal Medicine is a kind of sweet milk and might be the earliest milk wine.

Some ancient Chinese books have recorded matters relating to fruit wine production through the natural fermentation of fruit. Gui Xin Za Zhi (《癸辛雜 識》) by Zhou Mi (周密) of the Song Dynasty says that mountain pears stored

74

by local people in urns turned to alcohol. The preface to Pu Tao Jiu Fu (《蒲桃酒賦》) by Yuan Haowen (元好問) of the Yuan Dynasty says that a certain person who lived near a mountain ran away from the ravages of war and sought safety in the mountains. In his house was a pile of grapes stored in an urn. When fermented, the grape juice turned to alcohol under the action of the natural sugar of the grapes.

Notes
microorganism 微生物

中國最古老的穀物酒叫什麼名字？
What is the name of the oldest grain wine in China?

In ancient China, there was a kind of alcoholic beverage called li (醴) that was made from malted cereals. Some scholars think that li wine was similar to beer because of its low alcoholic content. Inscriptions on bones and tortoise shells preserve the records of li wine. In the Zhou Dynasty, alcoholic beverages were classified into two types: rice wine and li wine. One chapter in The Classic of History (《書經》) says, "If you want to brew rice wine, use qu (曲); if you want to brew the li wine, use malt (若作酒醴，爾惟麴糵)." It seems that there were two different technical processes in use for the production of the two types of wine during the Zhou Dynasty. After the Han Dynasty, li wine came to be neglected by rice wine made by qu, a kind of distilled yeast.

Notes
malt 麥芽 ; cereal 穀類植物

在中國歷史上誰最早提出禁酒？
Who first raised a prohibition against alcoholic drinks?

Chinese dynasty history begins with the Xia Dynasty (2070 B.C.-1600 B.C.). Yu the Great was the founder, and he was probably the first to prohibit alcoholic drinks. Book of Shang (《尚書》) and Classic of Poetry (《詩經》) contain the earliest sayings related to the morality of drinking alcohol. They say that alcoholic drinkers should keep social morality and they should not indulge in drinking. A chapter entitled Document of Prohibition Against Alcoholic Drinks《酒誥》 in Book of Shang represents Confucian teaching on the morality of alcoholic drinks. It says that alcoholic drinks are not permitted except on occasions when a ceremony is held to worship deities. In addition, people should not gather together just to drink alcohol.

At the beginning of the Western Han Dynasty, Xiao He (蕭何), the first prime minister, issued a law that said, "four liang copper penalty will be imposed on a group of three or more who gather to drink without a special reason." One liang is a unit of weight equal to 50 grams. Throughout times, the prohibition of alcoholic drinks was common. Some were for politic reasons, and some to control of grains. For the most part, grains were used to ferment wine in ancient times, and governments decided whether to lift their ban on the brewing of alcohol or not depending whether or not the grain harvest was bountiful.

Notes
prohibition 禁止；morality 道德；indulge 沉迷於；ceremony 儀式；bountiful 慷慨的

生產白酒的主要原料是什麼？
What is the principal ingredient for strong clear liquors in China?

For centuries, China has been producing a wide range of strong clear liquors. The principal ingredient is gaoliang (高粱), a grain belonging to the sorghum family. China was the first country to distil liquor with sorghum. Sorghum and corn have very similar composition, but sorghum is better than corn for making liquor. Famous sorghum liquors include Maotai (茅臺) in Guizhou Province, Fenjiu (汾酒) in Shanxi and other well-known liquors in Sichuan. Maotai is used for toasting at banquets. Drinkers are advised to take Maotai in small sips, and not to drink it on an empty stomach.

> **Notes**
> sorghum 高粱；toast 舉杯為……祝酒；stomach 胃

中國古人飲酒有哪些禮節？
How did Chinese behave when drinking in ancient times?

In ancient China people often followed a formal drinking etiquette. When hosts and guests drank together, they would kneel down face to face and touch the ground with their foreheads. It was the way to respect each other. When junior and senior members drank together, the juniors would first of all kneel down and kowtow, and then they would be seated in order of their positions. The juniors couldn't drink the wine before the elders. They had to wait until the elders completed their alcohol.

Usually there are four steps in the ancient drinking etiquette:

> A host and a guest perform a courtesy gesture by kneeling down face to face.

> The host pours a bit of alcohol down to the ground in appreciation of the kindness of Earth for providing grains and foods.

> The guest sips alcohol and expresses his/her appreciation of it to the host.

> At last, both the host and guest take up their cups and drink the alcohol.

Notes

etiquette 禮儀；kneel down 跪下；courtesy 禮貌；appreciation 感謝

在宴會上飲酒有哪些禮節？
How do Chinese behave when drinking at a banquet?

At a banquet, it is not polite to drink wine or liquor by oneself. Hosts and guests usually exchange toasts and speeches. Liquor may be served for toasts. Beer and soft drinks are also available for the same purpose. At the beginning of a banquet, the host is likely to make a short speech to welcome the guests and propose a toast in their honor. At this time, the guests need only accept these gestures graciously.

Generally after two or three dishes have been served, guests will respond to the toasts. Other individuals on the host's side normally take the lead in toasting guests seated closest to them. These toasts may involve only two people or everyone at the table. When there is more than one table, the host, after his opening remarks, will often go to each additional table to toast each individual. The chief guest is expected to follow this same custom.

Towards the end of the meal, the senior guest should give a return speech of gratitude for the hospitality and propose an appropriate toast. Usually before the meal ends, the host thanks the guests for coming or offers a final toast. As a rule, toasts are necessary at banquets. If you really can't drink, you can fill your wine glass with tea instead. If you happen to be the "object" of numerous toasts, it is perfectly acceptable, moreover, to raise your glass to your lips and lick the wine lightly.

<u>Notes</u>
gesture 舉止；graciously 優雅地；additional 另外的；gratitude 感謝；
lick 舔

現在飲酒有哪些禮節？
Nowadays how do Chinese behave when drinking?

Traditionally, Chinese drink wine only when eating. It is believed that alcohol should be consumed slowly to enhance the pleasure. Drinking in China has long been associated, moreover, with establishing new friendships or personal, political or business relations. When drinking, Chinese often play drinking games. The goal is not to get drunk, but for fun. The aim is to heighten drinking atmosphere. Typically, Chinese do not frequent western-style bars, and public drunkenness rouses look of disapproval and displeasure from others.

At a friendly meal or dinner party, the host is permitted to merely sip his or her drink-or not drink at all-in order to stay sober and properly manage the party. Hosts may also choose to join their guests in drinking if they are still able to take care of the banquet's duties.

Ganbei (乾杯) is a popular toast term in China, which means "empty your glass" or "bottom up." Guests may respond to the host by calling for a ganbei toast. Women, particularly if they are not important guests of the party, are generally excused from the ganbei ritual. Of course if the host or some other party member proposes a "sip" toast, anyone in the party can still go "bottoms up." When toasted, it is especially polite to follow suit, usually during the banquet. Drinking in China expresses interest or pleasure during the dinner party, but also demonstrates prowess, particularly among males.

A common saying goes, "If you respect each other, drink up your wine; if you don't respect less, just sip (感情深，一口悶；感情淺，舔一舔)." As the host drinks first, sometimes he will turn his cup upside down to show there's no wine in his cup. After this, the guests will also finish the wine in their cups. The more the guests drink, the happier the host is, so refusing to drink is regarded as impolite unless you have a good reason such as high blood pressure, an upset stomach, etc. In this case, joining the toast with water or soft drink is acceptable. Another popular way of limiting the amount you drink is not to fill your cup or glass to the top.

Notes
enhance 增加；atmosphere 氣氛；drunkenness 酒醉；rouse 驚醒；disapproval 不贊同；sip 小口喝；bottom up 乾杯；follow suit 跟著做；prowess 非凡的能力

飲酒有哪些獨特的方式？
Are there any unique ways of alcoholic drinking?

● 勸酒　Persuade Others to Drink More

Chinese hosts always want their guests to drink more. On special occasions, like a dinner banquet or feast, they repeatedly invite their guests for toasts in a hospitable attempt to overwhelm the guests with alcoholic beverages. The more the guests drink, the happier the host is. It is not a guest's job to drink himself or herself to the point of discomfort. But if the guest drinks too little, this may also upset the host.

● 文敬　A Toast in a Gentle Way

As the beginning of a dinner party, a host makes the first toast after giving a short opening speech. Sometimes he will turn his cup upside down to show no liquor is left in the glass. While this happens, guests stand up and usually drink their liquor off. During the party, the host often leaves his seat and goes to each table to clink the glasses to each guest and then drink a toast to them.

● 回敬　Drink a Toast in Return

As a host toasts, guests will respond. Even if the host or some other participants propose a "sip" toast, everyone in the party should do a "bottom up." - Generally guests should graciously accept these gestures. Towards the end of the meal, the senior guest should give a return speech of gratitude for the hospitality and propose an appropriate toast.

● 互敬　Toasts among Guests

These toasts may involve guests at the table. Usually the one who proposes the toast will give various excuses or reasons, which sound so convincing that it is hard to reject a "bottom up." Throughout toast exchanges, participants at a table continue talking with each other.

● 代飲　A Substitute Toast Drinker

Toasts are used not only to express interest or pleasure in the event, but also sometimes to demonstrate drinking prowess. So when a host or a guest is the "object" of numerous toasts, it is acceptable to have a substitute to drink on his behalf, since sometimes joining the toast with water or a soft drink is not desirable. For example, at the wedding party, a bridesmaid and bridegroom-bestman usually serve as ideal substitutes to drink wine on behalf of the bride and bridegroom.

Notes

repeatedly 反覆地；upset 打亂，攪亂；additional 另外的；graciously 和藹地，殷勤地；gesture 手勢；appropriate 適當的；reject 拒絕；prowess 非凡的能力；acceptable 可接受的；substitute 代替；bridesmaid 伴娘；bridegroom 新郎

飲酒時會玩什麼遊戲？

What drinking games do people play?

Chinese people sometimes play drinking games with friends. The goal of the game is not to get drunk; drunkenness is the penalty for the loser.

Common drinking games include the Rock-Paper-Scissors. According to this game, the rock beats the scissor, the scissor cuts the paper, and the paper wraps up the rock. Two players throw out the signs of either object, and if both players show the same sign, they continue the game until one player loses and has to drink.

The Finger Guessing Game is also well known. Two players give a sign for a number using their right hands while shouting out a number from zero to ten. The numbers from each player's hands are added together. If the sum matches either player's announced number, he/she wins. The player who loses has to drink.

The Food Chain is yet another two-player game. Each player begins by banging chopsticks on the table. The two players then touch chopsticks and call out one of the following:stick, tiger, rooster, or worm. According to the game's rules, the stick beats the tiger, the tiger eats the rooster, the rooster eats the worm, and the worm eats through the stick. If the two players say the same item, they keep chanting the items until someone loses and has to drink.

Fajiu（罰酒）, literally meaning "drinking as a punishment," occurs when someone arrives late to a feast or banquet. The latecomer usually takes three cups of liquor as a lighthearted penalty.

Notes
penalty 懲罰；chant 反覆（單調）地唱；light-hearted 隨便的

你能告訴我幾句李白寫的飲酒詩嗎？

Would you please introduce some poems written by Li Bai on wine drinking?

Ancient Chinese men of letters might write poems or monographs after tasting liquor. The Tang Poet Li Bai（李白）is one of the greatest poets in Chinese history. It is said that he enjoyed drinking very much, and some of his poems describe the pleasure he felt before or after drinking. Below are extracts from such a poem.

For the moment, drinking wine(《將進酒》)

Happiness is to be savored to the full. The golden cup must not face the moon untouched. Heaven born, my talents will find a place; A fortune spent in gold will come back again. So roast the sheep and kill the cattle, And down three hundred cupfuls in a single breath For the moment's pleasure.Inquiring of the moon, wine cup in hand.

Notes
monograph 專題論文；literature 文學；savor 品嚐

你能告訴我幾句杜甫寫的飲酒詩嗎？

Would you please introduce some poems written by Du Fu on wine drinking?

Du Fu（杜甫）was another well-known poet of the Tang Dynasty. He frequently used his poetry to expose social injustice and voice the suffering of the people. He came to Chengdu in 759, where he lived in peace and composed over two hundred poems. Some of these are associated with wine drinking.

A Friend Visits(《客至》)

So far from town, the food is very plain. And all we have to drink is this home brew.

If you like, I'll call across the fence to my old neighbor. To enjoy with us to finish off the last few drops!

> **Notes**
> expose 揭露；injustice 非正義

你能告訴我幾句蘇東坡寫的飲酒詩嗎？
Would you please introduce some poems written by Su Dongpo on wine drinking?

Su Dongpo (蘇東坡) who is also known as Su Shi (蘇軾), was the leading poet of the Northern Song Dynasty. Some lines in his ci-poems are cited below:

How fair are the lakes and hills of the southern land, Its plains spreading out like a golden strand!How often, wine-cup in hand, have you been here? To make us linger drunk, though we appear? Written for Chen Xiang at the Scenic Hall.

(Tune:"The Beautiful Lady Yu"《虞美人》)

How long will the bright moon appear? Wine-cup in hand, I ask the sky.

(Tune:"Prelude to the Melody of Water"《水調歌頭》)

> **Notes**
> strand 海濱；prelude 前奏；melody 歌曲

你能告訴我一些名酒的情況嗎？
What are the characteristics of some famous winesor liquors?

During national commodity fairs, experts judge the quality and taste of hundreds of alcoholic beverages and give awards to those they judge to be outstanding. Below are some alcoholic beverages, which are well-known across the country.

● 茅臺酒 Maotai

Maotai Liquor has long been regarded as the No.1 liquor in China, and one of the most famous liquors in the world, along with the Scottish Whisky, French Brandy and Russian Vodka. Maotai, being distilled in the town of Maotai near the Chishui River (赤水) in Guizhou Province, is older than the town itself. It has heavy fragrance and taste. At the Panama International Exposition of 1915, it won a gold medal for its excellent quality and unique flavor. At present, the Maotai Distillery combines traditional methods with advanced scientific processes to ensure that Maotai continues to enjoy its worldwide fame and recommendation.

● 瀘州老窖特曲 Luzhou Laojiao Tequ Liquor

Tequ (特曲) Liguor is the most prestigious liquor produced in Luzhou, Sichuan Province, followed by touqu (頭曲) and erqu (二曲) liguors. The three alcoholic beverages are all made with a kind of yeast called daqu (大曲). Tequ is a home-brewed liquor that has a long tradition. The distillery was set up in the Ming Dynasty and has now lasted over 400 years. At the end of the Qing Dynasty, there were more than 300 households involved in the production of tequ. Traditionally solid-state yeast and the special longquan water (龍泉水) are used in the process. The water tastes slightly sweet, but is also a bit acidic. The liquor is commonly stored in cellars for many years before being blended into laojiao liquor. Laojiao tequ has a heavy fragrance, tastes mellow and is a bit sweet. After drinking, one feels refreshed and can enjoy a long aftertaste. In 1915, this product won a gold medal at the Panama International Exposition. At present, Luzhou Laojiao Tequ stands side by side with Maotai as an outstanding liquor.

● 五糧液 Wuliangye Liguor

This liquor is produced in Yibin, Sichuan Province. Wuliang means "five food grains." The main five grains are good-quality rice, glutinous rice, sorghum, wheat and corn, but its original name was simply Grain Liquor. As early as in the Ming Dynasty, the Grain Liquor became famous in Sichuan. In 1915, it won a gold medal at the Panama International Exposition. In 1929, the name was replaced by wuliangye. In 1988, the distillery received both the product-quality certificate from the national government and the Quality-control Prize from the National Ministry of Commerce; and in 1991, the liquor was put on the list of Top Ten Chinese Liquors.

The liquor is a translucent beverage that has heavy fragrance. It tastes mellow, sweet and refreshing. Wuliangchun（五糧醇）, wuliangchun（五糧醇）and fruit wines are other products produced by the same distillery.

● 汾酒 Fenjiu Liquor

This liquor, being one of the most famous Chinese liquors, won a gold medal at the Panama International Exhibition in 1916. The high-quality of the liquor is due in great part to the natural water of wells located at the xinghuacun（杏花

村 , the Apricot Blossom Village) in Shanxi Province, particularly from a well-known as the Thousand-year-Well where the water tastes sweet and pure. The central Shanxi Plains abound in sorghum, moreover, which guarantees a good supply of the principal ingredient. Fenjiu Liquor looks clear and tastes soft and sweet. It may contain 38%, 48% or 53% alcohol, and it has light fragrance and taste.

● 郎酒 Langjiu Liquor

This liquor is produced in Gulin County, Sichuan Province. It is unique in Sichuan that it has the same heavy fragrance and taste of Maotai. By the end of the Qing Dynasty, a local distillery in Erlang (二 郎) Town, Gulin County, produced a liquor called Huisha Langjiu Liquor (回沙郎酒) that gained considerable reputation in Sichuan and Guizhou. Erlang is only 70 km away from the birthplace of Maotai in Guizhou Pro-vince with the Chishui River (赤水) flowing between the two areas. Due to its nearness to the Maotai Distillery, Gulin uses the similar brewing-techniques. In addition its raw materials include top-quality sorghum and wheat. In 1984, at the annual National Wine Appraisal Conference, Gulin Langjiu Liquor won a gold medal and was put on the list of the Top Ten Chinese Liquors. At present, the distillery has developed a series of products to satisfy the needs of different consumers with alcoholic contents of 53%, 43%, 39%, 28%, and 25%.

● 紹興黃酒 Shaoxing Yellow Wine

This wine takes its name from its color. It is made in Shaoxing City (紹興), Zhejiang Province and is also called Shaoxing Rice Wine. As one of China's eight traditional famous wines, it is made from high-quality glutinous rice and wheat, along with the pure water from the Jianhu Lake. It is noted not only for yellow color, but also for its mellow fragrance and good taste. It is said that its production in Shaoxing has a history of about 2,500 years. At present, Shaoxing wineries there produce 250,000 tons of the Yellow Wine per year, and their products include Jiafan Wine (加飯酒), Yuanhong Wine (元紅酒), Shanniang Wine (善釀酒), Huadiao Wine (花雕酒) and Xiangxue Wine (香雪酒) as the leading producer and exporter of rice wine in China.

<u>Notes</u>
commodity 商品；candidate 候選人；whisky 威士忌酒；vodka 伏特加酒；distillery 釀酒廠；re-commendation 推薦；prestigious 有名望的；acidic 酸的；mellow 芳醇的；exposition 展覽會；glutinous 黏的；certificate 證明書；refreshing 清涼的；apricot 杏；guarantee 保證；considerable 相當大的；appraisal 評價；description 描寫；exporter 出口商

第四章
漢字與書法
Chinese Characters and Calligraphy

　　漢字是記錄漢語的文字，它對發展中華民族的優秀文化產生了重大作用。本篇介紹的內容是漢字的起源、漢字的演變、中國書法以及漢字的改革。

學習漢字難嗎？

Is it difficult to learn Chinese characters?

Chinese characters are not an alphabet as Western languages used. Each character represents a separate word, and Chinese characters indicate both the meaning and the sound for a whole word. The writing system is not a convenient device lying ready at hand for overseas learners to pick up and use. In English, there are 26 alphabetic symbols. English native speakers can make tens of thousands of words with comparative ease. In Chinese, each character must be laboriously memorized. Language learners often wonder how many characters they need to learn in order to have a reading knowledge of Chinese materials other than classic literature. Various estimates have been given, ranging from 3,000 to 5,000.

Statistics show that the majority of the 50,000-60,000 existing characters are not in common use.

> **Notes**
> alphabet 字母表；indicate 指出；symbol 象徵；comparative 比較的；
> laboriously 費力地；estimate 估計；statistics 統計

漢字的起源有哪些傳說？

Is there any legend about the origin of Chinese characters?

Chinese script has at least a history of four thousand years. We are not certain of the date of its invention. There have been various stories about the origin of the Chinese characters. In remote antiquity, ancient people made records by tying knots with a rope. Another story says that there was an ancient legendary figure whose name was Cangjie (倉頡). He worked as Emperor Huangdi's historiographer. It was said that Cangjie had four eyes, and he was good at observation. He often watched the footprints of birds and beasts as well as the appearance of stars. His long-term observation inspired him to create the earliest written characters.

Notes
script 書寫體；antiquity 古代的；historiographer 歷史家；observation 觀察

漢字起源於圖畫嗎？
Did Chinese characters come from drawings?

These legendary stories cannot be accepted as the truth. However, in ancient China, characters began as simple drawings of natural objects-trees, water, mountains, horses, and humans. The earliest characters are thus "pictographic" in quality. In Banpo Village (半坡) in Xi'an and other places, archeologists discovered symbols engraved on the unearthed potteries which date to the period of the Yangshao Culture (仰韶文化), a matriarchal culture of the early Neolithic Age. More than 4,000 years ago, ancient people in the present Tai'an (泰安) area of Shandong Province engraved symbols on pottery which belong to a late period of the Dawenkou Culture (大汶口文化). Experts believe that these pictographic symbols may be the earliest forms of Chinese written characters.

At present, philologists think that symbols engraved on the Yangshao pottery are not a written language. However, the symbols engraved on the Dawenkou pottery unearthed in the Tai'an area may be the earliest forms of Chinese written characters. In this view, Chinese characters have existed for more than 4,500 years.

> **Notes**
>
> pictographic 繪畫文字的；archeologist 考古學家；matriarchal 母系氏族的；Neolithic 新石器時代的；pottery 陶器；philologist 語言學者

甲骨文是如何被發現的？
How were ancient inscriptions on bones or tortoise shells discovered?

The ancient inscriptions on bones or tortoise shells were characters used for divination practice during the Shang and Zhou dynasties (商周時代). Up to the present time, 4,600 characters have been discovered on unearthed bones or tortoise shells. Toward the end of the Qing Dynasty, peasants in Xiaotun (小屯) in Anyang County (安陽縣), Henan Province kept finding fragments of the bones and shells of ancient animals as they ploughed their fields. They thought that they were "dragon bones" which could be used for medical treatment. Therefore, more and more peasants went into the fields and they turned up the soil, hoping that they could pick up more bones of this kind and sell them to medicinal herb stores.

Several decades later, in 1899, a man by the name of Wang Yirong (王懿榮) was sick and was about to take some Chinese herb medicine from a herb store. Wang saw some bone fragments and discerned some inscribed figures which looked very much like ancient writing. Wang was the president of a college in Beijing under the Qing government. Being well-learned scholar, Wang knew that these fragments were not "dragon bones." He went back to the store and purchased some more bones for his study. At the same time, he was informed that these bones were all from Henan. Through his careful study, Wang came to realize that the symbols engraved on the bones were script used before the Qin Dynasty. At a considerable price, he bought the whole lot of bones and shells that bore inscribed figures and designs. He named these symbols "Tortoise Shell Characters (龜版文字)." This important discovery opened up the way to the study of the Shang and Zhou dynasties in the fields of socio-politics, economics and culture.

> **Notes**
>
> inscription 銘文；divination 占卜；fragment 碎片；discern 分辨；
> socio-politics 社會政治

什麼是「六書」？
What are the Six Categories of Chinese Characters?

In ancient times, Chinese characters fell into the Six Categories. The first four categories include "pictographs (象形)," "self-explanatory characters (指事)," "complex ideograms (會意)" and "semantic-phonetic characters (形聲)." The first four categories indicate the methods of forming the characters. The final two are "associative transformations (轉注)" and "phonetic loan characters (假借)." These two categories refer to the usage of characters.

> **Notes**
>
> pictograph 象形文字；explanatory 解釋的；ideo-gram 表意文字；
> semantic 語義的；phonetic 語音的；as-sociative 組合的；trans-
> formation 轉變；loan 借出

為什麼要了解漢字？
Why do we need to understand Chinese characters?

The Chinese language is an institution, rather than a tool of society. With their unusual script, Chinese characters developed a unique culture. The acquaintance with Chinese characters will bring interest, pleasure and a lifelong reward. Learning the characters will help you open up a door through which you are able to appreciate the most enduring cultural achievements of China.

> **Notes**
> institution 制度；unique 獨一無二的；unusual 獨特的；acquaintance 了解；appreciate 欣賞；enduring 持久的

你對方言了解多少？
How much do you know about dialects in China?

China has seven major dialect groups. Each group subdivides into many dialects. The people of each province have a special dialect; the people of each city, each town, and each village have their own special dialect as well. In many countries, a person using a southern vernacular can understand a person with a northern dialect. However, two people who speak Chinese even within the same dialect group do not necessarily completely understand each other. The general situation is that one can understand perfectly people speaking the same local dialect, but intelligibility decreases as the speakers come from more and more distant regions.

Mandarin, or putonghua, is referred to as the common spoken Chinese, and it is spoken mainly in Northeast and Southwest of China. This widespread spoken Chinese is based on the Beijing dialect. Putonghua is usually considered more formal and is required when speaking to a person who does not understand local dialect.

Over 90% of Chinese people speak Mandarin, but they may very likely also speak another dialect. The local dialect is generally considered more intimate and is used among close family members and friends and in everyday conversation within the local area. Chinese speakers will frequently code switch between putonghua and local dialects. Parents generally speak to their children in dialect, and the relationship between a dialect and putonghua appears to be mostly stable. Most Chinese know that local dialects are of considerable social benefit, and when they permanently move to a new area, they will attempt to pick up the local dialect. Usually learning a new dialect is done informally through a process of immersion and recognizing sound shifts.

Notes

dialect 方言；subdivide 把……再分；necessarily 必然地；in-telligibility 可理解性；decrease 減少；in-timate 熟悉的；considerable 相當大的；permanently 永久地；immersion 沉浸；recognize 認可

中國書法的起源是什麼？
What is the origin of Chinese calligraphy?

The origin of Chinese calligraphy is not very precise. Chinese writing originated approximately 4,500 years ago. It is thought that the written language began with ancient pictures, representing exactly what they looked alike. It is thought that calligraphy came after the invention of the language. Early periods of Chinese history reveal that calligraphy was viewed as a matchless and independent visual art form rather than a mere ornamental art. The lines of the Oracle Bone Script seem thin, stiff and straight. The lines of the Bronze Script seem thick, and characters are well-rounded in form. Primitive calligraphic works were inscribed on bones or pieces of pottery by sharp tools-a sort of metal brush, or "hard" brush as the Chinese say.

Notes

calligraphy 書法；originate 發源；approximately 大概；represent 表示；matchless 無與倫比的；visual 視覺的；ornamental 裝飾的；primitive 原始的

如何欣賞中國書法？
How does a Chinese scholar appreciate Chinese calligraphy?

Calligraphy is an art dating back to the earliest days of history, and it is widely practiced throughout China to these days. Although it uses Chinese words as its tool of expression, one does not have to know Chinese to appreciate its beauty. As of all the arts in China, the fundamental inspiration of calligraphy, is from nature. The medium of all the graphic arts is line-straight and line-curved or combinations of straight and curved lines. Chinese people value calligraphy for the sake of harmonious nature of its lines or groups of lines, strokes are deliberately formed in direct imitation of a natural object, and the Chinese brush effectively reproduces the movements of clouds and trees.

Chinese calligraphy should be beautifully executed in form for its aesthetic sense. Perfect harmony between mind and hand is required for Chinese calligraphy. At the moment of writing, an artist exerts his emotional energy to vitalize the harmony and reveal great refinement.

Principles of beauty in calligraphy include asymmetrical balance, momentum, dynamic posture, simplicity, suggestiveness, imagination and universality. These aesthetic principles govern the composition of Chinese characters and reflect the basic ideals of the Chinese mind in the fine arts.

Dou Meng (竇蒙) of the Tang Dynasty (618-907) described different styles of calligraphy, and these have been regarded as criteria for the appreciation of Chinese calligraphy.

Some of criteria say as follows:

➤ A work of ability presents a thousand possibilities.

   能：千種風流曰能

➤ Mysterious work stirs the imagination.

   妙：百般滋味曰妙

➤ A carefully executed work demands both inspiration and technique.

   精：功業雙絕曰精

➤ A carefree style has no fixed direction.

   逸：縱任無方曰逸

➤ A well-balanced composition indicates serenity.

   穩：結構平正曰穩

Notes
vehicle 工具；fundamental 基礎的；inspiration 好辦法；medium 手段；graphic 繪畫的；curved 草寫的；combination 聯合；imitation 模仿；deliberately 故意地；execute 製作；aesthetics 美學

的；exert 用（力）；vitalize 給予……活力；asymmetrical 不均勻的；mo-mentum 動力；dynamic 有活力的；suggestiveness 引起聯想；imagination 想像力；com-position 構成；criteria 準則；mysterious 神祕的；serenity 平靜

筆有哪些種類？
How do we categorize brushes?

Traditionally a brush pen, an ink-stick, paper, and an ink-stone are indispensable to traditional Chinese scholars who call them the "four treasures of the study（文房四寶）."

There are several ways to categorize Chinese brushes. One category depends on the type of hairs on the head of a brush. As for an ancient-styled brush, its hairs may be the hairs of a rabbit, goat, wolf, fox, rat, horse, deer, pig, chicken or other animals. Some of those hairs are listed as hard hairs, and the others as soft hairs. Therefore, there exist a hard-hair brush（硬毫）, a soft-hair brush（軟毫）, and a brush with mixed hairs（兼毫）.

The handle of a brush is usually made of bamboo, wood, sandalwood, nanmu wood, or pear-wood. The other materials include ivory, rhinoceros horn, ox horn, jade, crystal, silver, and porcelain. Some individual calligraphists enjoy having brushes inlaid with precious materials like mother-of-pearl inlay, ivory and jade.

As for traditional Chinese painting, brushes are subdivided into landscape-painting brushes, flower-and-plant painting brushes, figure-painting brushes, ribs-of-leaves drawing brushes, clothing-line drawing brushes, color-drawing brushes, etc.

什麼是墨？
What is ink-stick?

The ink-stick is the unique pigment of Chinese traditional painting and calligraphy. Legend says that King Yi first invented the ink-stick about 2,800 years ago, yet archaeologists have detected ink marks on the back of inscribed bones or tortoise shells dating back to the Shang Dynasty. It was during the Han Dynasty that artificial ink was produced. "Yumi-mo（愉糜墨）" ink-stick was considered the most famous ink-stick at that time. It was produced at the present site of Qianyang County（千陽縣）, Shan'xi Province（陝西省）. Its raw materials consist of pine, oil and lacquer. Before the Five Dynasties, the ink-production center was located in North China. Then, it gradually moved to the South. At present, the most well-known South ink-stick is "hui-mo（徽墨），" produced in Huizhou（徽州）, Anhui Province. This ink-stick, being made of burnt pine soot, is as hard as stone and does not deteriorate during at least ten years. Generally, ink sticks fall into three major categories based on the main materials which used in ink production: ① the pine-soot ink-stick, ② the oil-soot ink stick, ③ the oil-soot and pine-soot ink-stick.

Notes

pigment 顏料；archaeologist 考古學家；in-scribe 刻；soot 煤煙，煙灰；deteriorate 變壞

什麼是安徽宣紙？
What is xuan paper in Anhui?

Paper is a Chinese invention, and it is widely accepted that paper was invented by Cai Lun (蔡倫) of the Eastern Han Dynasty. After the Eastern Jin Dynasty, paper was extensively used instead of bamboo slips and silk, and in the Tang and Song Dynasties, the paper production industry became prosperous.

During the Tang Dynasty Jing County of Anhui produced a kind of writing paper for Chinese painting and calligraphy. Jing County was under the official administration of Xuanzhou Prefecture (宣州), and its paper was usually transported to Xuanzhou before it was distributed elsewhere. Gradually people called this type of paper as xuan paper.

Xuan paper absorbs ink well and shows clearly the lines and strokes. It has great tensile strength, and it retains its quality for a long time. Artists prefer using xuan paper mainly because their paintings and calligraphy can last many years. But xuan paper is expensive, so beginners often use coarse paper for their daily calligraphy or painting practice.

There are numerous types of xuan paper. One category includes three types of xuan paper: shengxuan paper (生宣), shuxuan paper (熟宣) and semi-shuxuan paper (半熟宣).

Sheng means "unprocessed" or "unrefined." The paper of this type is made without going through any refined process. Shengxuan paper easily absorbs and seeps ink or water, so freehand landscape paintings drawn on the paper of this type clearly show rich variations and line shades of ink strokes.

Shu means "processed," or "refined." The paper of this type is made through a refined process. During the process a xuan papermaker dissolves alum in water and then brushes shengxuan paper with the alum water. Shuxuan paper is tougher than shengxuan paper, and its water or ink absorbency is weak. Due to these facts, shuxuan paper suits meticulous brushwork of traditional Chinese paintings and calligraphy.

Semi-shu means "semi-refined." It is the third type of xuan paper, and its water absorbency is somewhat between that of shengxuan paper and shuxuan paper. Landscape painters tend to use semi-shuxuan paper not only because the paper of this type exhibits the variations of ink strokes, but also has no much water or ink absorbency.

Notes

bamboo slip 竹簡；transport 運輸；absorb 吸收；tensile 可伸展的；coarse 粗的；unprocessed 未處理的；unrefined 未精煉的；variation 變化；dissolve 使溶解；alum 明礬；absorbency 吸收性；semi-refined 半精煉的

什麼是硯？
What is ink-stone?

When the ink slab was invented is rather controversial.

Archaeologists have discovered from the ruins, dating back to the primitive society, simple stone ink-slabs on which pigments were ground by a pestle (研磨器).

During the Han Dynasty, artificial ink-sticks gradually replaced pestles, and stone, pottery, lacquer or copper ink-holders came into being. Most popular were the round-shaped and three-or-four-legged ink-stones (圓形三足式、四足式石

硯). During the Wei Dynasty. porcelain ink-holders came into being. However, most ink-holders were made of stones.

Chinese ink-stones are flat and hard and are shaped into beautiful objects. Since the Tang Dynasty, ink-stones have been classified into three main categories: Duan Ink-stone from Guangdong (廣東端硯), Hongsi Ink-stone from Shandong (山東紅絲硯) and Tao Ink-stone from Gansu (甘肅洮硯).

The regular process is that calligraphist drops water on the ink-stone, and then grinds an ink-stick against it. Gradually the water becomes inky black for use in calligraphic practice.

> **Notes**
> controversial 有爭議的；archaeologist 考古學家；pigment 顏料；
> pestle 杵；inky 漆黑的；calligraphic 書法的

練習中國書法有什麼好處？
What is the benefit of practicing Chinese calligraphy?

The calligraphy practice can mould a person's temperament.

When you are in low spirits, try to write down Chinese characters for a while with a Chinese brush. Soon you will cheer up. When you are hotheaded and your emotion is too strong to break control, try to practice calligraphy. Then you will calm down.

Calligraphists enjoy a long life. The practice is a good form of physical training because it requires concentration of mind, a calm temperament and easy breathing. The practice is similar to Chinese Taijiquan (太極拳 , Shadowing Boxing). Before you start writing, you should not distract your mind by looking at or listening to any other thing. You must keep calm, and while you write, your calmness and writing should operate harmoniously in co-operation.

> **Notes**
>
> temperament 氣質；hotheaded 暴躁的；con-centration 專心；
> breathing 呼吸；distract 使分心

什麼是中國篆刻？
What is Chinese seal engraving?

Chinese seal engraving, a combination of calligraphy and engraving, has a history of over 2,000 years. Most of the earliest ancient seals can be traced back to the Warring States Period. At that time the ancient seal, either official or private, was called the "xi (璽)" in Chinese. The script on the seal obverse was cut in relief or in intaglio.

After the Qin emperor unified the country, xi was referred only to the "imperial seal." Another Chinese character, "yin (印)" emerged as a general term for the seals used by ministers, lower ranking officials, or individuals in non-governmental circles. The style of engraved seal characters was similar to the one of the Small Seal Script (小篆) adopted during the Qin Dynasty.

During the Han Dynasty, the xi continued to be referred to royal seals, and yin to other types of seals. Later, some other terms were used. For example, "zhang (章)" was referred to seals used by military generals, and "yinxin (印信)" to personal seals. In the Western Han Dynasty, seals were usually cast, but during the Eastern Han Dynasty, people chiseled seals instead.

From the Warring State Period to the Northern and Southern Dynasties, the main materials for seal engraving were jade, gold, elephant tooth, and animal horns. This period was considered to be "the Period of Ancient Seal Engraving Art." The Qin Seal (秦印) prevailed from the late Warring States Period to the early years of the Western Han Dynasty, and its seal characters were named the Qin Seal Script (秦篆). The Han Official Seal (漢官印) was referred to a type of seal used from the Han Dynasty to the Northern and Southern Dynasties. Its engraved characters were neat and tidy, the style of the characters was dynamic, and the structure was upright or square.

From the Sui to the Yuan Dynasties, calligraphy and paintings came to assume the highest ranks as classical arts among the many arts of China. Artists, scholars and connoisseurs tended to stamp seals somewhere on a piece of calligraphy or painting for their own enjoyment and connoisseurship. Accordingly, the shoucang seal (收藏印 , the connoisseurship seal), the zhaiguan seal (齋館印 , the refined seal inscribed with the names of scholars'study or living rooms), and the xianwen seal (閒文印 , a type of seal inscribed with either poetry, prose, an idiom or a famous remark that contains the person's personal philosophy or literary inclination) was increasingly fashionable as a form of aesthetic composition. Meanwhile, during the Yuan Dynasty when the Mongols ruled ancient China, the Yuan seal featured both Chinese and Mongolian characters.

The art of seal engraving developed substantially during the Ming Dynasty. By the mid-Ming, it had become a unique seal-engraving art. Wen Peng (文彭 , 1478-1573) of the Ming was the most celebrated seal engraver, and engravers over the following generations held him up as the founder of artistic seal engraving. On the basis of the achievements of the Ming Dynasty, the art of seal engraving continued to advance during the Qing Dynasty and in modern times.

The feature of engraved characters is a combination of the Large Seal Script (大篆) and the Small Seal Script (小篆). In addition, the combination has been added with other script patterns like inscriptions engraved on bones or tortoise shells, and inscriptions cast on sacrificial vessels, bronze mirrors, and ancient coins.

Chong (沖) is a traditional technique used by a Chinese engraver to engrave characters. Chong means "engrave something with a forward thrust or cut forcibly as if by a bunch." In the Qing Dynasty some new styles began to evolve among the chong technique. One of the techniques was called sedao-engraving (澀刀). Exactly what sedao means has been difficult to determine, but it shows that the engraved strokes of sedao-style may not have flowed smoothly, but have some "broken lines (殘破)."

Notes

relief 浮雕；intaglio 凹雕；cast 鑄造；chisel 鑿；prevail 流行；
dynamic 充滿活力的；connoisseur 鑑賞家；connoisseurship 鑑賞，
鑒定力；inclination 愛好；substantially 實質上地；thrust 強行推入；
forcibly 強有力地

第五章
中國繪畫
Chinese Painting

　　中國畫簡稱「國畫」，是中國各族人民共同創造的傳統繪畫。中國畫屬於東方繪畫體系，有鮮明的中華民族特色。本篇介紹的內容是源遠流長的中國畫及其藝術特點。

中國畫起源於何時？

What is the origin of traditional Chinese painting?

When did Chinese painting start? Who started Chinese painting? It is hard to trace it back to its roots. For thousands of years, this issue has puzzled historians and scholars in the field of the history of Chinese arts. Many historians think that Chinese character writing and painting have the same origin. In ancient China, characters began as simple drawings of natural objects-trees, water, mountains, horses and human beings. They were engraved on pottery, bones, bronzes or mountain rocks. Some pottery vessels were painted with decorative patterns or human faces, animals and plants. Experts believe that these pictographic symbols may be the earliest forms of Chinese written characters. According to this view, these symbols constituted primitive Chinese painting and date from the Neolithic Period, around 6,000 to 7,000 years old ago.

Records of Famous Paintings of Dynasties (《歷代名畫記》) by Zhang Yanyuan (張彥遠) of the Tang Dynasty said that Chinese painting originated in the legendary period and that pictographic symbols unified painting and character writing. In his view, only when pictographic symbols and character-writing split, did Chinese painting start to become an independent art.

Notes
puzzle 使迷惑；historian 歷史學家

你如何理解傳統中國畫藝術？

How can you understand the art of traditional Chinese painting?

Chinese painting is a pure art. It is lyrical enough to stand on an equal footing with poetry and contemplative thought. It has incomparable refinements of design and reveals subtle insights into nature and human beings. Painting in the traditional style involves essentially the same techniques as calligraphy. It is done with a brush dipped in black or colored ink; oils are not used. The line drawn by a brush has remained the core medium of Chinese painting throughout its history. Painters give ever-greater emphasis to the brush-line itself, taking it as their primary descriptive and expressive means.

In dynastic times, painting and calligraphy were the most highly appreciated arts in court circles and were produced almost exclusively by amateurs-aristocrats and scholar-officials who alone had the sensibility and leisure to perfect the technique necessary for great brushwork. A piece of painting normally consists of the painting itself, calligraphic writing and seal stamps. As with calligraphy, paintings by famous painters have been greatly valued throughout China's history. They are mounted on scrolls which can be hung or rolled up, but some are done in albums or on walls, lacquerwork, and other media.

Notes

lyrical 抒情詩般的；contemplative 沉思的；in-comparable 無可匹敵的；refinement 優雅；essentially 實質上；expressive 有表現力的；album 相簿；media 媒介物

你能夠簡單介紹一下中國傳統繪畫的歷史嗎？

Can you give a brief introduction of the history oftraditional Chinese painting?

Chinese painting originated in the remote period, dating back to 6,000 to 7,000 years ago. At the primitive stage, from the Shang and Zhou dynasties to the Spring and Autumn Period and the Warring States Period, paintings decorated bronze ritual vessels and other bronze wares; and the concept of "beauty" was first applied, not to art, but to ancestral sacrifices.

Paintings on silk first appeared during the Warring States Period. But after the invention of paper in the 1st century A. D., silk was gradually replaced by this new, cheaper material.

Wall painting developed during the Qin and Han dynasties. Apart from wall paintings in palaces and temples, there were a great number of Chinese murals in the tombs of that period. During the Three Kingdoms Period, the main subject of painting was Buddhist figures and paintings executed according to Daoist concepts.

Beginning in the Tang Dynasty, the landscape painting came to the fore. The purpose was not to reproduce exactly the appearance of nature, but to grasp an emotion or atmosphere in such a way as to catch the "rhythm" of nature. In the Song Dynasty, landscapes of more subtle expression appeared. Emphasis was placed on the spiritual qualities of the painting and on the ability of the artist to reveal the inner harmony between human and nature.

The Yuan Dynasty is known for its outstanding ink-wash paintings. During the Ming and Qing dynasties, painting developed along two distinct lines. One, represented by Wang Shimin（王時敏）and Wang Jian（王鑒）, faithfully followed old masters. The other, represented by Zhu Da (朱耷) and the Yangzhou School (揚州畫派), emphasized the expression of personal feeling. The latter's unique endeavors and appealing taste have been accepted by famous modern artists like Qi Baishi (齊白石), Xu Beihong (徐悲鴻) and Pan Tianshou (潘天壽).

<u>Notes</u>
ancestral 祖先的；landscape 風景；fore 前部；atmosphere 氣氛；ink-wash 水墨的

什麼是「文人畫師」？
What are literati painters?

Literati painters were amateurs. They painted as a means of self-expression, much as the same way they wrote poetry; both forms were the inheritance of the Neo-Daoism era of the Six Dynasties. Many fewer literati were accomplished painters than poets; but there were always many literati who painted on the side, while serving as scholar-officials.

Literati painting was conceived as mode through which the Confucian junzi (君子 , noble person) expressed his ethical personality. It manifests concern little for technical showiness. Literati painters specialize in plain ink paintings, sometimes with minimal color. They emphasize the idea that the style with which a painter controls his brush conveys the inner style of his character. Brushstroke is seen as an expression of the spirit more than matters of composition or skill in realistic depiction.

While literati poetry developed fully during the Tang Dynasty, painting did not become central to literati until later. During the late Song, literati and academic painting become two distinct streams. Interestingly enough, however, although academic paintings were often far more skilled in technique, many felt and still feel that the "amateur" ink paintings of the literati are the highest form of art in China.

Notes
inheritance 繼承；distinct 明顯的

什麼是「院畫畫師」？
What are academic painters?

Academic painters were highly skilled craftsmen. Many were educated to some degree. They used colors for realistic or highly conventional representations of people or things and they focused on spectacular, sometimes applying gold leaf, or other techniques. Their whole effort was aimed at achieving marvelous effects. The imperial court employed some men painters, and other academic painters made their way in the world by selling their paintings to wealthy patrons and customers. They were professionals, both in their virtuoso skill and in their dependence on permanent employment as painters and on selling their paintings to live.

After many centuries, academic painting came to focus on human and animal figures as the most developed forms of visual art in ancient China. However, landscape painting entered a period of sudden development during the Tang and early Song dynasties; and academic painting took a new and different turn during the latter part of the Song Dynasty. Professional painters then began increasingly to explore smaller and more intimate forms of painting, even when depicting broad landscapes. In reducing the scale of their paintings, they also developed innovative ways, using abbreviated lines and ink washes to represent landscape features which the Northern Song masters had rendered with intense detail. Although academic painters achieved simplicity with the use of their fertile imagination and great effort, the skills they employed were more accessible to literati, who were, after all, masters of calligraphic brushwork.

Notes
realistic 現實的；conventional 習慣的；re-presentation 代表；
virtuoso 精湛的；marvelous 令人驚嘆的；permanent 永恆的；
innovative 創新的；accessible 可（或易）接近的

書法對繪畫有什麼影響？
What is the influence of calligraphy on painting?

Chinese calligraphy was a separate art form in ancient China, and it exerted great influence on literati painting. Beginning with the period of the Six Dynasties (222-589), expressing oneself through distinctive written characters constituted an important characteristic of being a well-bred member of the elite. A number of men became famous for their fine calligraphy, and examples of their styles were preserved through carvings, which traced their brushstroke in stone. Over time, men of literary learning tried to master one or more of these classical styles and improve their unique individuality on them. This medium of handwriting became an important way of expressing one's nature and reading the character of others.

Notes
exert 發揮；individuality 個性

元朝文人畫有什麼特點？
What are the features of the literati painting of the Yuan Dynasty?

In 1279, the Yuan Dynasty unified China under Mongol rule. Chinese literati ultimately learned how to live with Mongol rule, and many members of the educated class cooperated in continuing the management of government along the Confucian lines of the traditional imperial state. Nonetheless, many members of the elite did not want to involve themselves with the ruling Mongols and they sought ways to avoid service. A certain number of these men devoted themselves to painting and established a tradition of literati visual art. The Yuan literati applied their control of brushwork to the development of a new perspective on what art could achieve. The efforts at making things look realistic completely vanishes. Mountains, trees, and grass are depicted with extreme simplicity, not care for relative size; the sky is covered with writing. The interest has shifted from the landscape to the painter, and painting became an act of reinterpreting nature, which is simply the focus for the painters'self-expression.

This has amounted to a fundamental shift, and it is central to literati painting. Actually Chinese landscape becomes art not devoted to Nature itself. It is devoted to man's response to Nature. Now it clearly becomes a means for expressing the artist's unique self and perspective, reflecting one's moral self-cultivation and stance towards society.

In addition, the use of name stamp became established at this time. The addition of stamped name impressions, in itself an art, further enriched the artistic content of Chinese painting.

你對明代繪畫知道多少？

What is known about the painting of the Ming Dynasty?

During the Ming Dynasty, literati paintings were prized above academic paintings by most educated people who understood the goal of revealing the inner character of the painter and depicting of nature, man, or various objects in such way as to communicating a sense of virtue, strength of purpose, or sensitivity towards the conditions of human life.

The most notable center for painting in the Later Middle Ming was Suzhou, where the Wu School (吳門畫派) flourished (1460-1560). Designations like "Wu School" are Chinese classifications based on the artist's residence, style or social status. One of the most famous of all literati painters was Shen Zhou (沈 周 , 1427-1509) who stood at the beginning of the wu tradition. Although deeply influenced by the Yuan painting, he gradually developed a style of his own that conveyed genial warmth and a sense of ease and naturalness. Wen Zhengming (文 徵 明 , 1470-1559) studied painting under Shen Zhou. He painted in many different styles during his long and productive life, and some of his paintings are influenced by painting styles which trace back to the Tang painting. The paintings of these two masters became so important that they chose to focus their entire lives on the mastery of their art, rather than pursue government careers. In the increasingly urban and educated society of the Ming, these artists actually made considerable income from their work, either in the form of cash "gifts" or of

117

other goods "traded" for their art.

Literati circles at the highest levels often included groups of close friends and painters. Often literati painters would present paintings to friends with an invitation to write poetry and short essays on them. In this way, paintings sometimes seem to become more group expressions than mere individual expressions of the painter, capturing an essential Confucian element of society.

Notes

designation 稱號；classification 分類

清朝繪畫有什麼特點？
What are the features of the painting of the Qing Dynasty?

Three principal groups of artists were working during the Qing Dynasty. The first was that of the traditionalists, orthodox painters who sought to revitalize painting through the creative reinterpretation of past models. Outstanding among these were four artists all named Wang (Wang Shimin, 王時敏; Wang Jian, 王鑒; Wang Hui, 王翬 and Wang Yuanqi, 王原祁). Wang Shimin and his friend Wang Jian (1598-1677) were the senior members of this school, but they were outshone by their brilliant pupils-Wang Hui (1632-1717) and Wang Yuanqi (1642-1715).

The second group was that of the individualists, who practiced a deeply personal form of art. The most original work was done by men who refused to serve the new Qing Dynasty. One group of Ming loyalists lived in Anhui Province. These artists emulated Ni Zan (倪瓚 , 1306-1374) for his minimalist compositions and "dry-brush" painting style features that became hallmarks of the so-called Anhui School (新安派). The other main group was the Nanjing Masters (金陵八家), which included Gong Xian (龔賢 , 1618-1689), Fan Qi (樊圻 , 1616- ？), and Ye Xin (葉欣 , 1640-1673).

The third group was that of the courtiers, officials and the professional artists who served at the Qing court. Two of the most outstanding artists of the early Qing period were descendants of the Ming royal house： Zhu Da (朱耷 , 1626-1705) and Zhu Ruoji (朱若極 , 1641- 約 1718), both of whom became better known by their assumed names-Bada Shanren (八大山人) and Shi Tao (石濤). Yangzhou's mercantile elite supported a diverse array of artists who worked in two distinct pictorial traditions. One group of artists, later known as the "Eight Eccentrics of Yangzhou (揚州八怪)," drew inspirations from the highly individualistic works of Shi Tao.

Notes

traditionist 傳統主義者；revitalize 使恢復生氣；emulate 模仿；
minimalist 極簡抽象派藝術家；hall-mark 標誌 descendant 子孫；
eccentric 古怪的人；in-dividualistic 個人主義（者）的

如何分類中國繪畫？
How can we classify traditional Chinese painting?

Chinese brush painting can be classified into three main categories: landscape painting, bird and flower painting, and figure painting. Each classification can be further divided according to painting techniques as follows:

● Landscape painting

> Boneless landscape. Instead of drawing out the outlines, colors are directly applied to creating the form.

> Monochrome ink landscape.

> Light umber landscape. Umber and other light shades of colors are added to a landscape done primarily in ink.

> Detailed with color. Outlines are carefully drawn to create precisely the forms; then rich colors are applied layer by layer. Gold may be added for outlining.

● Figure painting

> Detailed with color.

> Outlining.

> Freestyle sketch, or expressionistic drawing. Personal expression is valued in this kind of painting. Whether or not one creates precise forms is not important.

> Wash. Light shades of colors are applied to a painting outlined in ink.

● Bird and flower painting

> Detailed with color.

> Outlining. After outlines are drawn in ink, light ink washes are added sparingly for highlighting.

> Freestyle sketch.

> Boneless method.

➤ Flower-outline and leaf-wash style. Flowers (or a part of the painting) are outlined and filled with colors, while leaves are dotted or dabbed with washes.

什麼是中國傳統繪畫的技法？
What are features of the techniques of the traditional Chinese painting?

The techniques of traditional Chinese painting are divided into meticulous style（工筆）and freehand style（寫意）. The former requires great care, grace, strict composition and fine elaboration. The effect is highly decorative. The latter style generalizes shapes and displays rich brushwork and ink technique.

In traditional Chinese painting, lines play a decisive role in the formation of images; and variations in lines are determined, in the main, by the method of using brushes. Ink occupies an exceedingly important position in traditional Chinese painting, with black being the main color. The use of ink involves processes such as showing the shades and texture of rocks and mountains by light ink strokes and applying dots and coloring.

Images are primary. Brushwork and ink depict images; colors only enrich them. What gives ink-and-wash paintings their unique appeal is their use of darkness or light, density or dilution to present the light and color of various objects. Special effect is formed through the interaction of water, ink and xuan paper. Even a painting executed a long, long time ago still looks fresh and full of vitality today.

Traditional painting stresses the intrinsic colors of the object, varying the shades on the basis of the intrinsic colors. Its effect grows out of the content and is subordinate to the requirements of the theme. It can exaggerate to the fullest extent and boldly change the intrinsic colors of the object to bring out the theme and express the artist's ideas or achieve an ideal artistic effect. Color is mostly used after finishing the basic modeling with brushwork and ink. It involves variations of brightness of the intrinsic colors; contrasting harmonious relations among various intrinsic colors; and the coordination of brushwork and ink techniques.

Notes
meticulous 小心翼翼的；generalize 歸納；ex-ceedingly 非常地；
dilution 稀釋；intrinsic 本身的

中國傳統繪畫和西方繪畫的不同點有哪些？
What are the differences between traditional Chinese painting and Western painting?

In the West, the human form has been the point of central interest throughout most of history, from the sculpture of the Greeks through Medieval and Renaissance paintings of the Holy Family and the 17th and 18th century portraiture in the French and English schools. Landscape as a major theme emerged comparatively late, in association with the Romantic Movement. In China it was otherwise. Landscape painting came to assume the highest place as the classical art par excellence. Although man was the main focus of philosophy, artists in ancient China from the eighth century or earlier found their inspiration in nature; and landscape painting was the most satisfying way to represent nature as a whole, feel a sense of communion with nature, and know oneself as a part of an orderly cosmos.

The other important difference is related to the viewpoint and perspective of the painter in Western and Chinese art. The eye of the Western artist takes in the scene from the level of an average-sized man, five or six feet above the ground. The Chinese artist works from a raised viewpoint, on a hillside opposite the scene. He has no fixed viewpoint, and that his gaze can rove at will, both horizontally and vertically.

Classic Western art works are executed in oil on canvas, whereas Chinese paintings are done by means of water-soluble ink on silk or highly absorbent paper. When oil paints are employed, it is possible to paint out a portion of the canvas and redo it in a new version, but with ink and watercolors, the stroke once drawn is beyond recall and can not be altered.

Notes
medieval 中世紀的；comparatively 比較地；com-munion 融洽關係；absorbent 能吸收（水、光等）的；rove 徘徊；canvas 油畫布

如何保存字畫？
How do we preserve the calligraphy and paintings?

Environmental pollution causes damage to calligraphy and paintings. In cities, the air has high acid and alkali elements due to car exhaust and industrial pollution. These harmful elements and dust usually deposit onto the paper on which calligraphy and paintings are executed. If these things remain on the paper for a considerable period of time, they will erode calligraphy or paintings. Following are some necessary points that help you preserve your calligraphy and paintings.

➤ It is better to clean paper-based calligraphy and paintings once a month. If you use a hairdryer for this effort, first of all, hold the hairdryer 10 to 15cm away from the paper and let the end of the hairdryer face the paper at an angle of 30 degrees. Sweep the paper with a soft brush while the hairdryer works, blowing out natural wind towards the paper. A chicken feather duster is also available to gently brush off the dust. Don't use a piece of rag for the cleaning.

➤ Hang calligraphy and paintings twice a year,each time lasting no more than two months. Then store these artworks for the rest of the time.

➤ Store these artworks in places, which are fireproof, bookworm-resistant and moisture-proof. Mothballs or camphor balls are commonly used for protection against bookworms. The wooden case, made of camphorwood, is an excellent choice for the storage of calligraphy and paintings because camphorwood itself has a mothproof attribute and fine air-tightness.

➤ Place all the artworks to be suspended inside the case, with a desiccant agent, mothballs or camphor balls below no matter what kind of box or case is used for storage.

➤ The suitable temperature for storage is between $14^{\circ}C$ and $18^{\circ}C$; the suitable humidity is between 50% and 60%. Avoid high temperature, high humidity and heavy pressure.

Notes
pollution 汙染；alkali 鹼的；exhaust 排出的氣；hairdryer 吹風機；fireproof 防火的，耐火的；bookworm 蛀書蟲；moisture-proof 防

潮氣；camphorwood 樟腦木；mothproof 防蛀的；air-tightness 密封；suspend 懸掛；desiccant agent 乾燥劑；mothball 樟腦丸；hu-midity 溼氣，溼度

第六章
中國傳統棋牌
Traditional Chinese Chess Games

博弈是東方文化生活的重要組成部分，它不但不同於一般的消遣遊戲，而且還影響和陶冶著人們的道德觀念、行為準則、審美趣味和思維方式。本篇介紹圍棋、中國象棋、麻將的起源及其主要特點。

人們一般如何看待棋盤遊戲？
What do you think of the board game?

For thousands of years, people have been planning attacks, captures, chases, and conquests in a variety of different board games. Most such games commonly involve hunts or war tactics, races or chases, capturing or blockading a fortress. There are folk entertainments that have evolved through the centuries, and they exhibit endless local variations. These games have the fascinating similarities and differences that give each game its unique appeal as vital to a culture as music, dance and tale telling. Like other forms of entertainment, they do not singly give pleasure, they positively influence people's morality, behavior and the way of thinking. New board games are invented almost daily and continue to attract new devotees and reveal new possibilities.

In China, board games have been long played in peoples' recreational life. Along with zither playing, calligraphy and painting, board games constitute one of the four major forms of traditional Chinese art. In link with the Chinese tradition of rational culture, board games combine military strategies with philosophy, poetry and arts. They nurture wisdom, grace, generosity and a sense of indifference to the fame of winning or loss. Traditional games like weiqi (圍棋 , I-GO) and xiangqi (象 棋 , Chinese chess) give rise to careful thought and enlightenment that expand infinitely.

> **Notes**
> capture 占 領；chase 追 逐；conquest 征 服；blockade 封 鎖；
> variation 變化；fascinating 極美的；similarity 相似之處；devotee

什麼是圍棋？
What is weiqi?

Weiqi（圍棋）is the Chinese name for the classic board game usually known in English as Go (from the Japanese go). It has never been as popular in terms of mass support as xiangqi (Chinese Chess), but in recent years professional players have emerged in China to challenge the top Japanese masters, and from 1970 onwards public interest in weiqi has grown in China.

A full-size weiqi board has a grid of 19 horizontal and 19 vertical lines. The lines are thin and black, and the grid contains 361 intersections. 180 white round pieces and the other 181 black pieces are used. These are called "stone pieces." The basic rules are charmingly simple and easy to learn. Two players use their respective stone pieces to compete for territory on the surface of the board, in turn placing their pieces on the grid intersections. These pieces are not moved, but they may be captured, singly or in groups, by a player when he surrounds them. The winner is the player holding more of the board at the end of the game, which comes when both players agree that it is over.

Notes
emerge 出現；grid 格子；intersection 交點；charmingly 令人高興地；respective 分別的；territory 領土

你對圍棋的歷史知道多少？
What is the history of weiqi?

It is generally thought that the weiqi's equipment (black and white stones) is in existence for purposes of divination before the game rules were hit upon, and that some forms of the game have been around for 4,000 years. Accounts of weiqi quote a legend saying that a man named Yao (堯) invented weiqi in order to instruct his son Dan Zhu (丹朱). Between the Spring and Autumn Period and the Warring States Period, weiqi developed rapidly. Later, in the Han Dynasty both 17×17 and 19×19 boards co-existed. In the Three Kingdoms Period, it seems that weiqi experienced one of its times of peak interest. Between the Jin Dynasty and the South and North Period, the present full-size weiqi board began to be formalized. During the South Period, weiqi-ranking sets began to be used. Players who were competent were ranked, from one to nine, the highest rank. Weiqi was thought to illustrate the classical military theory of Sun Zi (孫子) and subsequent military strategists, and during the Tang Dynasty, weiqi experienced another time of peak interest. At that time, it was regarded by literati as one of their important intellectual pursuits. During the later Song Dynasty, weiqi began to lose its linkage with military thought and came to be regarded simply as a skilled competitive game. Along with full-time professional weiqi players, many of literati enjoyed playing it. Moving forward to 16th and 17th centuries, we find a large amount of materials concerning game strategies that show that weiqi was played at a level of proficiency beyond today's amateurs.

Weiqi was taken to Japan before the year 1000, and it was cultivated at court and in certain Buddhist sects. In the 1950s, a professional weiqi system was established in Korea, when weiqi master Cho Nam-chul returned from professional training in Japan. Today weiqi is more popular in Korea than anywhere else in the world. It is estimated that from five to ten percent of the population regularly plays it.

> **Notes**
>
> equipment 設備;co-exist 共存;formalize 使正式;competent 有能力的;linkage 聯繫;literati 文人;competitive 競爭的;proficiency 精通;amateur 業餘

圍棋的基本規則是什麼？
What are the basic rules of weiqi?

The essential rules of weiqi are as follows:

➤ Two players take turns placing black and white stones on the board's points of the line intersections. Black moves first in an even game. In a handicap game, black (the weaker player) has a number of stones on the board, and white starts the game.

➤ The object of the game is to surround and control more points or territory than your opponent.

➤ Tactical rules:

· A single stone may be placed on almost any empty intersection. Stones can't be moved after being placed, but they may be captured and removed from the board by the opponent.

· A group of stones consists of stones connected via straight lines but not diagonals.

· When one places a stone on an empty board, it usually has four empty spaces surrounding it. Stones on the edge have three, and those at the corners have two. These are called liberties.

· The number of liberties in a grouping is constituted by the total number of empty spaces connected to any stone in the group.

· If a stone of the opposite color is placed on the last liberty of a stone or group, that stone or group is captured and removed from board.

· Stones may not be placed on points where there is no liberty, unless placing a stone there would capture one or more stones, thus creating a liberty.

· An "eye" is a blank space (or a group of blank spaces) inside a group of stones. An opponent cannot place a stone within a single-spaced eye unless it is the final liberty of a group. In this case he kills the group. A group that has two separate eyes or more is impossible to kill.

· The game is over when both players pass, having no more profitable moves to make.

· All "dead" stones (stones not part of "living" groups) are then removed.

· Scoring: Each player's score is calculated by the number of points under the color's control. Captured stones are placed within the territory of the player who lost them, thus reducing his territory. "Dames" are neutral points, or points between boundary lines that belong to neither player. They are not counted.

The winner is the player with the higher score.

There are a small number of subtle variations for these rules. These variations affect scoring, but do not much change the character of the game.

什麼是象棋？
What is xiangqi?

Xiangqi is the classic Chinese popular board game, usually known as Chinese Chess or Elephant Chess. It is played on a board nine lines in width by ten lines in length. The pieces, marked with an identifying character, are placed on the points of line intersections as in weiqi. There are two opposing sides- red, which moves first, and black. The central row of squares is called the "river." Each side has a palace that is three lines by three lines in the center of that side against the back edge of the board. Each side has 16 pieces, red or black. Each side has one general (將 / 帥), two guards (士 / 仕), two ministers or elephants (象 / 相), two horses (馬), two chariots (車), two cannons (炮) and five soldiers (卒 / 兵). The battle may take place simultaneously all over the board, and give-and-take between offensive and defensive play are more obvious in xiangqi, thus having more of a general mass appeal.

你對象棋的歷史知道多少？
What is the history of xiangqi?

Xiangqi is evolved from an ancient Chinese game called liubo (六 博), which was invented some 3,500 years ago. It is said that it was invented by King Zhou of the Zhou Dynasty. In early times, xiangqi was also called "xiangxi" (象 戲 , the Elephant Games). There are two possible reasons. First of all, the game pieces of general and soldiers in liubo were made of ivory and so called xiangqi, xiang meaning "elephant." Secondly, Chinese were known to incorporate elephants in military battles. The legendary Huang Di of 4,000 years ago allegedly had a fleet of elephants in his army, and it is recorded that elephants were used in combats during the Han Dynasty.

During the Northern and Southern Dynasties, a king called Wudi (武帝) of the Northern Zhou State was good at xiangqi, and he wrote a book entitled Way to Play Elephant Game (《象經》). During the Tang Dynasty, xiangqi evolved into a game of generals, horses, chariots and soldiers that was more complicated than previous games. In the Song Dynasty, xiangqi developed rapidly, and the modern game began to take shape. New pieces, such as the cannons, the guards and the elephants were added. Between the Ming and Qing dynasties, the red and black sides each had its own typical pieces, marked with identifying characteristics. For example, one side had the general, and the other side the king; one side had the elephant, and the other side the minister.

Notes
combat 戰鬥 ; complicated 複雜的 ; previous 以前的

象棋的基本規則是什麼？
What are the basic rules of xiangqi?

Like international chess, Chinese chess is easy to learn, but difficult to play. The basic movements are as follows:

- ➤ 老將守深宮：The general only moves one point horizontally or vertically. It cannot move diagonally, and it cannot leave the palace. The king and the general cannot face each other on an open file.
- ➤ 斜士保駕鑾：A guard moves one point diagonally. It has one restriction in that it cannot leave the palace. This means that there are only five points which it can occupy.
- ➤ 象走田：An elephant moves two points diagonally. It may not leap over occupied points. Moreover, elephants are confined to their home side of the river. Due to these limitations, the elephant can see only seven points on the board. The symbols on red and black elephants differ, but their moves are the same.
- ➤ 車行一線：The chariot moves in a straight line, forward, backward, or sideways.
- ➤ 馬走日：A horse moves one point at a right angle with its original position and the one point outward-diagonally. It may not leap over occupied points. That is, if the first point of a move is blocked by a piece, then the horse may not move in that direction.
- ➤ 隔子飛炮：A cannon moves like the chariot. It captures an opponent piece by jumping over one piece. But it may never jump over more than one piece in a given move.
- ➤ 兵卒步步直向前：The soldier can move only one point forward at a time.

Once a soldier crosses the river, it acquires the power to move sideways, but it can never move backwards. When it reaches the opposing back rank, moreover, it can only move sideways.

> **Notes**
> angle 角度；limitation 限制；cannon 炮；opposing 對面的；file 縱列

什麼是麻將？
What is the majiang?

Majiang is a social game of Chinese origin that enjoys worldwide popularity. The English name is simply the transliteration of the Chinese name. It is played with four players. Majiang game pieces (tiles) and scoring rules used in China have slight regional variations.

Tiles maybe are made of bamboo, wood, ivory, bone, or a kind of plastic used in domino games. The game itself bears resemblance to Rummy, a Western card game, but it is much more sophisticated and versatile. It allows for diverse strategies and demands greater concentration. It provides constant new challenges and maintains players'interest even after countless hours of play. Majiang can be played as a social game between friends or in a competitive tournament. It is easy to learn, but impossible to master it completely.

> **Notes**
> transliteration 音譯；plastic 塑料製品；domino 西洋骨牌；Rummy 一種紙牌戲；versatile 多用途的；diverse 不同的；countless 數不盡的；competitive 競爭的；tournament 錦標賽

如何辨別麻將的牌名？

What do majiang pieces consist of?

A majiang set is usually composed of 144 pieces which consist of small rectangular tiles or blocks faced with various characters and designs. There are 108 suit tiles, which are marked with circles, characters or bamboo; 28 honor tiles, which are marked with winds and dragons and 8 flower or seasonal tiles as follows:

➤ The 108 suit tiles are made up of three suits numbered one through nine, with circles, characters or bamboos (條子、餅子、萬子), four of each number.

➤ The 16 suit tiles are marked with four winds-east, south, west, north (東風、西風、南風、北風), four for each wind.

➤ The 12 suit tiles are marked with three dragons-white, green, red (白板、發財 / 綠發、紅中), four for each dragon.

➤ The eight flower or seasonal tiles are marked with four flowers-spring, summer, autumn and winter or plum blossom, orchid, chrysanthemum and bamboo (春夏秋冬或梅蘭菊竹), two for each flower or season.

> ### Notes
> rectangular 長方形的；suit 組；orchid 蘭花；chrysanthemum 菊

你對麻將的歷史知道多少？
What is the history of majiang?

The early evolution of majiang is lost to us. The only certain thing that can be said is that it developed from an old Ming-Dynasty domino-type game called madiao (馬吊牌) which employed 40 cards numbered one to nine plus four flower cards. Tiles replaced cards because the cards tended to get blown away when playing at windy places. During the Qing Dynasty, various different tiles came to be used, and the game was played with 108 pieces. At some later date, as many as 160 tiles were used to play a variant of the game, but the number was subsequently reduced to make the game more playable. Majiang in its modern form is, in all probability, no more than 150 years old. In the 1920s, the game was introduced to the Western world.

But when it is played in other parts of the world, the rules may differ greatly. Thus players, previously unknown to each other, meet a lengthy discussion of the rules to be used is almost inevitable. The rule variations can be categorized in three major groups: Chinese, Japanese and American, each consisting of matching tiles according to different layouts.

Notes
subsequently 其後；playable 可玩的；pro-bability 可能性；
lengthy 冗長的；inevitable 不可避免的

第七章
中國武術
Chinese Martial Arts

　　武術是打拳和使用兵器的技術。武術是中國傳統體育項目之一。本篇介紹的是武術的起源與發展、武術的種類以及中國武術的奧妙。

什麼是中國武術？
What are Chinese martial arts?

Wushu literally means "martial methods" and was historically called "wuyi (武藝)" or "martial arts." Throughout human history, wushu have been created and developed for self-defense and survival. Chinese wushu training aims to improve peoples physical ability, health and willpower. It gives individual excellent exercises, an exciting competitive sport, and a basis for self-defense and sparring.

In the West, Chinese martial arts are usually referred to as "gongfu (功夫)." However, the term does not specifically mean "Chinese martial arts." Rather, gongfu is a philosophy applied to any time-honored pursuit of excellence. It can refer to any endeavor in which a person, over time, refines his or her skills and art through diligent practice as a cook, photographer, artist, and so on. In short, gongfu literally means "hard work," or "learned skill" through painstaking effort. At present, however, gongfu commonly indicates the enormous variety of martial arts native to China. It is widely thought that there are currently more than 1,000 distinct styles of wushu in China.

Notes
self-defense 自衛；willpower 意志力；photo-grapher 攝影師

140

你能簡述中國武術的歷史嗎？

What is the history of Chinese martial arts?

Traditional Chinese martial arts originated during primitive times when people made attack and defense movements as they hunted. In terms of technique, these early methods were crude and relatively unorganized.

During the Warring States Period, soldiers from different states practiced wushu in winter. One kind of martial art constituted a dance performed during ritual services. The earliest contest of wushu appeared during the Spring and Autumn Period and the Warring States Period and was usually held during the Spring and Autumn.

During the Qin and Han dynasties, there were one-man and two-man pattern of wushu in use, including patterns imitating the movements of various creatures. One of these patterns was the Five-Animal Exercises（五禽戲）which appeared during the Eastern Han Dynasty. During the Tang Dynasty, warriors were chosen and officers promoted through wushu competition. Shaolin martial art became popular at that time. During the Song Dynasty, a school was set up to train military officers in wushu, and it was practiced and preserved also within family clans and religious temples. Down to the Yuan, Ming and Qing dynasties, various forms of wushu were well established in China as well as Korea, Japan, and many other countries.

> **Notes**
> unorganized 無組織的；imitate 模仿

中國武術如何分類？
How can we categorize Chinese wushu?

Styles of Chinese martial arts may be broadly categorized as the Northern style and the Southern style with reference to the geographical regions divided by the Yellow River. The Northern style wushu originate from north of the Yellow River; the Southern style from south of the river.

Another categorization divides into external wushu and internal wushu. External wushu use muscular force, speed and sheer strength to produce power. It is known from its area of origin, such as Northern Shaolin Boxing (北少林拳) or Chang Boxing (長拳). Internal wushu uses "wise force (巧力)" to overcome its opponents. It combines qi (氣) energy with muscle strength to produce power; and its best known styles are Taijiquan (太極拳), Xingyiquan (行意拳), and Baguazhang (八卦掌). Training the internal wushu often includes standing meditation and special exercises to foster qi. Some experts think, however, that this categorization is not accurate because any good wushu style should have a healthy balance of both internal and external principles and no wushu, regardless of its technique or training, is purely internal or external.

Notes
categorization 分類；muscular 肌肉（發達的），強健的

還有其他的武術分類嗎？

Are there other categorizations of wushu?

Wushu is also known as fighting strategies, which fall into categories of unarmed and armed combat. Unarmed combat refers to the boxing arts (拳術) and functions as the basis of wushu training. The main forms include Chang Boxing, Southern Boxing (南拳), Taijiquan and Shaolin Boxing. Armed combat refers to martial arts that use weapons (兵器). Although there are more than 400 different types of ancient Chinese weapons, there are only 18 standard weapons used in wushu competition. Some popular weapons include broadsword, straight sword, spear, staff, double-sword, nine-section whip and three-sectional staff. Sometimes a practitioner will create a variation involving two of the same types of weapons.

Modern wushu competition performances fall into six categories:

➤ Empty hand forms.

➤ Weapon forms.

➤ Choreographed routines (involving two or more people).

➤ Group practice.

➤ Sparring competition.

➤ Qigong power demonstration.

> **Notes**
> choreograph 從事編舞；routine 固定劇目

什麼是長拳？
What is Chang Boxing?

This system is the foundation for all of the traditional styles of external wushu. It is based on the combined techniques of various forms of Northern Boxing. Chang Boxing is characterized by an open posture, fast, powerful and agile movements, high kicks, jumping and acrobatic techniques. Chang Boxing is very exciting to watch and very demanding to practice. It is well suited for the child or young adult wishing to greatly enhance their strength, speed, agility, flexibility and endurance while developing practical defensive and offensive skills.

> **Notes**
> agility 敏捷；flexibility 靈活性；endurance 忍耐

什麼是形意拳？
What is Xingyiquan (Form and Will Boxing)?

Xingyiquan is a famous internal fighting style created by a Chinese general around 1127 A. D. It is as a powerful straightforward style emphasizing offensive movement; it imitates the fighting techniques of twelve animals-the dragon, tiger, monkey, horse, water lizard, chicken, harrier, swallow, snake, Chinese ostrich, eagle and bear. Mastery of these animal forms yields a variety of simple, effective fighting techniques; and Xingyiquan training increases one's qi (energy) and muscular strength and produces incredible power and vitality.

Xingyiquan uses five basic techniques:piquan (劈拳 , splitting or cutting fist), zuanquan (鑽拳 , drilling fist), bengquan (崩拳 , crushing fist), paoquan (炮拳 , cannon fist) and hengquan (橫拳 , crossed fist). Various drills and two-man sparring set-patterns are used to give practitioners the initial feeling of how to apply each technique and transform one technique to another.

Notes
harrier 獵兔狗；ostrich 鴕鳥

什麼是八卦掌？
What is Baguazhang (the Octagon Palm)?

Baguazhang is literally translated as "eight-diagrams palm" or "octagon palm" and it is one of the three primary Neijiaquan (內家拳) or internal styles of boxing of China. Baguazhang uses many distinctive methods that contain unfathomable changes of palm. It was created during the Qing Dynasty and is still practiced daily and enjoyed by wushu artists in China and overseas.

The foundation of Baguazhang is meditative walking in circle and the "Single Changing Palm (單換掌)" exercise that was developed in Daoist monasteries over 4,000 years ago. As a meditation practice, it allows one to achieve a stillness of mind in the midst of intense physical activity.

Baguazhang emphasize the use of spiral movements and sophisticated footwork and fighting angles. Technically, the correct performance of this exercise increases the practitioner's energy through simultaneous circle walking, performance practice and breath control.

Notes

octagon 八邊形；unfathomable 深不可測的；meditative 沉思的；
breathing 呼吸；simultaneous 同時發生的

什麼是太極拳？
What is Taijiquan?

As a major form of Chinese wushu, Taijiquan is one of the most popular and widely practiced health exercises in the world. It combines posture, physical activity, relaxation, coordinated breathing and mental focus, and it thus has beneficial effects on balance, flexibility, cardiovascular, respiratory function and immune system. Taijiquan was born towards the end of the Ming Dynasty, and there are several schools, includingthe Chen Form（陳式太極拳）, the Yang Form（楊式太極拳）and Simplified Taijiquan（簡化太極拳）. The first two forms focus on attack and defense, which determine the movements. Their common movements of foot-stamping, running, jumping and explosive exertion do not fit the sick, the old or the weak. Simplified Taijiquan is a new form based on the first two styles. It possesses 24 movements and is easy to learn, simple in structure and beneficial to people of all ages and conditions.

Notes

postural 姿勢的；relaxation 放鬆；coordinate 使配合；cardio-
vascular（病等）心血管的；respiratory 呼吸的；immune 免疫的；
explosive 爆發性的；exertion 費力；beneficial 有益的

長期習練太極拳對身體有益處嗎？

Does regular Taijiquan practice benefit health?

Taijiquan has a reputation as a good treatment for chronic ailments, and this reputation is not groundless for it has the following health benefits:

➤ Each movement is executed in the mind, so Taijiquan requires one to concentrate one's mind on practice without distracting thoughts. Such concentration has proved to be effective and beneficial for the central nervous system.

➤ Regular practice is conducive to the good health of cardiovascular system in the prevention of hypertension and arteriosclerosis.

➤ One breathes slowly and evenly in pace with rhythmic movements. Sometimes this requires deep breathing controlled by the diaphragm. Regular practice helps to improve the elasticity of lung tissue, resulting better lung ventilation and the metabolism of carbon dioxide.

➤ The movements are conducted in a slow and continuous flow, so regular practice helps strengthen bones and tendons.

➤ Regular practice helps elderly people maintain the health of their kidneys.

➤ Practice helps the metabolism of fat and protein as well as the change of calcium and phosphorus in non-organic salts.

Notes

chronic （病）慢性的；ailment 病痛；reputation 名聲；distract 分散注意力；arteriosclerosis 動脈硬化（症）；diaphragm 橫膈膜；elasticity 彈性；ventilation 通風；metabolism 新陳代謝；carbon 碳；dioxide 二氧化物；calcium 鈣；phosphorus 磷的

練太極拳的基本要求是什麼？
What are the basic requirements for Taijiquan practice?

Exercisers should bear the following points in mind:

➤ Keep the head and neck roughly perpendicular with the floor, as if suspended by a piece of thread.

➤ The mouth is slightly opened or barely closed. Grit the teeth gently, not tightly. The tongue rests on the upper palate, or the tip of the tongue touches it. Swallow saliva when necessary.

➤ The eyes look shut, but, in fact, they are not. They always follow the dominant moving hand.

➤ Don't throw out the chest or hunch the back. Bend both shoulders slightly inward to make the chest relax and extend the back naturally.

➤ Relax both shoulders. Keep elbows loose and suspended. When you push your hand, protrude the palm slightly and extend fingers with the finger-joints slightly bent. When you draw your hand back, flex the wrist and fingers slightly.

➤ Footwork should bear a close resemblance to the walking movement of a cat, or a lotus broken, but its fibers still joined.

➤ Generally inhale in unison with the movements of standing up, bending the arms or lifting the legs. Exhale inunison with the movements of squatting, extending the arms, dropping a foot or ending each form.

➤ Exercise should be done in a quite and flat place where the air is fresh, preferably early in the morning or late in the evening.

As a Chinese proverb goes, "Small gains in 100 days, and big gains in 1,000 days!" Persist in Taijiquan practice if you want to get the maximum benefit from it.

> **Notes**
>
> perpendicular 垂直的；suspend 懸掛；grit 咬緊（牙）；palate 上顎；
> swallow 嚥下；protrude 伸出；flex 屈曲；inhale 吸入；squat 蹲；
> preferably 更好地；maximum 最大量

武術的道德要點是什麼？
What are the main points of wushu ethics?

In ancient China, human beings were regarded as the most valuable treasure of nature. Man is respected as one of "The Four Greats," together with Heaven, Earth and Truth (Natural Law). Those who respect human life will love life and understand wushu. Moral principles provide the basis for maintaining a stable relationship between man and man, as well as man and society. The following are the main points of wushu ethics that students of wushu must follow.

➤ They shall respect these principles and never do anything harmful to Chinese cultural traditions.

➤ They must cultivate a sense of justice, diligence, persistence, honesty and hard work.

➤ They must try to master everything that is taught, and both teacher and student must take care of each other and treasure their mutual friendship.

➤ They should keep improving their skills and refrain from being arrogant and imperious or showing off their wushu skill while belittling others. Everyone should learn from one another to improve and be united and cooperative with one another.

➤ Their practice aims at self-defense and the improvement of one's physical conditions. They should not bully the weak or contend with anyone out of personal grudge. No bullying of the innocent is allowed, but it is encouraged to take up the cudgels to uphold justice and truth.

➤ The practice of wushu is a hard task; it takes time and requires arduous effort. Thus, steadiness and persistence are required. One must try to fully understand the essentials and inner meaning of each routine.

Notes

diligence 勤勉；persistence 堅持；arrogant 傲慢的；belittle 輕視；cooperative 合作的；grudge 怨恨；bully 威嚇；cudgel 棍棒；arduous 艱巨的

第八章
中國絲綢
Chinese Silk

　　中國是世界上最早種桑養蠶、取絲織綢的國家，絲綢之路一直是中國古代最長的陸上國際商路。在古代，透過這條古路中國絲綢大量地運往其他國家。本篇介紹的內容是絲綢的歷史、絲綢之路以及繡品和錦品。

你能簡要介紹中國絲綢生產的歷史嗎？
What is the history of Chinese silk production?

The cultivation of the silkworm can be traced back to the 3rd century B. C. It was said that Leizu（嫘祖）, a legendary figure of prehistoric China, started the planting of mulberry trees and raising of silkworms. According to archeological discoveries, silk and silk fabrics emerged at least 5,500 years ago.

As early as the 4th century B. C., local people in Sichuan Province were able to produce a kind of plain silk cloth called bo（帛）; and silk brocade was first produced in Chengdu, Sichuan.

In the Zhou Dynasty, a special administration was set up to manage sericulture and silk production; and from 138 to 126B. C., Zhang Qian（張騫）carried a diplomatic mission to the west under imperial order along what was called the Silk Road. From that time on, sericulture and silk production techniques gradually spread to many other countries.

Down to the Song Dynasty, the center of silk production gradually shifted to areas south of the Changjian River from areas along the Yellow River; and in the Northern Song Dynasty, the brocade industry advanced into large-scale workshops. During the Ming and Qing dynasties, Suizhou and Hangzhou became important bases for silk production, and many markets and towns were fully engaged in the sake of silk sales.

Notes
silkworm 桑蠶；sericulture 養蠶（業）；bro-cade 錦緞

關於絲綢的發現有什麼傳說嗎？

Are there any legendary stories related to the discovery of silk?

Legend has it that once there lived a father with his daughter. They had a magic horse, which could not only fly in the sky but also understand human language. One day, the father went out on business and did not come back for quite some time. The daughter promised the horse that if he could bring back her father, she would marry him. Several days later, her father arrived home, riding the horse, but he was unwilling to let his daughter marry a horse and so he killed the innocent animal. Then a miracle happened! The horse's skin carried the girl up into the sky. They flew and flew away and at last stopped on a tree. The moment the girl touched the tree, she turned into a silkworm. Everyday, she spun out long, thin silk that expressed her feeling of longing for the horse.

Another story says that some ancient Chinese women discovered silk by chance. Once, as they picked fruit from trees, they found a special kind of fruit that was white in color. They tasted it, but it was hard to eat. So they boiled the white fruit in hot water, hoping it might taste better, but it still tasted awful. The women lost their patience and began to beat it with large sticks. Unexpectedly, they discovered silk and silkworms, for the white hard fruit was cocoons!

> **Notes**
> innocent 無罪的；cocoon 繭

桑蠶的作用是什麼？
What is the function of the silkworm?

The silkworm is not a worm, but a caterpillar, the larva of a moth. Its diet consists solely of mulberry leaves, and it is native to Northern China. It is called silkworm because it spins its cocoon for raw silk. The cocoon is made of a single continuous thread of raw silk from 300 to 900 meters (1,000 to 3,000 feet) long. If the caterpillar is left to eat its way out of the cocoon naturally, it cuts the threads short, and the silk will be useless. So silkworm cocoons are usuall thrown into boiling water, which kills the larva and makes the cocoons easier to untwist. This operation has continued for thousands of years.

> **Notes**
> caterpillar 毛蟲；larva 幼蟲

你能簡述一下絲綢之路的歷史嗎？
What is the history of the Silk Road?

The Silk Road originated in the 2nd century B. C. when Emperor Wudi of the Han Dynasty sent Zhang Qian, a court official to the Western Regions to seek allies against Xiongnu（匈奴）, a nomadic tribe that frequently raided the border regions of the Han. On his way, the Xiongnu captured Zhang Qian and detained him for ten years. At last, he escaped, and continued his journey to Central Asia. The local rulers, however, had no intention of allying with the Han Empire against Xiongnu. In his trip Zhang Qian collected information about local geology, products and culture of Central Asia, and when he returned to the Han capital, he reported everything to the emperor. In 119B. C., he made his second trip to the Western Regions, escorted by a caravan of 300 persons. It was this time that silk products were first transported to the other regions.

During the Tang Dynasty, trade was prosperous along the route, but only 30 percent of the trade was silk. Several thousand foreign merchants, students, artists and people of different religious beliefs came to China through the route for friendly exchange and trade in various fields.

After the Tang Dynasty, trade on the route gradually declined as a sea route rose up from the east coast of China. In the late 15th century, many goods and materials were shipped along the sea route. Moreover, the Persians also mastered the art of sericulture, so the import of silk from the East was reduced.

Notes

nomadic 游牧的；detain 拘留；geology 地質學；escort 陪同

請告訴我古絲綢之路的具體路線好嗎？
What is the route of the Ancient Silk Road?

The Han Dynasty Silk Road began from the Han capital, Chang'an (長安), the present site of Xi'an (西 安). The route took traders westwards into Gansu Province where it passed through Lanzhou (蘭州), Tianshui (天水) and Jiuquan (九泉). It advanced along Hexi Corridor (河西走廊) until it reached Jiayuguan (嘉峪關)-the giant barrier of the Great Wall and the first key point of the route: Dunhuang (敦煌).

When the Silk road entered Xinjiang (新疆) from the Hexi Corridor, it broke into three main roads. The southern road ran west along the northern foot of the Kunlun Mountains (崑崙山) and on to Kashgar (喀什噶). It then went over the Pamirs and arrived in India; or it passed through Afghanistan and Russian Central Asia and reached Arabia or the coast of the Mediterranean.

The central road extended west along the southern foot of the Tianshan Mountains (天山) and Aksu (阿克蘇). It then crossed the Pamirs and continued on to Mari in Russia.

The northern road went along the northern foot of the Tianshan Mountains and reached the Yili River Valley (伊犁河谷) before it advanced to areas near the Black Sea.

The three routes of the Silk Road ran between mountain ranges, traversed desolate desert areas, and wound over snow-capped peaks in Xinjiang. It was the only way for China to get in touch with the West between the 2nd century B.C. and the 10th century A.D. Although sections of the Silk Road have long been buried by desert sand, the dry local climate has preserved sites and relics for several thousand years. Some relics are as good as they were centuries ago.

Notes
corridor 走廊；Mediterranean 地中海的；snow-capped 積雪蓋頂的

什麼是中國手工絲繡？

What is handmade Chinese embroidery?

Embroidery is a traditional handicraft art with a long tradition. Embroidery products, made from soft satin and colored threads, are stitched by hand, and the varied stitching methods create unique local styles.

The discovery of silk is as early as 5,000 years ago, and the production of silk thread and fabrics gave rise to the art of embroidery. In 1958, a piece of silk was found in a tomb of the State of Chu dating back to the Warring Sates Period (475 B. C.-221B. C.). It is embroidered with a dragon-and-phoenix design, and it is the earliest piece of Chinese embroidery ever unearthed.

There are four famous kinds of embroidery in China. They include Sichuan Embroidery (蜀繡) from Sichuan Province, Suzhou Embroidery (蘇繡) from Suzhou area, Xiang Embroidery (湘 繡) from Hunan Province and Yue Embroidery (粵 繡) from Guangdong Province. The four local embroideries borrow elements from each other, but look different. Suzhou Embroidery is famous for its extremely delicate stitches, Xiang for its rich colors, and Yue for its complicated patterns.

Local folk arts provide patterns for different embroidery style, and traditional Chinese landscape painting also offers favorite subjects. Designs on embroidery include flowers, birds, landscapes, fish, worms and human figures. The products themselves are used as quilt covers, pillow covers, back cushions, tablecloths, scarves and handkerchiefs. During the Daoguang Period (道光年間) of the Qing Dynasty, Sichuan embroidery industry took big strides forward. Its needlework displayed even stitches, bright threads, and close and soft texture. Each county-level government set up an embroidery management office to take charge of the local embroidery business. Their main products were official clothes, gifts and dowries, as well as colorful daily clothes and necessities.

> **Notes**
>
> embroidery 刺繡；stitching 縫紉；quilt 被縟；pillow 枕頭；cushion 坐墊；stride 闊步

什麼是雙面繡？
What is double-sided embroidery?

Current embroidery methods carry forward solid old traditions, but it also makes some innovations in stitching and modeling. Traditional embroidery needlework displays patterns only on one side, but presently artists produce two-sided embroidery pieces, stitching different patterns on either side of the same satin cloth. In some amazing designs, one side displays a cat, and the other a fish. Both figures are done on a single piece of transparent fabric and both are completed at the same time.

> **Notes**
>
> needlework 縫紉；刺繡；satin 緞子

如何鑒賞中國手工繡品？
How can we appreciate Chinese handmade embroidery?

Have you ever seen such a lovely fish or a cat on a piece of silk cloth? The fur or scales look quite real. You can see the individual hairs, and the eyes look at you. Just imagine embroidering such a delicate figure with finely silk threads and tiny needles! There are no ugly knots and things on the back, and they are usually done by hand.

The art of Chinese painting has been applied to embroidery. An artist works indoors using indirect lighting to illuminate her or his canvas, which is mounted on a frame. Famous paintings are reproduced precisely with needles and silk thread! The result looks like a painting from distance, but embroidery at close range.

The following three points are to be noted:

➤ Quality is of the utmost importance. To create a high quality piece, an artist needs to split a single silk thread into several thinner threads and embroider layer after layer with threads of a variety of colors in an attempt to reach the wonderful final effect. The work is extremely time-consuming and requires much hardwork and patience.

➤ Artistic Value. Most collected embroidery pieces that are considered top quality are based on classic paintings.

➤ Size. It usually takes an artist or group of artists several months or even years to complete a high-quality large piece. The larger the size of an embroidered piece, the higher is its value.

Notes
embroider 繡（花紋）；illuminate 照亮；time-consuming 費時的

什麼是中國「錦」？
What is silk brocade?

Brocade is a kind of silk fabrics woven with raised patterns resembling embroidery. It has a unique look, colorfully luxurious, and is amazingly soft to the skin. Handmade brocade evolved over more than 20 centuries, but at present, it has given way to the modern textile industry. It is manufactured under automatic control, using a jacquared loom equipped with electronic devices. Brocade factories specialize in making fabrics, which can be used for traditional products or modern vests, skirts or jackets. There are four local-styled brocades, which are known across the country. They include Shu Brocade (蜀錦) from Sichuan Province, Yun Brocade (雲錦) from Nanjing, Song Brocade (宋錦) from Suzhou and Zhuang Brocade (壯錦) from the Guangxi Autonomous Region.

> **Notes**
> luxurious 豪華的；amazingly 令人驚奇地；auto-matic 自動的；
> jacquared 提花織機

中國的四種地方「錦」有什麼區別？
How do these four Chinese local brocades differ?

Yun Brocade. Yun means "cloud," and this style looks like colorful clouds due to the high-quality of silk and exquisite skill. From the Yuan to the Ming dynasties, Yun Brocade was mostly used for imperial garments.

Song, or Suzhou Brocade. This style disappeared at the end of the Ming Dynasty, but soon revived at the beginning of the Qing Dynasty. Being characterized by harmonious colors and geometrical patterns, it falls into large and small types according to size. The large brocade, also called Heavy Brocade, is mainly used to mount pictures; the Small Brocade is used to decorate small articles.

Zhuang Brocade of the Zhuang ethnic nationality. Local articles, including quilt covers, tablecloths, and scarfs, are woven by weaving machine, and its patterns include figures, flora and fauna and geometrical patterns.

Shu Brocade of Sichuan Province. Towards the end of the Eastern Han Dynasty, a device was invented in Sichuan to weave raised designs on fine silk. This new technique greatly enhanced the quality of silk products, and Shu Brocade became an important article of tribute to the imperial court. In the Tang Dynasty, it was produced with a large number of marvelous patterns. There were designs lined with flowers, the red lion and phoenix, and pairs of pheasants or sheep or other animals that highlighted the central feature. At that time only high officials and nobles lords could afford the brocade.

Notes
garment 衣服；geometrical 幾何圖案的；flora 植物群；fauna 動物群；marvelous 非凡的

蜀錦有沒有流行的圖案？
Are there any fashionable patterns of Shu Brocade?

Fangfang Brocade (方方錦 , check-patterned brocade). First, a loom is used to weave a single-colored brocade base. On this colorful warp and weft, silk threads are woven into check-shaped patterns. Finally a flower is added to each check.

Yuehua Brocade (月華錦 , moonlight brocade). Groups of colorful warp and weft silk threads are interwoven according to designated patterns. The weaving visually transforms from light to dark colors. Then decorative patterns are added by means of tow-to-thread spinning.

Huanhua Brocade (浣花錦 , fallen flower and flowing river). Plum, peach and other flowers are woven on brocade fabrics, and the overall pattern takes the form of a pleasant scene with fallen flower and flowing river.

Pudi Brocade (鋪地錦), which means adding flowers to a brocade fabric. First, the brocade base is woven into geometric figures with small flower patterns. These support large flowers, which are added to make their pattern look more splendid.

> **Notes**
> loom 織布機；warp 經（紗）；weft （紡織物的） 緯線

如何養護絲綢？
How do we maintain silk fabrics?

Tapestry satin, soft satin, silk brocade, georgette, light and thin silk yarns, or raw silk can't be washed in water. Dry-cleaning is advised. However, there are some washable silk fabrics. The following are some necessary points that may help you wash these fabrics.

➤ Don't mix together dark-colored and light-colored silk fabric clothes or silk materials when washing them.

➤ Wash immediately sweat-wetted pure silk clothes or soak them in fresh water. Make sure not to wash them in warm water at the temperature of 30°C and above.

➤ Use acid detergent or light alkaline detergent while washing silk fabrics. It is best to use a kind of special-silk-fabric-detergent.

➤ Washing by hand is advised. Don't twist silk fabrics hard or scrub them with a stiff brush. After washing, gentlypress water out of silk fabrics by hand or with a towel. Dry these fabrics in the shade.

➤ Iron-press washed silk fabrics when they are 80% dry, and don't spray water directly on silk fabrics. Iron the interior covering rather than the exterior of silk clothes. The temperature at the flat of the iron should be between 100°C and 180°C.

➤ Fold silk fabric clothes up in good shape and storage them in a closet. It is inadvisable to put camphor or camphor balls in the same closet.

Notes

tapestry 絨繡，織錦；georgette 喬其紗；dry-clean 乾洗；washable 可洗的；twist 捻，搓；iron-press 熨，燙平；closet 櫥櫃；inadvisable 不可取的

第九章
中國陶瓷
Chinese Pottery and Porcelain

　　陶瓷是陶器和瓷器的合稱。中國陶瓷歷史悠久，種類繁多，製作精美，是中國古代人民的偉大發明。在唐宋以來一千多年的時間裡，中國陶瓷源源不斷地輸送到海外，為中國文化增添了光彩，為世界文明做出了貢獻。本篇主要介紹陶器、瓷器的特點。

什麼是中國陶器？
What are Chinese pottery and porcelain?

Pottery and porcelain refer to all products that are made of a mixture of clay, feldspar and quartz, through shaping, drying and firing. Chinese pottery and porcelain go back to distant antiquity and have played an important role in cultural development of Chinese society. China is among the first countries in the world to use pottery, and China has been recognized as the "home of porcelain," the word "china" being synonymous with porcelain. Throughout the ages, China's porcelain has been admired and valued by the world for its usefulness and beauty.

Notes
feldspar 長石；quartz 石英

在中國，最早的陶器有什麼特點？
What are the features of the earliest pottery vessels in China?

The earliest pottery vessels so far found in China are those unearthed at the sites in Xinzheng, Wu'an and Yuyao counties. The vessels found at the Hemudu site have large quantities of organic matter such as grass, powdered leaves and seed hulls from a grass family mixed with the clay. Firing turned the organic matter to charcoal, which made the pottery black. These vessels were entirely hand-made and fired at a fairly low temperature. The walls of the vessel body were rather thick, and their appearance was simple and irregular. Jars were often uneven in thickness, and the color was not properly curved. Some were even distorted in appearance, which indicates that the art at that time was very primitive.

原始社會彩陶的特點是什麼？
What are features of painted pottery in primitive society?

Primitive cultures produced painted pottery utensils, especially during the periods of the Yangshao Culture, Daxi Culture and the Qujialing Culture. Potters also produced painted cauldrons, tripods and ovens for cooking, as well as rings, beads and other small objects for use and ornaments. These designs were well arranged and graceful. Most were painted on a red pottery background.

Primitive dwellers on the Central Plains used parallel lines, circles, checks, waves and herring patterns in accordance with the shape of the vessels. Pottery unearthed in Huaxian County, Shanxi Province, has a pattern of standing swans and flying wild birds; vessels found in Banpo Village have patterns of wild deer and long-tailed aquatic birds with fish in their beaks. One pottery basin was painted with the smiling face of a man who wore a fish-shaped headdress.

During the period of the Longshan Culture, the pottery manufacture changed from clan ownership to family ownership. Pottery vessels achieved regularity of shape. The paste was even, and some vessels'walls were as thin as eggshell. This kind of pottery is known as "eggshell black pottery (蛋殼陶)." The black color was due to a relatively high charcoal content. Utensils and vessels made of black pottery include bowls, basins, plates and others, such as the gui (簋), a three-legged cooking vessel with a handle, and jia (斝), wine goblets, which were new products that did not exist in the Yangshao Period.

> **Notes**
>
> The Daxi Culture 大溪文化；The Qujialing Culture 屈家嶺文化；
> cauldron 大鍋；tripod 三腳架；dweller 居住者；herring 鯡魚；
> aquatic 水生的；manufacture（大量）製造；regularity 規則性；
> eggshell 蛋殼；goblet 高腳杯

瓷器與陶器有哪些區別？
What is the difference between porcelain and pottery?

Chinese pottery and porcelain go back to distant antiquity and have played an important role in cultural development of Chinese society. Porcelain differs from pottery in the following respects:

➤ Common clay can be used to form the basic material of pottery. Porcelain requires specific materials including pure white gaoling clay, feldspar and quartz.

➤ A pottery base body is usually fired into a fixed shape at a fairly low temperature between 800°C and 1,100°C (degrees centigrade). Porcelain has a coating of vitreous glaze that is fired at a temperature of at least 1,200°C until tough crystals appear. Common clay made for a pottery base body cannot become porcelain, but instead will be melted into glassiness when fired at a temperature of 1,200°C and above.

➤ A pottery base body is opaque, and even its wall is as thin as an egg-shell. A porcelain base body appears semitransparent regardless of wall-thickness.

➤ A pottery base body is not fired completely due to the low temperature of the heat during the firing process. This process results in a porous material that produces an unclear ringing sound when struck. A porcelain base body is non-porous for it is fired completely due to the high temperature of the heat during the firing process. Accordingly, porcelain produces a clear ringing sound like the sound of struck metal.

➤ There are two types of pottery, one being glazed and the other unglazed. In the Han Dynasty diverse types of glazed pottery were manufactured in large quantities. There are two types of porcelain glaze. One type of glaze is used to coat a porcelain base body. Both the coating and the body are together fired at a high temperature. The other type is called a low-temperature glaze, which is used to coat an unglazed porcelain base body after the body has completed its high temperature heating. The newly-coated body is fired again at a low temperature.

➤ Mankind shares the invention of pottery, and China is among the first countries in the world to use pottery. Porcelain is often called china because it was first made in China.

Notes
glassiness 玻璃質；regardless of 不管……；non-porous 無孔的；
mankind 人類；invention 發明

瓷器是什麼時候發明的？
When was Chinese porcelain invented?

Academic circles still debate when this occurred. Some scholars think that porcelain originated in the Wei and Jin dynasties; others look to the date of the origin within the Eastern Han Dynasty or the Three Kingdoms Period. The most recent viewpoint, based on new data and chemical findings from 1972, claims that porcelain goes back to the Shang and Zhou dynasties.

China's earliest porcelain was proto-celadon which dates back to the Shang and Zhou dynasties. Its paste is called "china clay." Vessels excavated from a Western Zhou tomb in Tunxi (屯溪), Anhui Province, for example, have a paste that contains a substance similar to the fine clay still used today in Jingdezhen Kilns (景德鎮窯). The only difference between the remote and present pastes is that the older is not so carefully washed and refined.

> **Notes**
> proto-celadon 原始青瓷；excavate 發掘（尤指古物）

什麼是青瓷？
What is celadon?

From the Shang and Zhou dynasties, Chinese porcelain is called proto-celadon. Down to the Warring States Period, porcelain is termed "early celadon." Its glaze is fairly thick and glossy, and its color a rather dark blue-green.

Complete sets of celadon vessels were manufactured as early as at the beginning of the Western Han Dynasty. In addition to the blue-green glaze, vessels have pale grey, yellowish green and brownish black glazes.

During the Tang Dynasty, celadon manufacture reached a high degree of perfection. The most important manufacturing site is that of the Yue Kilns (越窯) in Yuezhou (越州), South China. These kilns were the early center of celadon production. Yue celadon is described as "jade like," "ice like" or "the color of infused tea." Its pale blue-green glaze was translucent and lustrous. Yue celadon was also a tribute item to the reigning imperial court.

During the Song Dynasty, Longquan Kilns (龍泉窯) in Longquan County and several other counties in Zhejiang Province became the center of celadon manufacture in South China. These kilns remained in existence for 700 years from the Song to the Qing Dynasty, and some of the products were shipped overseas.

Notes

dark blue-green 深青綠色的；pale grey 淡灰的；yellowish green 淡黃綠色的；brownish black 褐黑色的；lustrous 有光澤的

什麼是白瓷？
What is white porcelain?

While the kilns in South China manufactured celadon porcelain, white porcelain was produced in North China. It emerged during the Northern and Southern Dynasties, and its china clay and glaze were white in color. White porcelain vessels have been unearthed from the tomb of Fancui (范粹墓) in Northern Qi (北齊) in Anyang County (安陽), Henan Province, representing China's earliest white porcelain so far discovered.

During the Tang Dynasty, the quality of white porcelain was greatly improved. Xing porcelain (邢窯白瓷), produced at the Xing Kilns (邢窯) at the site of Neiqiu (內丘), Hebei Province, was the most important white porcelain of the Tang Dynasty. Some scholars describe the white glaze of the porcelain produced at the Xing Kilns as "silver-like" and "snow-like."

Down to the Song Dynasty, ding white porcelain (定窯白瓷), produced at the Ding Kilns (定窯) at the site of Quyang (曲陽) in Hebei Province, gradually replaced the xing white porcelain of the Tang. Ding porcelain is spotlessly white, with some decorative patterns added. White porcelain had far-reaching prospects and gradually became China's prime porcelain product. Its white color also served as the bottom color for painted porcelain.

Notes
decorative 裝飾的；prospect 景象

什麼是彩瓷？
What is painted porcelain?

Generally speaking, prior to the Yuan Dynasty, celadon and white porcelain were the main porcelain products in ancient China. During the Yuan Dynasty, colored porcelain rose in numbers, and it thus remained as a main form of porcelain from the Yuan to the Qing dynasties. The porcelain vessels of the Yuan had already varied patterns of scrolls, leaves, sunflowers, peony, fruits, dragon, phoenix, flowing streams, etc; but a rich variety of painted designs opened great prospects for painting on Ming porcelain.

"Blue-and-white" porcelain (青花瓷) made its first appearance at that time. Potters used cobalt oxide as the main coloring agent in the pigment. They used to draw on the clay shapes. Then potters used a white glaze to cover the drawings before firing the clay at a high temperature. The result was blue-and-white porcelain. There were also other forms of painted porcelain, including under-glaze red porcelain (釉裡紅), polychrome over-glaze decor porcelain (五彩瓷) and soft-colored over-glaze decor porcelain (粉彩瓷).

Notes
cobalt 鈷；polychrome 多色的

什麼是唐三彩？
What is the tri-color pottery of the Tang Dynasty?

The emergence of tri-color pottery brought China's age-old traditional pottery industry to a new high. Tang tri-color is the general name for color-glazed pottery of the Tang Dynasty. Its colors include yellow, green, brown, blue, black and white; but yellow, green and brown are the major colors. The body is made from white clay. After the clay mold is fired into a fixed shape, a mineral frit is applied. These minerals contain elements of copper, iron, cobalt and manganese. The body is then fired again at a temperature of around 900 degrees centigrade, allowing the different colors to permeate.

Tri-color pottery is used mainly for burial utensils, and rarely used for items of daily use. Most tri-color human figures are female. They range in size from a dozen centimeters to over one meter tall and wear gorgeous, fashionable costumes. Their full figures and round faces are in conformity with the criteria of beauty of the Tang Dynasty.

Of the animal figures, horses and camels account for the greatest number. Tang horses are robust and handsome. As they throw back their heads or rear up, their inner strength is depicted in outward appearance. The Tang camels are presented in a walking position or with their heads held high, as if whinnying.

Notes

emergence 出現；tri-color 三色的；frit 熔塊；manganese 錳；permeate 滲入；gorgeous 燦爛的；conformity 遵從；robust 強健的；whinny 嘶叫

你對中國古代向海外運輸陶瓷的歷史了解多少？

How much do you know about the overseas transportation of pottery and porcelain in ancientChina?

Before the Han Dynasty, China already traded silk for products from West Asian countries. In the 2nd century B. C., Zhang Qian of the Western Han Dynasty went twice on diplomatic missions to the western regions and established ties between China and a number of countries west of the Pamirs (帕米爾高原). Large quantities of silk fabrics flowed along the road leading to Central Asia. It is an east-west caravan road of 7,000 kilometers, famous as the Silk Road. China's pottery and porcelain were transported west along this road.

Up to the 16th century, the Silk Road was China's main caravan route for the export of porcelain to the West. However, Chinese sea navigation also goes far back into history. During the Han Dynasty, sea travels between China and Japan became more frequent, and in the South, sea navigation developed between Chinese and Indian Ocean ports. Since the early Tang Dynasty, around the 7th century, Chinese pottery and porcelain has exported by sea in large quantity, and the Tang court appointed an official at Guangzhou to be in charge of sea navigation and foreign trade. At the same time, overseas merchants who visited the Tang Empire purchased large quantities of pottery vessels and porcelain and shipped them abroad. Since the Tang Dynasty, the sea route continued to expand to various countries in Asia, Africa, Europe and other regions. Later, people called this route as "The Pottery and Porcelain Sea Route (海上陶瓷之路)."

Pottery and porcelain are easily broken. In ancient China, horses and camels were the main means of transport along the Silk Road, and in addition, the road transportation couldn't assure the safety of pottery and porcelain. Therefore, many famous kilns were built along the coastal areas for sea shipment, and the main ports included Guangzhou, Quanzhou, Xiamen and Macao.

Notes

diplomatic 外交的 ; caravan 商隊 ; navigation 水上運輸 ; shipment 裝運

第九章　中國陶瓷 Chinese Pottery and Porcelain

第十章
中國醫藥學
Traditional Chinese Medicine

　　中國醫藥學是中國文化的一個寶庫，它對中華民族的繁榮昌
盛發揮了重大作用。中國醫藥學有自己獨特的理論和體系，本篇
主要介紹中國醫藥學的基本特點和部分獨特的治療方法。

你能簡介中醫的歷史嗎？
What is the history of traditional Chinese medicine?

Traditional Chinese Medicine has a long history. In remote antiquity, when our ancestors searched for food, they found that some foods had specific properties for relieving or curing certain diseases. While warming themselves around a fire, they discovered that warming a patient with hot stone or earth wrapped in bark or an animal skin can relieve the symptoms of certain diseases. They noted by chance that pain in one part of the body was alleviated when some other part was pricked. This treatment with bian shi (扁石 , stone needles) and bone needles came into being.

During the Warring State Period, about 200 B. C.-300B. C., a book called Medical Classic of the Yellow Emperor (《黃帝內經》) appeared. This book explains the foundations of human health and illness with illuminating discussions of the doctrine of yin-yang and the Five-elements (五行學), the description of the human body and its organs, qi and blood, pathogenic agents, concepts of disease, principles of diagnosis, and a variety of therapies.

400 years later, Zhang Zhongjing (張仲景) from the Eastern Han Dynasty wrote a book entitled Treatise on Febrile Diseases and Miscellaneous Diseases (《傷寒雜病論》). This book first provided theoretical basis for Chinese medicine, along with therapeutic principles for diagnosis and treatment based on an overall analysis of symptoms.

There were well-known physicians in ancient times, including Bian Que (扁鵲) of the early Warring States Period and Hua Tuo (華佗) of the Eastern Han Dynasty. They were honored as miracle workers for their skill in medical treatment. In the following 1,000 years, medicinal theory and practice continued and advanced; and many medical experts and books emerged in large numbers. At present, there are 13,000 types of Chinese medical books.

Notes

property 屬性；relieve 減輕；symptom 症狀；prick 刺（穿）；diagnosis 診斷；pathogenic 引起疾病的；miscellaneous 各種各樣的；theoretical 理論的；the-rapeutic 治療的；physician 內科醫生

什麼是「三寶」和「氣」?
What is san bao and qi?

Nature includes air, water, and earth. In the same way, the Chinese medicine assumes that the human body possesses qi（氣）, moisture and blood. Qi refers to "energy"; it is the force behind all bodily movement. Moisture refers to the liquid substance that protects and nurtures tissue. Blood is the basic substance from which bones, nerves, skin, muscles and organs are produced.

According to Chinese theory, there are three treasures, that is san bao（三寶）. These are jing（精, essence）, qi, and shen（神, spirit）. Shen represents consciousness and our higher mental faculties. Qi is the root of jing and shen. When qi accumulates, it produces jing, and when jing accumulates, it in turn makes shen wholesome. One basic notion of Chinese medicine is that qi must circulate through living organisms, and when this circulation stops, disease results. So many treatments are to get qi to flow properly and to prevent it from being blocked.

<u>Notes</u>

moisture 溼氣；motivate 激發；consciousness 意念；accumulate 累積；wholesome 強健的；organism 生物

什麼是陰陽學說？
What is yin and yang?

Yin and yang derives from Daoism which regards them as "the fundamental principles" or "forces in the universe." In Chinese theory, everything contains these two contracting principles.

Heaven is considered as yang; the earth is yin. Yin and yang are not simply oppose to each other; they coexist in interdependence. Thus, there would be no earth without heaven. Moreover, yin may transform into yang and vice versa. In the human body, the upper part is yang, the lower part yin; the exterior is yang, the interior yin; the back is yang, the abdomen yin. With regard to internal organs, the heart, liver, spleen, lung and kidney are yin, while the six intestinal organs are yang. These are the gallbladder, the stomach, the large intestine, the small intestine, the urinary bladder and the triple warmer.

The harmony of yin and yang produces good health; disharmony leads to disease. Therefore, traditional Chinese doctor uses acupuncture, herbs and food to help correct an yin-yang imbalance until the body returns to a healthy state. For example, a preponderance of yang (陽盛) may lead to the hyper-function of an organ or heat manifestations (熱症). So cooling drugs are used to inhibit the excessive yang. On the contrary, a preponderance of yin leads to manifestation of cold or weakness in function of an organ. In this case, warming drugs are used to restrict the predominance of yin.

Notes

derive 衍生出；component 成分；interior 內的；abdomen 腹部；organ 器官；bowel 腸；gallbladder 膽囊；intestine 腸；urinary 泌尿的；interdependence 互相依賴；vice versa 反之亦然；dis-harmony 不一致；im-balance 不均衡狀態；preponderance 優勢；hyper-function 作用亢進；manifestation 顯示

什麼是五行學說？
What is the theory of the Five Elements?

The Five Elements are five basic substances of natural phenomenon. These include wood, fire, earth, metal, and water. In accordance with their different properties, functions and forms, traditional Chinese medicine attributes the liver to wood, the heart to fire, the spleen to earth, the lung to metal and the kidney to water. This attribution understands the physiology and pathology of the human body in interrelation with a person and physical nature. The Five Elements are in-terrelated as follows: Wood begets fire, fire begets earth, earth begets metal, metal begets water, and water, in its turn, nourishes wood. In turn, wood subdues earth, earth subdues water, water subdues fire, fire subdues metal, and metal subdues wood. The same applies to the human physiology: the liver (wood) stores blood to nourish the heart (fire); the heat of the heart (fire) warms the spleen (earth); the spleen (earth) transforms and distributes food essence to replenish the lung (metal); the lung (metal) dredges the water passages to help the kidney (water); and the vital essence of the kidney (water) nourishes the liver (wood). A traditional doctor thus first seeks to nourish the spleen before curing illness in the lung.

> **Notes**
>
> attribution 歸因; physiology 生理學; in-terrelation 相互關係; subdue 制服; replenish 把……裝滿; dredge 疏濬; passage 通路

中西方醫學對病的不同觀念是什麼？

What are different attitudes between Chinese and Western medical practitioners towards disease?

According to Chinese cosmology, all is born from the marriage of yin and yang. Harmony between the two produces good health; disharmony leads to disease. One of the major assumptions of traditional Chinese medicine is that disease is due to an internal imbalance of yin and yang, and so the strategy is to restore harmony and traditional Chinese doctors use acupuncture, herbs and special food to help correct yin-yang imbalance until the body returns to a healthy state. Another assumption is that each organ has a mental as well as a physical function, and all parts of the bodily whole are intimately connected.

Western medicine assumes that a disease is due to external forces such as a virus or bacteria. It is based on the Cartesian philosophy that the body represents one functional system, and the mind another. It recognizes that each system may affect the other, but it sees disease as either primarily physical or mental.

治病有什麼傳統的方法？
What are traditional methods for treating illness?

Traditional Chinese physicians use numerous ways to treat illness by restoring the desired balance between yin and yang and among qi, shen, blood and bodily fluids. These include acupuncture, herbology, moxibustion, food therapy, cupping, qigong exercises, coin-rubbing and others.

Moxibustion is a traditional therapy utilizing moxa or mugwort. Mugwort is aged and ground up to a fluff. Then the fluff is further processed into a stick that resembles a cigar, and it is used to warm area of the body and acupuncture points.

Dieda（跌打）means "fall and strike." Practitioners of dieda specialize in healing traumas due to sports'injuries, such as bone fractures, cuts, bruises,etc. It is not strictly a branch of medicine, but a spin-off from the long history of Chinese martial arts. Practitioners may also use more typical Chinese medical therapies if an internal injury is involved.

Notes

fluid 液；herbology 草本植物；moxibustion 艾灸；moxa 艾；mugwort 艾蒿；fluff 絨毛；fra-cture 骨折；bruise 碰傷；injury 傷害

你能告訴我一些針灸知識嗎？
Could you tell me something about the acupuncture?

An acupuncturist usually inserts acupuncture needles at critical points in the human body for multi-medicinal purposes. It is thought that there exists a web of pathways called channels (經絡) that link all parts of the body, and more than 360 acupuncture points are located at these channels. Qi or vitality flows through these channels and passes these points to support tissue, muscles and organs, and when qi is blocked at critical points, the function of tissue, muscles and organs will be weakened, so an acupuncturist inserts acupuncture needles at these points to help qi flow, correct qi imbalances, and raise the level of internal energy.

Notes
acupuncturist 針灸師；insert 插入；critical 關鍵性的；channel 路線；weaken 使變弱

針灸痛嗎？
Does acupuncture cause pain?

Patients have different sensations. They may feel sore, numb, warm or swelling; but many say they feel relaxed when the needle is inserted beneath their skin. Many doctors commonly use six to eight needles during treatment at most of times, but they may use ten or more needles if two or more symptoms need acupuncture treatment at the same time. For instance, if a patient has both back pain and a headache, the acupuncturist treats him or her for both symptoms at the same time. Some acupuncturists insert as many as 30 or more needles at the same time.

Normally, each treatment takes 20 to 30 minutes, however, this depends on the sensitivity and condition of the patient as the disease is treated. Generally speaking, the success of a treatment depends on the experience and skill of the acupuncturist on a correct diagnosis of symptom, accuracy in hitting acupuncture points, timing, the depth and angle of insertion, etc.

Notes

sensation 感覺；swelling 腫脹；headache 頭痛；sensitivity 敏感性；insertion 插入

人們如何在家中熬製中藥？

How do people decoct herbal medicine at home?

A patient receives small packages at a pharmacy of traditional medicine in accordance with the prescription of his or her doctor. These contain various dry herbs, and the patient usually puts them in a pot, adds water until they are completely soaked, and heats them in a pot over a fire. When the water begins to boil, the heat is immediately reduced, but the fire is kept simmering for 30 or 40 minutes. Then the herbal water is poured out into a bowl; and the herbs themselves remain in the pot, which is refilled with water and placed over the fire again. The whole process is repeated three times until enough concentrated herbal tea is produced.

The doctor usually concocts a remedy from one or two main ingredients appropriate for the illness. Then he or she adds other ingredients to adjust the formula to the patient's yin and yang condition to cancel out toxicity or side-effects of the main ingredients. Unlike western medication, the balance and interaction of all the ingredients are more important than the effect of individual ingredients. A key to success, moreover, is the treatment of each patient as an individual.

> **Notes**
> package 包裹；pharmacy 藥房；prescription 藥方；simmer 熳；concentrated 集中的；formula 公式；appropriate 適當的；toxicity 毒性；side-effect 副作用

「本草」是什麼意思？
What is bencao?

Herbal medicine is the mainstay of traditional Chinese medicine. The knowledge of the medicinal herbs was originally handed down verbally. With the birth of the Chinese characters, medical books began to appear, and many were printed. They are called bencao（本草）, which means that plants are the basis of medicinal healing. At present, there are about 300 types of medical books in existence. These include the earliest book, Shennong Bencaojing（《神農本草經》）, Shennong Herbal Medicine Classics which was written during the Eastern Han Dynasty. Another famous work, Bencao Gangmu（《本草綱目》，Compendium of Materia Medica), written by Li Shizhen（李時珍）of the Ming Dynasty. It lists 1,892 herbs with 1,160 pictures and 11,000 drug prescriptions. At the beginning of the 17th century, foreign scholars began to translate this work into English, Japanese, French and other languages.

中國的食療法有什麼功用？
What is the function of Chinese food therapy?

Food therapy in China employs a combination of foods and herbs to make medicinal concoctions for the treatment of illness and the prolongation of life. It has a recorded history of more than 3,000 years and is the most basic treatment in Chinese medicine to prevent and cure disease. Herbs are the primary foodstuff for nourishing the body in precise and well-defined ways, and these herbs usually combine fresh, natural foods. There are hundreds of recipes in circulation, and many are used in households on a regular basis. These can be classified according to the following categories: health promotion, sickness prevention, disease control and aids for recuperation. They are less expensive than drugs and generally have no adverse side effects.

常見藥膳有哪些？
What are some common medicinal foods?

Stewed brews are common medicinal dishes. A long, slow simmering process extracts the essential nutrients from ingredients into the soup, and the effect on brews is quick and it is easiest for the body to digest and absorb. Such brews are suitable for people of all ages and even the weakest person living on a fluid diet can benefit from nutritional brew.

Another popular form of medicinal food is watery porridge. This is prepared by cooking rice into a semi-solid form with herbs and water. It is easy to digest as a meal replacement.

Typical dishes include Sewed Squab with Chinese Caterpillars, Mandarin Fish Grains with Pine Nuts, Soft-Shelled Turtle with Cordyceps, Mutton with Candied Dates, Stewed Pigeon with Ginseng and Cordyceps, Duck with Chinese Caterpillar Fungus, and others.

<u>Notes</u>
nutrient 營養物；nutritional 營養的；porridge 粥，糊；replacement 代替；squab 乳鴿；caterpillar 毛毛蟲；cordyceps 冬蟲夏草屬；fungus 菌類植物

第十一章
中國古書
Ancient Chinese Books

中國的圖書有著悠久的歷史。本篇介紹的是中國最古老的文字紀錄,以及後來的簡書、帛書和流傳至今的部分名著。

書籍產生以前人們用什麼方法記事？

What ways were used to keep a record of eventsbefore books came into existence?

Western bibliophiles know of the clay tablets of the Sumerians, the papyrus scrolls of the Egyptians, and the parchment texts of the Greeks. In the Shang Dynasty, ancient Chinese engraved inscriptions on tortoise shells or animal bones. Some people say that the Oracle Bone Script (甲骨文) was the earliest "book" in China. Later, people tended to engrave inscriptions on bronze ware or stones. So some say that the Bronze and Stone Scripts are "books."

When we use the word "book" today, we mean a bound text. To a certain degree, the oracle bone, bronze and stone scripts function as "books," but most of these are not bound together. In addition, they are not used for the purpose of disseminating knowledge. They are only the record of some characters.

Notes

bibliophile 藏書家；Sumerian 蘇美爾人；papyrus 紙莎草紙；
parchment 羊皮紙；bind 裝訂

簡冊是中國最早的書籍嗎？

Was jiance the earliest books of China?

Jiance means "texts written on bamboo or wooden slips." The ancients at that time wrote characters on bamboo or wooden slips with Chinese brushes. Then, in accordance with their meaning, they bound all the slips together with a thick cord of hemp, silk or cowhide. When did bamboo or wooden slips start to be used? They might have been used during the Shang and Zhou dynasties. From the Spring and Autumn Period to the Han Dynasty, bamboo and wood remained as the main writing materials. In 1975, more than a thousand bamboo slips were unearthed in Yunmeng County (雲夢縣), Hubei Province. These date back to the Qin Dynasty and constitute a considerable amount of Qin's law documents. In the 1980s, some 50,000 wooden slips from the Han Dynasty were unearthed at sites in Tianshui (天水), Gansu Province. These provide firsthand material that enables us to know the social order in detail during that period.

The slips from the Qin and Han dynasties differ in length. The laws and classic scriptures were written on longer slips, while biographies and essays were written on short ones. Chinese characters were written vertically from top to bottom on one face of each slip. During the Han Dynasty, there were usually 60 characters written on one slip. However, some slips had only one or two characters, and some others just over ten.

The bound slips could be rolled up into a cylindrical shape. Usually a bamboo or wooden slip book came in bundles. People in ancient China read bound slips from right to left, and they rolled up them from left to right.

> **Notes**
> slip 片條；cord 細繩；hemp 麻類植物；co-whide 牛皮革；biography 傳記；essay 論說文；vertically 垂直地；cylindrical 圓柱的；bundle 捆

什麼是帛書？
What is boshu?

The ancient Chinese used brushes to write characters or copy books on silk fabrics. This is called boshu which means "an ancient book copied on silk fabrics." From the Spring and Autumn Period, silk had also been used as a writing material. In 1973, archeologists unearthed more than 20 books copied on silk fabrics from Tomb No.3 at Mawangdui (馬王堆) in Changsha (長沙), Hunan Province. The total amount of characters is some 120,000. The books include Book of Changes (《易經》), Way and Virtue (《道德經》) and Strategies of the Warring States (《戰國冊》). Most strikingly, these books differ greatly from the copies of these books used today.

Silk fabric is a better material for character writing, compared with bamboo or wooden slips. In addition, books copied on silk fabrics are soft, light, and portable. However, silk remained expensive at that time because the silk output was quite low. So only imperial courts and rich families used it, and only to a limited extent.

Notes
fabric 織物；strikingly 顯著地；similar 相像的；portable 便於攜帶的；
expensive 昂貴的 ；output 出產

什麼是《百家姓》和《三字經》？
What are Bai Jia Xing and San Zi Jing?

In ancient China, Chinese children first studied the Chinese characters with Bai Jia Xing (《百家姓》, The Hundred Family Surnames) and San Zi Jing (《三字經》, The Three Character Classic). Then, they studied Si Shu Wu Jing (《四書五經》, The Four Books and Five Classics) and other classic books.

San Zi Jing was a required text for all Chinese children in ancient China. They would recite it as a group, accompanied by the swaying of the body to give the proper rhythm. It was written in the 13th century, and it is thought that the text was written by Wang Yinglin (王應麟 , 1223-1296), a renowned Confucian scholar of the Southern Song Dynasty. It is written in couplets of three characters (syllables) for easy memorization. The complete text is less than 1,200 characters, and it manages to express the main features of the Confucian tradition. The following is a part of the classic in translation:

At birth, everyone is naturally good.

Initially, they are similar in character; as time goes on, they become different.

If this lacks proper teaching, their nature becomes bad.

The right way to teach demands absolute concentration.

(人之初，性本善；性相近，習相遠。苟不教，性乃遷；教之道，貴以專。)

Bai Jia Xing has profound influence. It was written during the Song Dynasty in the 10th century, and it lists all of the known Chinese surnames in use at the time, which amount to438. Who created Bai Jia Xing? When did the book first come into being, and where was it published? To this day, all those remain a mystery. According to textual researches by academics, a master copy of Bai Jia Xing might exist even before the Song Dynasty.

In this text the surnames are given in a prescribed order and arranged in the form of a poem to facilitate memorization by school children. The surname leading the whole collection is zhao, the surname of the ruler of the Song Dynasty. The next several surnames also appear to be related to other important personages of the era.

Since the book was produced, many other new surnames have been created. However, the surnames of The Hundred Family Surnames still account for 90% of all Chinese surnames in use.

Notes

surname 姓；accompany 陪同；sway 搖擺；rhythm 節拍；attribute 把……歸因於；memorization 熟記；profound 深刻的；academic 學究式的；prescribe 規定；exception 例外；era 時代

什麼是「四書五經」?
What is Si Shu Wu Jing?

Si Shu Wu Jing means The Four Books and The Five Classics. In the Confucian tradition, The Four Books and The Five Classics have been regarded as the cardinal texts which one must learn to understand the authentic thought of Confucianism.

● The Four Books (四書) are as follows:

➤ Great Learning (《大學》) is originally a chapter in Classic of Rites (《禮記》). It is the first of The Four Books and gives a fundamental introduction to Confucianism. The way of great learning consists in manifesting one's bright virtue, loving the people, remaining in perfect goodness (大學之道，在明明德，在親民，在止於至善).

➤ Doctrine of the Mean (《中庸》) is the name of another chapter in Classic of Rites. The purpose of this book is to demonstrate the usefulness of the golden means to gain perfect virtue.

194

➤ Analects of Confucius (《論語》) is a book of concise sayings attributed to Confucius and recorded by his disciples.

➤ Book of Mencius (《孟子》) is a book of conversations between Mencius and some kings of his time, probably written by Mencius'disciples.

The Four Books were singled out, grouped together, and published in 1190 A.D.by Zhu Xi (朱熹), a Neo-confucian philosopher. The Four Books remained especially important as the basis of study for all civil service examinations from about 1300 to 1900.

● The Five Classics (五經) are as follows:

➤ The Book of Odes (《詩經》) is made up of 305 ceremonial and folk verses written over a period of about 500 years during the Western Zhou Dynasty and the Spring and Autumn Period. These poems are actually songs based on musical types, and they have had a profound influence on the later development of poetry.

➤ The Book of History (《書經》) is a collection of documents and speeches alleged to have been written by rulers and officials of the early Zhou Dynasty and before.

➤ The Book of Changes (《易經》) is a book used for divination in the tradition of the oracle bones tradition. In one interrelated whole in symbolic form, it combines all of human life, fate and the physical elements of the cosmos. These are all represented by the Bagua Diagram (八卦) of whole and broken lines. The contents of the book include ancient cosmological beliefs of the Chinese antedating the separate philosophical schools.

➤ The Book of Rites (《禮記》) describes ancient ceremonial usages, religious creeds and social institutions from the middle Zhou Dynasty down to the first part of the Han Dynasty.

➤ Spring and Autumn Annals (《春秋》) is a historical record of the State of Lu, Confucius' native state, from 722 B. C. to 479 B. C. written (or edited) by Confucius.

Traditionally there are two divergent views about the relation of Confucius to The Five Classics. One maintains that Confucius himself wrote all of these works, while the othermaintains that he was the author of Spring and Autumn Annals, the commentator of The Book of Changes, the reformer of The Book of Rites, and the editor of The Book of History and The Book of Odes.

> **Notes**
> cardinal 主要的；authentic 可信的；originally 新穎地；Confucianism 儒學；manifest 顯示；doctrine 教義；demonstrate 證明；analects 論集；disciple 信徒；philosopher 哲學家；ceremonial 禮節的；verse 詩句；poetry 詩歌；allege 宣稱；interrelate 相互關聯；symbolic 象徵的；diagram 圖表；cosmological 宇宙論的；antedate 先於；philosophical 哲學的；creed 教義；commentator 註釋者；reformer 改革者

《孫子兵法》是一本什麼樣的書？
What Kind of books is Sun Zi Bing Fa?

Sun Zi Bing Fa is a book of military strategy and tactics written by Sun Wu (孫武), the great military strategist of the Spring and Autumn Period. The ancient editions of Sun Zi Bing Fa have thirteen chapters. However, in recent years, another edition was discovered in a Han tomb located in Shandong Province. Its edition has fifteen chapters. The book, which describes the art of war in ancient China, includes rich experiences from many different historical battles. In addition, it illustrates aspects of the society during the Spring and Autumn Period. Its expression seems simple, but it offers deep thought. The book is regarded as one of the great prose works of its time.

Notes

tactics 戰術；edition 版本；illustrate 闡明；prose 散文

《內經》是一本什麼樣的書？
What Kind of books is Nei Jing?

This book's full name is Huangdi Neijing (《皇帝內經》，Medical Classic of the Yellow Emperor). The current version of the book consists of two parts: the Plain Questions (素問) and the Divine Pivot (靈樞). Each part has eighty-one articles. Many historians and physicians throughout Chinese history verified that the major contents of Medical Classic of the Yellow Emperor appeared in the Warring States Period. It was added to during the Qin and Han dynasties and compiled in the early times of the Western Han Dynasty.

The book's authors are unknown. It includes the Yellow Emperor in its title because people in ancient China believed that only an ancient sage could have written such a good book. But the book consists of numerous short, medical essays by anonymous authors explaining the foundations of human health and illness along with the discussions of the yin-yang and five-agents doctrines, the human body and its organs, qi and blood, pathogenic agents, concepts of disease and diagnosis, and a variety of therapies. For the first time, health care took the form of "medicine." Reading this book not only offers a better understanding of the roots of Chinese medicine as an integrated aspect of Chinese civilization, it also provides a much needed starting point for discussions of the differences and parallels between European and Chinese ways of dealing with illness and the risk of early death.

Notes

version 版本；pivot 樞軸；physician 醫師；verify 證明；compile 彙編；therapy 治療；integrate 使結合；unknown 陌生的；sage 賢人；perception 感知；pathogenic 引起疾病的；concept 概念；parallel 相似處

《史記》的作者是誰？
Who wrote Historical Records?

Sima Qian（司馬遷，約前 145- ？）wrote Historial Records. He began to write it at the age of 42, completing it 11 years later. The records cover a period of 3,000 years, from the legendary age of the Yellow Emperor to the Han Emperor. It is the first comprehensive history in the form of biographical records in China. These records consist mainly of three sections, which contain more than half a million words. In the first section, an account of each emperor's reign is given. In the second section, Sima Qian wrote essays on music, calenda, astrology, rivers, canals, economics, and other topics. The third section presents biographies of many major and minor historical figures. The literary quality of this history has always been regarded as extremely high, and as a model of biographical literature, the records have had a strong influence on the literary development of later prose writing, including fiction and drama.

《漢書》的作者是誰？
Who wrote The Book of the Former Han Dynasty?

The Ban family wrote this book. Ban Biao（班彪）began writing the book, and his son Ban Gu（班固）constituted it, writing the bulk of the book. Ban Zhao （班昭）, Ban Gu's younger sister added a few chapters after Ban Gu's death.

This book records the historical period from the first year of Gaozu（高祖元年）, the first emperor of the Han Dynasty until the fourth year of Dihuang of the Xin Dynasty（王莽新朝地皇四年）. It covers a total of 229 years. As the book deals with the Former Han, it mainly borrows materials from Historial Records. Although Ban Gu's historical approach is not as enlightened as that of Sima Qian, he is also regarded as a great historian. He stressed objective historical facts, and the book has become the model for each dynasty's historians in composing official accounts of the events of the previous dynasty in ancient China.

你對明清章回小說了解多少？

How much do you know about episodic novels in the Ming and Qing dynasties?

The traditional Chinese novel developed as a literary form during the Ming and Qing dynasties. It is episodic in nature, relating the adventures of a large number of characters in a string of loosely connected events. Its thematic range is broad, including historical romances, chivalric tales, ghost stories, social satires and love stories. Most of the novels depend heavily on the ancient tradition of popular storytellers in the marketplaces and teahouses. This dependence results in two consequences. The first is that the long, episodic novels are strong in fascinating detail but weak in unified plot. The second is that the authors tend to be collectors, editors, and adaptors of earlier materials. There follows a few of the best-known novels that still remain popular among current Chinese readers.

> **Notes**
> episodic 情節不連貫的；adventure 冒險活動；loosely 鬆散地；romance 浪漫情調；chivalric 俠義的；satire 諷刺；dependence 依靠；consequence 結果；fascinating 極好的

《三國演義》是在講什麼？

What does The Romance of the Three Kingdoms talk about?

This novel is thought to have been compiled by Luo Guanzhong（羅貫中）between the end of the Yuan Dynasty and the beginning of the Ming Dynasty. It is based on existing written and oral accounts of the last years of the Eastern Han Dynasty and the Three Kingdoms Period of Wei（魏）, Shu（蜀）and Wu（吳）. The novel traces the rise and fall of the three kingdoms and shows the different approach of the three political groups in their aspirations to unite China and live in peace. It contains 400 characters, of which Cao Cao（曹操）, Liu Bei（劉備）, Zhuge Liang（諸葛亮）, Guan Yu（關羽）and Zhang Fei（張飛）have captured the imaginations of generations of readers. The language in the novel is a mixture of the literary and the vernacular, and it sounds easy and fluent. The novel has given rise to many other novels and stage plays related to The Romance of the Three Kingdoms.

> **Notes**
> account 記述；approach 接近；aspiration 志向；imagination 創造力；fluent 流利的

《水滸傳》是在講什麼？
What does Outlaws of the Marsh talk about?

Outlaws of the Marsh is also known as The Water Margin or All Men Are Brothers. This is the first novel that gives a detailed account of Chinese peasant uprisings in feudal society. Its authorship is uncertain, but the current edition has been attributed to Shi Nai'an（施耐庵）and Luo Guanzhong（羅貫中）. The author or authors collected materials from oral legends, storytellers'scripts and various dramas, providing continuity between unconnected episodes and improving the literary quality of the original material. The book relates the stories of 108 men and women who gathered at Liangshan（梁山）, in present Shandong Province, under the leadership of Song Jiang（宋江）during the Northern Song Dynasty. Day by day, this uprising becomes more powerful, and the government is unable to put them down. Eventually the emperor has to offer them amnesty and official positions. The book is divided into many chapters, describing 108 men and women one by one. Most of the chapters can be thought of as independent biographies, and they have been told and retold by generations of Chinese people.

Notes

outlaw 反叛者；marsh 沼澤；margin 邊緣；uprising 起義；feudal 封建的；authorship 著作者的身分；continuity 繼續不斷；unconnected 不連接的；amnesty 大赦

《西遊記》是在講什麼？
What does Journey to the West talk about?

Journey to the West is also known as Record of a Journey to the West. It was written by Wu Cheng-en（吳承恩, about 1500-1582）and contains 100 chapters. The story is based on the actual pilgrimage about a Chinese monk of 7th century A.C., Xuan Zang（玄奘）, to the source of Buddhism in India. The first part relates the adventures of Monkey King（孫悟空）, who by virtue of his enlightenment has acquired magic powers, such as the ability to jump 108,000 li (a li is one third of a kilometer) in one bound and the capacity to summon aid when in a tight spot. As he plucks out one of his own hairs and spits it out, it immediately turns into an army of monkeys. By these and other means, Monkey King defeats all the forces Jade Emperor sends against him. However, he is finally curbed by Buddha, who gives him the task to accompanying Xuan Zang to fetch scriptures from India and bring them to China. Zhu Bajie（豬八戒）and Sha Seng（沙僧）also join the journey to guard Xuan Zang. The description of numerous adventures on their journey occupies the remainder of the book.

In the last 500 years, this novel has had a profound influence on Chinese literature. Its romantic style, imaginative content and humorous expression have captured readers of past generations, and its stories have been adapted into dramas and cartoons that have won worldwide appreciation.

Notes

journey 旅行；Buddhism 佛教；acquired 養成的；magic 魔法；capacity 能量；pluck 摘；spit 吐；curb 控制；constructive 構造上的；remainder 剩餘物；humorous 幽默的；cartoon 動畫

《紅樓夢》是在講什麼？
What does A Dream of Red Mansions talk about?

A Dream of Red Mansions contains 120 chapters in all. Most scholars believe that the first 80 chapters were written by Cao Xueqin (曹雪芹 , about 1715-1764). This text first circulated under the title of Story of a Stone (《石頭記》). The novel's present title was the contribution of a later writer, Gao E (高鶚) who added a final 40 chapters along the lines of the original author's intention.

The novel focuses on the tragic love stories of Jia Baoyu (賈寶玉) and his beautiful cousins Lin Daiyu (林黛玉) and Xue Baochai (薛寶釵). It also depicts the gradual decline of the aristocratic Jia family. The author brings to life a host of young women, including young ladies and lowly maidservants. There is also an extensive cast of male and female characters from all levels of society both inside and outside the Jia family. In language, the novel lifts the vernacular of the traditional Chinese novel to its highest point, skillfully combining colloquial and vulgar speech with highly refined poetry and prose in the literary language. As a masterpiece of the world literature, it represents the peak of the development in the traditional Chinese realistic novel.

> **Notes**
>
> mansion 大宅；circulate 傳播；tragic 交通；aristocratic 貴族的；maidservants 女僕；cast 演員陣容；colloquial 口語的；vulgar 通俗的；refined 優美的

人們為什麼喜歡讀《唐詩三百首》?
Why do people enjoy reading The Collection of 300 Tang Poems?

In Chinese literature, the Tang Dynasty is considered the golden age of Chinese poetry. The Collection of 300 Tang Poems was compiled by Sun Zhu (孫洙) around1763. Sun compiled this collection due to his dissatisfaction with the then popular textbook called Poems by a Thousand Poets (《千家詩》). Sun made his own selection from a large number of Tang poems, most of which are the poets'best works. Moreover, most that he selected are written in relatively simple language and are easy to understand. Sun's collection became a "best seller" soon after its publication. Nearly every Chinese household owns a copy of the collection, and parents often encourage their children to memorize the poems. There is a popular saying that, "If you learn the 300 Tang Poems by heart, you can chant poetry though you are not a poet (熟讀唐詩三百首，不會作詩也會吟)."

> **Notes**
>
> dissatisfaction 不滿；selection 選擇；publication 出版

第十二章
中國古代神話
Ancient Chinese Mythology

本篇介紹中國古代神話的概況、特點、風格以及流傳至今的部分神話故事和神話人物。

中國古代神話的特色是什麼？
What is the feature of ancient Chinese mythology?

The ancient mythology has strong Chinese characteristics and is imbued with a sense of human vitality. The heroes are gods or deities, but they are also considered as Chinese people's ancestors such as Yu the Great (大 禹) and Huangdi (黃帝). The heroes and gods all love people in the world. Pangu (盤 古), Nüwa (女娲), Yi (羿) and Emperor Yu, for example, sacrifice themselves for the benefit of others. In addition, Chinese mythology contains the basic spirit of Chinese people who strive continuously to make new progress. Pangu, for example, creates the universe, and Jingwei (精 衛) fills up the sea. Generally speaking, Chinese myths constitute the roots of Chinese culture. They have deeply influenced philosophy, literature, arts and language.

> **Notes**
> imbue 使充滿；livelihood 生計；deity 神；ancestor 祖先

盤古是誰？
Who is Pangu?

In ancient Chinese mythology, Pangu was the first living being and the creator of the universe. According to Chinese cosmology, in the beginning there was nothing in the universe except formless chaos. Then this chaos began to unite into a cosmic egg, and Pangu emerged from the egg. He then set about the task of creating the world. He separated Yin from Yang. Yin became the earth, and Yang formed into the sky. This task took him eighteen thousand years. During this period, each day the sky grew ten feet higher, the earth ten feet wider, and Pangu ten feet taller. After eighteen thousand years had passed, the sky was ninety thousand li from the earth. Pangu died afterwards. His body became the mountains of the world, his blood the oceans and rivers, his left eye the sun, his right eye the moon, and his hair forests and grass.

> Notes
> creator 造物主；formless 無定形的；chaos 混沌

女媧是誰？
Who is Nüwa?

In Chinese mythology, Nüwa is the goddess who created human beings. As everyone knows, she had the upper body of a woman and the lower body of a snake. It is said that there were no men or women when the sky and the earth were separated. Nüwa felt lonely. One day while washing her face by a river, she began making tiny clay figures with yellow soil. As Nüwa placed each clay figure on the ground, it became alive and started calling Nüwa "Mama." On hearing this, Nüwa was extremely happy, and she named each of them. Nüwa continued making clay figures in this way until she was exhausted. Then she put a piece of rope in deep mud, raised the muddied rope high, and threw it on the ground. The mud on the rope splashed immediately and landed everywhere. The numerous splashed mud droplets turned into innumerable men and women. It is said that nobles are created from the yellow clay, and poor or lowly people from droppings of the rope.

Notes
exhaust 用完；muddy 使沾上爛泥；splash 濺；droplet 小滴

羿是誰？
Who is Yi?

There existed ten suns that appeared in turn in the sky during the period of Emperor Yao, a legendary ruler in ancient China. At the beginning, the ten suns each would take turns moving off into the sky for a journey of one day. Later they were tired of this routine. So the ten suns decided to appear all together in the sky in the daytime. The combined heat made life on the earth unbearable. Crops were dying out, forests were burning into flames, and the seas were boiling. Moreover, savage beasts came out to hurt people. So Emperor Yao sent Yi, a great archer armed with a magic bow and ten arrows, to frighten the disobedient suns. Yi first shot to death all the savage beasts. Then he started to shoot the ten suns. However, Emperor Yao thought that the sun was still useful to human beings. So he had someone take away one of Yi's ten arrows. Therefore, Yi shot down nine suns, and only the Sun we see today remained in the sky.

Notes
routine 慣例；unbearable 不能忍受的；flame 火焰；savage 凶猛的；
beast 獸；disobedient 不服從的

精衛為什麼要填海？
Why does Jingwei fill up the sea?

Once upon a time, Emperor Yan's (炎 帝) youngest daughter swam in the Eastern Sea. Suddenly a strong wind rose, and the surging waves drowned her. However, her spirit turned into a small bird. As she flew over the roaring sea, the bird cried sadly with a sound like Jingwei. People later named the bird Jingwei after her sound. The bird lived on a mountain near the sea. She looked like a crow, but had a colorful head, a white bill and two red claws. The bird hated the sea so much that she decided to fill up the sea. Every day she flew to and from between the mountain and the sea, carrying a twig or a pebble from the mountain and dropping it into the sea. It is said that she still carries out the same mission today.

The story describes the indomitable will of people who never stop in their mission until they reach their goal.

> **Notes**
> drown 把……淹死；roaring 咆哮的；pebble 小卵石；mission 任務

女媧為什麼要補天？
Why does Nüwa mend the sky?

A long time ago, Gong Gong (共工), God of Water, and Zhu Rong (祝融), God of Fire, had a battle. Zhu Rong won, and Gong Gong, in anger, struck his head against the Buzhou Mountain (不周山). The mountain collapsed, and down came the big pillars that held the Heaven. Half the sky fell in, leaving a big black hole. Consequently fires and floods occurred, and savage animals started to hurt people.

Nüwa was sad to see that the human beings which she had made underwent sufferings, so she melted rocks of five colors and used them to mend the sky. In addition, she cut off the legs of a giant turtle and used them as pillars to support the sky. She scared away all the savage beasts and blocked the flood with the ashes of reeds. Since then, people were able to live in peace.

Notes
collapse 倒塌；pillar 柱子；consequently 因此；undergo 經歷；melt 融化；reed 蘆葦

神農為什麼要嚐百草？
Why does Shennong try to taste hundreds of herbs and grass?

Shennong is also called Emperor Yan. According to Chinese myth, he invented farming and taught people how to cultivate crops, and establish markets for trade. He helped people change from a diet of meat, clams and wild fruits, to the diet based on grains and vegetables. During Shennong's time, people drank unboiled water and ate grass and wild fruits. As a result, they often got sick. So Shennong tasted all kinds of herbs that were suitable as remedies or medicinal herbs. It is said that he once identified more than 70 poisonous plants in a day. Due to him, people learned that medical herbs could cure diseases.

It is thought that Shennong lived from 2737 B.C. to 2697 B.C., nearly 5,000 years ago, so people often say that Chinese medicine has a history of 5,000 years. However, we have little information about how herbal medicines were used prior to The Shennong Herbal Medicine Classics (《神農本草經》), written during the Eastern Han Dynasty.

你知道嫦娥奔月的故事嗎？
Do you know the story of Chang'e Flying to the Moon?

Yi, the hero who shot down the nine of the suns, went to Mt. Kunlun (崑崙山) where he got some elixir from the Queen of the West (王母娘娘) and brought it back home. Unexpectedly his wife Chang'e ate it without his permission. Afterwards she felt herself light-footed as if she were floating on air. Gradually she couldn't help but fly up to the sky, and eventually she landed on the moon, where she lived forever. Because the moon was cold and lonesome, she was always homesick for her past life on the earth.

你知道夸父追日的故事嗎？
Do you know the story of Kuafu chasing the sun?

A long time ago, there was a tall man whose name was Kuafu and who lived on a mountain. Every day he saw the sun rise in the east, travel across the sky, and then go down in the west. Kuafu wished to chase the sun and visit the place where the sun hid itself in the west. So he started racing after the sun.

He ran very fast and succeeded to approaching the sun. But the closer he got, the more he became eagerly desirous for water to drink. He looked round and saw the two rivers-Huanghe（黃河）and Weihe（渭河）. He plunged into the rivers and soon devoured all the water. Afterwards Kuafu was still thirsty. He started to run northwards in hope to reach the Great Lake and drink more. Unfortunately, he died of thirst on the way. The cane he left became a forest of peach trees.

Notes
obviously 明顯地；approach 接近；desirous 渴望的；devour 吞沒；
unfortunately 不幸地

第十三章
中國戲劇藝術
Chinese Opera Arts

　　中國素有戲劇大國之稱。中國的戲劇藝術，歷史悠久，種類繁多。本篇介紹的是中國戲劇的起源、京劇和其他一些主要劇種的藝術特點。

中國傳統戲劇何時初具規模的？
When did the forms of traditional Chinese opera begin to be perfected?

Opera is the most ancient form of theater that still flourishes in China today. It combines acting, singing, poetry, dialogue and acrobatics. The origins of Chinese theatre go far back into history. Most elements of voice, instrumentation, dancing and acrobatics existed during the Han Dynasty. However, the operatic forms began to be perfected during the 12th century.

Notes

flourish 茂盛；dialogue 對話；acrobatics 雜技；instrumentation 樂器（演奏）法

傳統戲劇有什麼表演特點？
What are the performance features of the traditional opera?

It is generally believed that traditional Chinese opera has taken shape as an artistically advanced form of theatre. It conveys the idea of time and space to the audience through staged performances, and it features unique solo singing, refined acting, rich percussion and irresistibly funny comedians. A performance focuses on four traditional characters. Actors or actresses draw on the tradition in which they are well versed to give performances without previous thought or preparation. Originally, Chinese opera was performed before a simple backdrop, with the other three stage sides remaining open and empty. The setting itself was also extremely simple, but over centuries, actors or actresses have developed a set of sophisticated stylized stage symbolism. This includes a table, which might stand for an official's table, a hill or a bridge. The action is based on illusion. Gestures, footwork and other body movements express actions such as riding a horse, rowing a boat, opening a door, going up stairs, climbing a hill or traveling. In a word, each action of a performer is highly symbolic.

傳統戲劇的角色有什麼特點？
What is the feature of the character roles of the traditional opera?

Character roles in traditional opera are generally divided into four main types according to the sex, age, social status and profession of the character. They are sheng (生), dan (旦), jing (淨) and chou (丑).

Sheng refers to male roles. These can be subdivided into different types, including zhengsheng (正生), xiaosheng (小生) and wusheng (武生). Zhengsheng refers to a bearded, middle-aged or elderly man who plays the part of a positive character; xiaosheng refers to a young man whose gesture is unrestrained and footwork brisk; wusheng is a military general between 30 and 55 years old.

Dan refers to female roles. These can be subdivided into the following different types: laodan (老旦), qingyi (青衣), huadan (花旦) and wudan (武旦). Laodan refers to an old woman. Qingyi refers to a refined young or middle-aged woman, who is often in a dark pleated skirt and is portrayed as a positive character. Huadan refers to a girl or young woman in a jacket and pants. She appears shrewish or active. During the performance, she speaks more and sings less. Wudan refers to woman with martial skills. This character mainly shows her martial skills rather than singing or talking.

Jing refers to roles with painted faces. Jing or hualian (painted faces) refers to male roles that have a frank personality and unrestrained movement. Their facial makeup is multi-colored.

Chou, or clown, is a comic character which can be recognized at first sight for his special makeup (a patch of white paint on his nose). Chou is the main role in a comedy or a satirical opera. It can be subdivided into wenchou (文丑 , male clowns), wuchou (武丑 , clowns with martial skills) and danchou (旦丑 , female clowns). They mainly play the part of positive characters. But sometimes they also act as negative characters.

Notes
profession 職業；unrestrained 無限制的；pleated 起褶的；portray 表現；shrewish 潑悍的；martial 尚武的；personality 個性；satirical 愛挖苦人的；negative 反面的

傳統戲劇的臉譜有什麼特點？
What is the facial makeup of traditional opera?

When you are watching an opera, what impresses on you the most may be the "painted face." Facial patterns date far back in history. Ancient Chinese actors sometimes wore masks known as "dummy faces." Later, painted patterns replaced the mask. Facial patterns follow a set mode in composition, sketching and coloring. The patterns use multi-colored exaggeration and symbolism to suggest a character's personality, and painted faces become what the Chinese call "a mirror of the soul." From the painted faces, Chinese audiences can instantly tell the personality of characters on the stage.

Audiences have long become accustomed to the facial patterns and expression. Generally speaking, red face makeup (紅臉) refers to loyal and upright persons; black face makeup (黑臉) refers to faithful and straightforward persons; white face makeup (白臉) refers to imperious and treacherous persons; multi-colored face makeup (五彩臉) refers to ghosts and gods; the white makeup between eyes and nose (小花臉) indicates a clown's face'which appears funny and humorous.

> **Notes**
> dummy 假的；mask 假面具；facial 面部的；sketch 概略地敘述；exaggeration 誇張；instantly 立即；upright 正直的；straightforward 正直的；imperious 專橫的；treacherous 背叛的；humorous 詼諧的

臉譜按照圖案分類有哪些類型？
How many kinds can the facial makeup be divided into according to its pattern features?

In accordance with facial makeup patterns, the facial makeup falls into another four types as below：

Zhenglian (整臉, whole-face facial makeup)Zhenglian refers to a whole-face makeup pattern. Typically paint the whole face with one color, and then outline eyebrows, eyes, nose, and facial lines. It aims to display the personality of a character in a play.

Sankuai Walian (三塊瓦臉 , three piece facial makeup)This makeup refers to left-and-right-side makeup patterns produced on the basis of a whole-face makeup pattern. This type seems incomplete, and it is divided by the mouth and nose on the same face.

Huasankuai Walian (花三塊瓦臉 , flowered three piece facial makeup)On the basis of the left-and-right-side makeup patterns of sankuai walian, some more artistic lines have been added along the edge of these patterns until a sankuai walian facial makeup becomes fragmented.

Suilian (碎臉 , fragmented makeup)

This makeup refers to a variation of Sankuai Walian facial makeup. Flower-shaped lines are added along the edge of left-and-right-side makeup patterns. These lines have been exaggerated to such an extent that it misshapes the left-and-right-side makeup patterns.

> **Notes**
>
> character 人物，角色；incomplete 不完全的；fragmented 不完整的，無條理的；misshape 使造型不佳，把……弄成畸形

你對傳統戲劇樂器知道多少？

How much do you know about the musical instruments used in traditional Chinese opera?

Traditional Chinese opera commonly has a music band of string and percussion instruments. Some foreigners do not readily appreciate this art, for the opera tunes sometimes sound very shrill. The music is not intended to be melodic, as in the West. Rather, it is used to punctuate the performance with a strong rhythmical accompaniment. Each regional opera has its own typical band. The two main music instruments used in Beijing Opera are jinghu and erhu (京胡、二胡), two kinds of two-stringed bowed fiddles with a low register. Other instruments include yueqin (月琴, moon-shaped mandolin), pipa (琵琶, the Chinese lute), drums, bells, gongs and other instruments. The drumbeat sets the music tempo. The Kunshan Tune (崑腔) in Sichuan Opera is a melodic form, and a bamboo flute or vertical bamboo flute are the dominant melodic instruments. The clapper, consisting of wooden bars of unequal length，is used in Qinqiang Opera (秦腔) to produce a strong rhythm in harmony with clear loud voices of the actors.

In the older days, the band joined by some percussionists usually was in full view on stage. A drum-man conducted the band. Nowadays, the band has a fixed place on the stage, but out of sight of the audience.

Notes
shrilly 尖聲地；melodic 有旋律的；rhythmical 有節奏的；accompaniment 伴奏；fiddle 小提琴；register 音域；mandolin 曼陀林（一種撥絃樂器）；unequal 不相等的；harmony 和諧；percussionist 打擊樂器演奏者

京劇是如何產生的？
What is the origin of Beijing Opera?

Beijing Opera commands the largest following in China and is also the best-known form of Chinese opera abroad. During the mid-Qing Dynasty in the 17th and 18th centuries, Kunqu Opera (崑曲), characterized by soft singing and minimal orchestral accompaniment, such as the clapper or drum and a bamboo flute, rose to the status of national opera even in Beijing. In addition, Qinqiang Opera (秦腔) and Gaoqiang Melodic Form (高腔), a high-pitched singing style, were popular in Beijing. In 1779, on the occasion of Emperor Qianlong's (乾隆) 70th birthday, throngs of artists arrived in Beijing to give performances, and among these people were four Huiban Opera Troupes (徽班劇團) from Anhui. After their performances at the Qing court, the troupes stayed in Beijing and continued to perform their plays. Some accomplished dramatists made innovations in the Huiban Opera there. Their music was based on the erhuang melodic tradition of Anhui Opera (徽劇) and the xipi tradition of Hubei Opera (漢劇). It also incorporated some of the repertoire, tunes and music accompaniment of Qinqiang Opera and folk music. These joint operatic forms developed during a twenty-year period to become a new form of opera with distinctive features, and it came to be called Beijing Opera during the reign of Emperor Xianfeng (咸豐).

Notes

minimal 極微的；orchestral 管絃樂（團）的；high-pitched 聲調高的；innovation 創新；accomplished 有造詣的；incorporate 包含；operatic 似歌劇的；di-stinctive 有特色的

什麼是崑曲？
What is Kunqu?

Kunqu (崑曲) was originally called the Kunshan Tune (崑腔). In the Qing Dynasty, it was renamed Kunqu, and at present it is known as Kunju Opera (崑劇). Kunqu is one of the oldest extant forms of Chinese opera. Due to its influence on other Chinese theatre forms, it is known as the "teacher" or "mother" of a hundred operas, including Beijing Opera and Sichuan Opera. On May 18, 2001 it was listed as one of the Masterpieces of the Oral and Intangible Heritage of Humanity by UNESCO.

Kunqu was developed during the late Yuan Dynasty in Kunshan (崑山), east of Suzhou city. It was a dramatic form developed from Nanxi (南戲), the Southern Drama of the Yuan Dynasty, and its emergence ushered in the second Golden Era of Chinese drama. The famous romance-dramas included Peony Pavilion (《牡丹亭》) by Tang Xianzu from the Ming, and The Palace of Eternal Youth (《長生殿》) by Hong Sheng and The Peach Blossom Fan (《桃花扇》) by Kong Shangren from the Qing.

Kunqu combines acting, singing, dancing, dialogue, and acrobatics. Characteristically, it is noted for delicate tunes and elegant melodies. A bamboo flute, suona trumpet, pipa instrument, and traditional percussion are the dominant melodic instruments.

Some well-known plays written in the Ming and Qing dynasties are still performed on stage. In addition, many classical Chinese novels and stories, such as Romance of the Three Kingdoms, Outlaws of the Marsh and Journey to the West were adapted very early into dramatic pieces.

Notes

extant 仍然存在的；masterpiece 名作；in-tangible 無形的；heritage 文化遺產；humanity 人文學科；UNESCO（United Nations Educational, Scientific, and Cultural Organization）聯合國教科文組織；emergence 出現；peony 牡丹；eternal 永恆的；acrobatics 雜技；percussion 打擊樂器；melodic 有旋律的

川劇曲調有哪些特點？

What is the feature of the melodic forms in Sichuan Opera?

Sichuan Opera is the major form of local opera in Southwestern China, popular in Sichuan, Yunnan and Guizhou provinces. It appeared around the middle of the Qing Dynasty, and it has adapted four major melodic forms. One is kunshan Tune (崑腔), which originated in the southern Yangtze Basin and was later imported to Sichuan. It sounds gentle, clear, and fluent.

The second is huqing Voice (胡琴), a voiced form that derives mainly from the xipi (西皮腔) and erhuang (二黃腔) melodic families of Huiju Opera in Hubei Province.

The third is tanxi (彈戲), one of the oldest forms of opera in China. During the Ming Dynasty, it appeared in Shaanxi, Hunan and other areas. As it was introduced into Sichuan, local people called it Chuanbangzi Opera (川梆子). Chuan means Sichuan; bangzi indicates wooden clapper with bars of unequal length, which is used as an accompaniment to produce a strong rhythm in harmony with the clear, loud voices of the Chuanbangzi Opera.

The last one is gaoqiang (高腔), a high-pitched singing style. It is the most highly known style among the multi-tunes of Sichuan Opera. Its solo vocal range extends beyond the eight-bar music scale, and its melodic ornamentation sounds both elegant and energetic. Its high-pitched tune usually has no stringed accompaniment. Its solo vocalization moves quickly up or down the scale and skillfully gives a throbbing effect and embellishments to the tones. Sparse rhythmical emphasis from the wooden clappers usually accompanies the high-pitched melody, and choral effects from the band either repeats or elaborates on what the solo melody sings.

> **Notes**
>
> **adapt** 改編；**vocal** 歌唱的；**energetic** 精神飽滿的；**throb** 有節奏地震動；**embellishment** 裝飾

川劇變臉是怎麼回事？
What is the face-changing performance in Sichuan Opera?

In Sichuan Opera, some characters suddenly show their magical power by quick changes of facial patterns without makeup, jumping through burning hoops and hiding swords. Among these magic tricks, the face-changing is the most popular. An actor playing a bandit may change his faces nine times, each time to escape pursuers, and an evil sorcerer changes his face with his moods.

The face-changing is bianlian in Chinese, and it is an important intangible cultural heritage. Only a few masters have grasped this skill. They know how to change masks magically in quick succession. As they flourish their arms and twist their heads, their painted masks change again and again and again.

Face-changing got its start 300 years ago. At the beginning, actors changed the color of their faces during performances by blowing into a bowl of red, black or gold powder. The powder would adhere to their oiled skin quickly. In another method, actors would smear their faces with colored paste concealed in the palms of their hands. By the 1920's, actors began using layers of masks made of oiled paper or dried pig bladders. They could peel off one after another in the blink of an eye. At present, actors use full-face, painted silk mask. They can be worn in layers, as many as two-dozen thick, and be pulled off one by one.

> **Notes**
>
> hoop 箍狀物；bandit 強盜；sorcerer 巫師；intangible 難以確定的；heritage 繼承物；magically 不可思議地；succession 一連串；smear 塗抹；conceal 隱蔽；bladder 囊狀物

什麼是皮影戲？
What is Chinese Shadow Play?

Chinese Shadow Play is also known as Chinese Shadow Puppets. Originated in the Han Dynasty, the play became quite popular as early as the Song Dynasty. In the Ming Dynasty, there were 40 to 50 shadow show troupes in the city of Beijing alone. In the Qing Dynasty, the shadow play came to maturity in Chengdu. They mainly existed in counties across Western Sichuan, with Chengdu as its centre. Folk artists usually call it the "Chengdu shadow act under the leather lamplight." Zhou Xun (周詢) of the Qing Dynasty said, "The shadow play exists everywhere in China. However, the ingenious and exquisite workmanship in other places is not comparable to that of Chengdu (燈影戲各省多有，然無如成都之精備者)."

Chinese Shadow Play combines storytelling and entertainment, and demonstrates the style of harmony and exaggeration. In addition, it presents a unique artistic charm due to the fact that it has merged traditional forms of paper-cut, mural painting, stone carving, operas, music, etc.

The shadow puppets are brightly painted leather figures. Each puppet's trunk, head, and limbs are separately carved but joined together by thread so that each puppet part can be manipulated by the operator to simulate human movements. A talented operator can make puppet figures appear to walk, dance, fight, nod or laugh.

The "stage" for the shadow play is usually a white cloth screen on which the shadows of puppet figures are projected. Operators are all under the stage, manipulating rods that support separate parts of each puppet figure. A traditional puppet figure has six or seven parts supported by two or three rods. Sometimes one operator can skillfully manipulate more than three puppets at the same time.

Today, puppets are used to tell dramatic versions of traditional fairy tales and myths. In Gansu province, it is accompanied by Daoqing music; while in Jilin, it shows to the accompaniment of Huanglong music form and some of the basis of modern opera.

Notes
troupe 劇團；lamplight 燈光；ingenious 巧妙的；workmanship 技藝；storytelling 說故事；exaggeration 誇張；woodblock 木版；intricately 複雜地；manipulate 操縱；simulate 模擬；nod 點頭；to the accompaniment of 在⋯⋯伴奏下的

第十四章
中國古代建築
Ancient Chinese Architecture

　　在中國大地上有許多造型優美、色彩絢麗的古代建築,這些建築在世界建築史上占有重要地位。本篇介紹獨特的木結構、庭院式建築的平面布局、各種屋頂樣式及其豐富的色彩。

中國古建築有什麼基本特徵？
What is the basic feature of ancient Chinese architecture?

Visitors who come to China for the first time may be struck by some traditional Chinese buildings with their curved roofs, bold colors and intricate outlines. They may wonder how the Chinese ever came up with this unique architectural style. In order to appreciate ancient buildings in China, visitors should know the prominent feature of such buildings as follows:

➤ Most buildings are made of wood. A timber framework is a basic feature of ancient Chinese architecture.

➤ Courtyard composition and layout is another feature. A courtyard is a space enclosed by walls, or a yard surrounded by buildings.

➤ Varied roof patterns have been added to enhance the beauty of these ancient buildings.

➤ Paint is much used as an architectural ornament.

➤ Ancient Chinese buildings keep in harmony with their natural surroundings.

Notes
architectural 建築學的；architecture 建築學；intricate 錯綜複雜的；outline 外形；prominent 顯著的；framework 構架；enclose 圍住；surround 圍繞；surroundings 環境

中國古建築的木結構有哪些特點？

What are the features of the timber framework in ancient Chinese architecture?

Ancient Chinese buildings use timber extensively as a building material in addition to bricks and tiles. Chinese wood represents "life." Moreover, timber was easily available, transportable and practical at that time. The timber framework consists mainly of wooden vertical pillars and crossbeams. They are perfectly interlocked with brackets so that the whole weight of a house is transferred to its foundations through the pillars, beams, lintels and joists. Walls bear no load; they only separate space. The timber framework supports most of the weight of the house. There is an old saying that, "A house still stand even if its walls collapse（牆倒屋不塌）."

Two things are worth attention when you view ancient buildings. One is the wooden tenon（榫）, and the end of a piece of wood perfectly shaped to fit into a corresponding wooden mortise（卯）in another piece of wood. This technique was invented 7,000 years ago. The other is the system of support brackets, called dougong（鬥拱）. These are wooden brackets on the top of a column to support the crossbeam; they rise up level by level from each pillar. These brackets both support the structure and are also a distinctive and attractive ornamentation. This invention came into being about 2,000 years ago, during the Warring States Period.

> ### Notes
> extensively 廣大地；tile 瓦；transportable 可運輸的；practical 實際的；crossbeam 橫梁；interlock 使連鎖；bracket 托架；lintel 楣石；joist 托梁；tenon 榫；corresponding 相應的；mortise 卯；column 圓柱；crossbeam 橫梁

古建築的色彩有什麼特點？
What are the color features of the ancient Chinese architecture?

Paint is much used on buildings. Initially paint was used on wood to prevent damage from moisture, but gradually paint became an architectural ornament. Ancient palaces and temples tend to have brilliant colors like glazed yellow tiles, red walls and white balustrades. The shining colors make these buildings look grand and impressive. However, colors applied on garden-like buildings or commonplace houses tend to be quietly elegant. These colors give people a nice, cool sense.

The painting on ancient buildings functions as an ornament. In the Qing Dynasty, it commonly fell into three categories as follows:

➤ Hexiwucaihua (合細五彩畫， Hexi Five-color Decoration): This painting style is applied only to the key buildings in imperial palaces and altars. Usually, a dragon or phoenix is painted on green background, and paint lines are gilded with gold powder or gold foil.

➤ Xuanzicaihua (旋子彩畫， Circular Color Decoration): This style is extensively applied to government buildings, key buildings in temples, and the attached buildings of imperial palaces and altars. An artist tends to use bright designs and auspicious flowers. In addition, he outlines the designs in ink color and adds some running dragons and strokes. He then draws a pattern in the shape of the Chinese word gui (圭) on the either side of the design center. Inside the "gui" pattern are many other brightly colored designs developed from peony flowers.

➤ Suzhou decoration: This painting style originated in Suzhou; later it has developed into two schools: the southernand the northern. Southern suzhou decoration focuses on bright designs, and the northern on landscape, figures, flowers, pavilions, etc.

> **Notes**
>
> balustrade 欄杆；impressively 給人以深刻印象地；imperial 皇帝（或女皇）的；gild 把……鍍金；foil 金屬薄片；additional 額外的

佛教寺廟內主要有什麼建築？
What are the main buildings in a Buddhist monastery?

Chinese Buddhist architecture consists of temple, pagoda and grotto. It started during the Han Dynasty as Buddhism entered China. In ancient times, many Chinese emperors of different dynasties believed in Buddhism, so Buddhist monasteries or temples were constructed across the country. In the Northern Wei Dynasty, monasteries or temples accounted to more than 30,000 in number. Later, glazed tiles, exquisite engravings and delicate paintings were all used in Buddhist monastery construction. These monasteries and temples were fashioned after the imperial palaces and bore very little resemblance to temples in India or other Buddhist countries.

Chinese monastic buildings usually follow a north-south axis (中軸線). Generally each monastery or temple has three groups of buildings, separated by courtyards or walls. Each group has a main building, which stands on this axis, facing south. The names of the main buildings include the Temple Gate (山門), the Heavenly King Hall (天王殿), the Great Buddha Hall (大雄寶殿) and the Buddhist Scripture Library (藏經樓). Additional buildings are set up on either side of the axis. Living quarters, kitchens, dinning halls and storehouses are usually located on the right side of the main buildings, but buildings on the left side are for visitors.

Notes

construct 建造；account（在數量等上）占；ex-quisite 精緻的；resemblance 相貌相似；heavenly 天國的；storehouse 倉庫

道教寺廟的特點是什麼？
What are the features of a Taoist temple?

A Daoist temple evolved from the traditional square-shaped Chinese court-yard. The main halls usually stand on the north-south axis, serving as places for people to worship the statues of Daoist gods and conduct Daoist ritual ceremonies.

During the Eastern Han Dynasty, when Daoist was born, Daoist ascetics mostly lived in huts and even caves in remote mountains. From the Jin Dynasty to the Northern and Southern Dynasties, Daoist experienced reforms, and many temples were set up in cities or even in the capital under imperial orders. During the Tang Dynasty, Daoist, Buddhism and Confucianism influenced one another, and thus Buddhist and Confucian architecture had a great influence on Daoist temple construction. As a result, Daoist temples resemble those of Buddhism and Confucianism in design and many other aspects.

Daoist architecture falls into two styles: traditional and bagua（八卦）. The traditional style refers to a compound layout in which the main halls usually stand on a north-south axis and other buildings are on the two sides or at the back of the courtyard complex. The bagua style refers to that in which all buildings surround the danlu（丹爐）, a stove to make elixirs. The south-north axis appears very long, and structures flank the axis. This style symbolizes the notion that human beings follow the Earth, the Earth follows the Heaven, the Heaven follows the Dao (道), and the Dao follow itself.

Notes

worship 崇拜；conduct 實施；ceremony 禮儀；ascetic 苦行者；
design 構思；layout 布局；flank 位於……的側面（或兩側）

傳統村落整體布局有哪些環境特徵？
What are the environmental features of the general layout of a traditional village?

A village is likely to be constructed in harmony with natural surroundings. Local villagers always highly appreciate trees, hills or streams nearby. In their mind, natural surroundings have been imbued with cosmic vitality and a sense of life.

In ancient times, the Chinese believed that the movements of the sun and moon affected spiritual currents that influenced people's daily lives. This "cosmic breath" is known as Fengshui (wind and water). It is said that it was also affected by the form and size of hills and mountains, the height and shape of buildings, and the direction of roadways. Ancient people were aware of the importance of geomancy in the location and orientation of buildings and other structures.

An ideal location of a village should be in much conformity with the positions of the "Four Images" that are regarded as the lucky supernatural beasts. These are the Qanglong (青龍, the green dragon) that represents the east, the Zhuque (朱雀, the phoenix-like beast) the south, the Baihu (白虎 , the white tiger) the west and the Xuanwu (玄武 , the tortoise like beast with a snake winding round it) the north.

In accordance with the ideal environmental structure, the placement of a village generally observes one principle of "being situated at the foot of a hill and beside a stream (依山傍水)" where locals could cut woods in the hill for fuels and obtain water in the stream for drinking or washing. The other principles include "the main facade being southern or eastern (坐北朝南 / 坐西朝東)."

Safety is one of the concerns for the environmental structure. Wall or stockade is probably made around the village to escape from marauding animals and dangers brought by bandits or robbers.

Notes

surrounding 周圍的；imbue 浸染；cosmic 宇宙的；geomancy 占卜；orientation 方向；in conformity with 和……相適應；environmental 周圍的；fa.ade 建築物的正面；stockade 柵欄；maraud 搶劫；bandit 強盜；robber 盜賊

四合院有什麼特點？
What are the features of siheyuan?

Siheyuan is a residential courtyard. It is a traditional Chinese architectural form used extensively since the 12th century. In Beijing, most of the courtyards extant today were built in the Ming and Qing dynasties.

In ancient times, the courtyards were divided into those for princes, dukes, officials or common citizens. The princes'mansions of the Ming Dynasty consisted of front and rear sections, each section containing three main buildings along the south-north axis. In the Qing Dynasty, officials of the sixth and seventh ranks had major and minor halls of three jian (間), a room or area between adjacent pillars in a large hall and a single main gate painted with black iron rings. Ordinary citizens were not permitted to have rooms of more than three jian in size.

The normal arrangement of a "four-square" courtyard consists of a south-facing main hall（正房）, a north-facing southern hall（南房）and two halls along the east and west sides. The doors to these halls face toward the yard. Behind entrance gate the courtyard is a huge screen wall that prevents anyone outside from seeing what it is inside the courtyard.

Notes
extensively 大規模的；extant 尚存的；mansion 大廈；rear 後部；adjacent 毗連的；arrangement 安排；prevent 預防

古代庭院建築有什麼特點？
What are the features of ancient garden architecture?

An ancient Chinese garden is an artistic recreation of nature. It looks like a landscape painting in three dimensions due to a combination of structures and man-made landscape modeled after natural scenery. Most of the ancient gardens extant today were built in the Ming and Qing dynasties.

Garden architecture falls into two main types: the northern imperial gardens and the private gardens like those on the southern side of the Changjiang River.

Imperial gardens appear spacious, exquisite and grandiose. Built for royal families, they look magnificent. The most famous gardens include Beihai Park（北海公園）, the Summer Palace（頤和園）and the Yuanmingyuan Summer Palace（圓明園）in Beijing.

Private gardens are usually built in urban areas, near residences. They generally look small, but their overall layout is flexible, and their scenery tastefully delicate. In ancient times, they served as a place of retreat for gentleman-scholars to escape the chaos of the city. The most famous private gardens are located in Suzhou.

These two types of gardens are artistically common in some aspects:

➤ Each garden skillfully combines natural elements, such as rocks, water, trees and flowers, in an attempt to produce a harmony between man and nature.

➤ Each garden has pavilions built upon a lake or a pond so that half the structure is on land, while the other half is raised above a body of water.

➤ Covered corridors are another key element of ancient Chinese gardens. They are built to allow the owners to enjoy the garden in the rain and snow.

Notes

artistic 藝術的；recreation 娛樂；landscape 景色；dimension 容積；spacious 寬敞的；grandiose 宏偉的；urban 城市的；delicate 精美的；corridor 走廊

你對殿宇屋頂上的動物造型知道多少？
What is known about the animal figures on the roofs of ancient Chinese buildings?

On roofs, ancient Chinese palaces, temples and mansions have zoomorphic ornaments called wenshou（吻獸）. Some are on the main ridges, and some on the sloping and branch ridges. These, which are on roof ridges on the top of palaces, temples and other ancient buildings, form an important part of traditional Chinese architecture.

The monstrous figures at either end of the main ridges is called chiwen (鴟吻). It appears roughly like the tail of a fish and looks as if it were ready to devour the whole ridge. According to Chinese mythology, chiwen is one of the sons of the Dragon King who stirs up waves and changes them into rains. So chiwen are placed at either end of the main ridge for their magical power to conjure up a heavy rain to put out any fire. At the end of the sloping and branch ridges, there often stands a group of smaller animals. Their sizes and numbers are decided by the status of the owner of the building in the feudal hierarchy.

The largest number of zoomorphic ornaments is found on the Taihedian Throne Hall (太和殿) in the Forbidden City, all with unusual names. A god riding a phoenix (or rooster), the first animal, leads the flock. Behind the god, come a dragon, a phoenix, a lion, a heavenly horse, a sea horse and five other mythological animals. Qianqing Palace (乾清宮 , the Palace of Heavenly Purity) has nine animal figures; Kunning Palace (坤寧宮 , the Palace of Female Tranquility) has seven; the other twelve halls used to house the imperial concubines each have five.

Placing animal figures on roof-ridges has been a traditional practice for at least 2,100 years. It is believed that an immortal being and various beasts serve to protect sacred buildings and keep evil spirits far away.

Notes

ornament 裝飾品；zoomorphic 獸形的；monstrous 怪異的；devour 吞沒；conjure 施魔法；hierarchy 等級制度；phoenix 鳳凰；rooster 雄雞；mythological 神話的；tranquility 平靜；concubine 妾

數字「九」與皇家宮殿有什麼關係？

What is the relation between the number "nine" and imperial palaces?

"Nine" is the largest single digit number. In ancient China, this number had a special significance, symbolizing the supreme sovereignty of the emperor. For this reason, this number is often employed in palace structures and designs. For instance, ancient palaces generally consist of nine courtyards. The same is true for the Temple of Confucius (孔廟) in Qufu (曲阜), Shandong Province. The buildings of the Forbidden City in Beijing are traditionally measured as having a total floor space of 9,900 bays (a room spaces enclosed by four poles). Some even say 9,999 bays, but this may be an exaggeration. In the Forbidden City, nails on every door are arranged in nine lines with nine nails; and the doors, windows, stairs and fixtures are also in nines or its multiples. In addition, the watchtowers inside the four corners of the palace compound each have nine beam roofs, 18 columns and 72 ridgepoles. The three famous screen walls each have nine dragons.

The number "nine" is not only used on buildings. The New Year's dinner for the imperial household had 99 dishes. Stage performances had to comprise 99 numbers to celebrate the birthday of an emperor as a sign of good luck and long life.

Notes

digit 數字；supreme 至上的；sovereignty 主權；fixture 固定裝置；multiple 倍數；watchtower 瞭望臺；ridgepole 房屋的棟木；comprise 包含

古建築也反映了封建社會裡的等級制嗎？
Did ancient buildings reflect the social system offeudal China?

In ancient China, emperors, empresses, and princesses lived in imperial palaces. Undoubtedly the palaces rank as the highest class of building according to the ancient social system. The same class goes to the Majestic Buddha Hall (大雄寶殿) in a Buddhist monastery and the Three Trinity Hall (三清殿) in a Daoist temple. These buildings appear typically magnificent because they have yellow glazed tiles, multi-layer eaves, the wudian roof, decorative paintings, painted dragons, phoenix patterns, and giant red gates. The residence owned by government officials and rich businessmen is called the Large-type Housing Building (大式). These buildings have no glazed tiles, and brackets on top of the columns reflect the social system. The third grade residence is called the Small-type Housing Building (小式) used frequently by common people.

The raised base of the ancient architecture also reflects the social system of the feudal society. The ordinary base is simple and flat to support the small or large-type housing buildings. Another kind of the raised base is called the Xumi-Seat-Patterned Base (須彌座) which originally came from the pattern of the bottom base for a statue of Buddha. This Buddhist pattern came into the traditional Chinese architecture after Buddhism entered China. This structure supports important halls in the imperial palace complex as well as buildings in a monastery or temple. The purpose is to show the resident's noble status and rank. In addition, this base has white marble railings. The third kind of raised base is the superfine base that consists of multi-stone-floors; each floor is the Xumi-Seat-Patterned Base circled by jade stone railings. The multi-floor base is only used to support key halls in the imperial palace complex and some key buildings in a monastery or a temple like the Hall of Supreme Harmony (太和殿) in the Forbidden City and the Dacheng Hall in the Qufu Confucian Temple (曲阜孔廟 的大成殿). According to The Canon Collection of the Qing Dynasty (《大清會 典》), the raised base is limited to 0.67 meters in height for the residence owned by high officials of the third rank and above, and 0.33 meters in height is for the residence owned by officials of the fourth rank and below.

A jian (間) or bay is the area within 4 pillars; one jian is approximately 15 square meters. According to the ancient social estate system, a main hall in the imperial palace usually is a 9-jian hall. During the Qing Dynasty, the Hall of Supreme Harmony in the Forbidden City was expanded from 9 jian to 11 jian in dimension to show imperial power. Under the Ming Dynasty, the front, middle and rear halls owned by a top ranking duke were permitted to extend to 7 jian, and his front gate was limited to 3-jian in space. Officials of the first to fifth ranks could have 7-jian major and minor halls. Officials of the sixth and seventh ranks had 3-jian major and minor halls. Ordinary citizens were not permitted to have rooms of more than 3 jian in size although they were not limited to any specific number of rooms they could build. The Qing period saw many changes in these rules, but the system laid down by the Ming remained basically intact.

Notes

undoubtedly 無疑地；majestic 尊嚴的；multi-layer 多層；glazed tile 琉璃瓦；railing 欄杆；approximately 大約地；intact 完整無缺 的

什麼是亭臺樓榭？

Could you tell me something about a tower and a pavilion?

An ancient tower or pavilion is mainly built with wood. In some examples of their construction, not a single nail is used. Sets of brackets link up the joints of the wooden structures. Wooden teeth bite into points where wooden pieces or stuff meet.

In ancient times, a tower (樓) functioned as a storage house for books, scriptures, and portraits of famous people. A tower can beautify a garden or a scenic spot, offering visitors a space where they are able to look far into the distance. Famous towers include Yueyang Tower (岳陽樓) in Hunan Province and the Yellow Crane Tower (黃鶴樓) in Hubei Province.

A pavilion (亭) usually has a roof but no walls. Most pavilions have gently upturned eaves, splendid glazed tiles, and bright red pavilion posts. Green trees, grass, and water often encircle the pavilion, forming a beautiful landscape. The Chinese often say that a pavilion represents humankind's place in the universe. During the Qin and Han Dynasties, a pavilion was set up every 5 kilometers for convenience of people who walking by and might stop in for a rest or lodging. The pavilion functioned as a sentry box in border districts. Later on, the pavilion turned into a small-scale building in which a visitor could have a rest or overlook the scenery all around. In the Tang Dynasty, it was common to build pavilions in scenic places and gardens. The design of pavilions varies. The most common design is the square-shaped pavilion. A common feature of Chinese gardens is the waterside pavilion (臺榭) which is half built on land and half raised on stilts above a body of water to offer a view from all sides. Through a combination of natural and artificial elements, designers seek balance and harmony between man and nature in their design.

Notes
storage 儲藏；humankind 人類；stilt 支撐物

第十五章
儒學
Confucianism

　　中國的儒教博大精深，是中國文化的重要組成部分，對中華
民族的文化、心理、倫理道德等方面影響很深，在世界上也有很
大的影響。本篇介紹的內容是孔子的生平、儒教的影響、孔子的
主要思想以及儒教的一些特點。

你了解孔子的一生嗎？
What is known about Confucius'life?

According to Chinese tradition,Confucius (551 B. C.- 479 B. C.) was a thinker, political figure, and educator. Records of the Historian (《史記》) by Sima Qian collected tales about him. Based on these tales, his ancestors were members of the Royal State of Song (宋國貴族). Later, his great grandfather, fleeing turmoil in his native Song, moved to Lu (魯國), somewhere near the present site of Qufu in southeastern Shandong Province.

There the family became impoverished, and the young Confucius had to undertake jobs as an accountant or cared for livestock. We do not know how he was educated, but tradition has it that he studied ritual with the Daoist Master Lao Dan, music with Chang Hong, and the lute with Music-Master Xiang (相傳曾問禮於老聃，學樂於萇弘，學琴於師襄). In his middle age, Confucius is supposed to have gathered about him a group of as many as 3,000 disciples whom he taught. At the age of 50, his talents were recognized by the state, and he was appointed Minister of Public Works and then Justice Minister. But he apparently offended members of the lu nobility and was forced to leave office and go into exile.

In the company of his disciples, he left the State of Lu and traveled from state to state to offer his advice to rulers on how to improve their management of state affairs. At the same time, he looked for an opportunity to put his ideas into practice, but this opportunity never came. In any case, by most traditional accounts, he returned to Lu in 484 B. C. and spent the rest of his life teaching and editing Book of Songs (《詩》), Book of Documents (《書》), and Spring and

Autumn Annals (《春秋》). The best-known of which is Analects (《論語》), a collection of his sayings that was compiled and edited in its modern form during the Han Dynasty. Confucius died in 479 B. C., aged 72.

> **Notes**
> thinker 思想家；ancestor 祖宗；turmoil 混亂；impoverished 窮困的；undertake 從事；accountant 會計；livestock 家畜；talent 天才；offend 冒犯；nobility 貴族

儒教的影響有多大？
What influence has Confucianism had?

Confucius is the most famous sage of China. More than any other single man, he, through his followers, produced the principle basis of the Chinese tradition of ethics and political theory that had thus deeply influenced Chinese society and culture. Over the centuries, this influence spread also to Korea, Japan and other countries.

Confucianism is wholly considered more of an ethical philosophy than a religion. However, it is debatable if the system founded by Confucius should be called a religion. It prescribes a great deal of ritual, but little of this can be interpreted as worship or meditation in a formal sense, and Confucius occasionally made statements about the existence of other-worldly beings that sound agnostic to western ears.

> **Notes**
> ethics 倫理學；debatable 可爭論的；meditation 沉思；occasionally 偶爾地；agnostic 不可知論的

孔子思想的基本內容主要有哪些？
What are the basic concepts in Confucian thought?

Li（禮）, courtesy. Courtesy is originally believed to have originated in Heaven. Confucius redefined li to refer to all actions done by a person to build an ideal society in everyday life. In practice, Confucius tried to revive the etiquette of earlier dynasties.

Xiao（孝）, filial piety. This had long been considered as one of the greatest virtues and had to be shown towards both the living and the dead. It denotes the respect and obedience that a son should show to his parents, especially to his father. Confucius extended this code of conduct to broader patterns of obedience-the wife obeys the husband; the younger brother the elder brother; the subject the ruler.

Zhong（忠）, loyalty. This was traditionally the equivalent of filial piety on a different plane, and the relationship between a ruler and his ministers. It was not only stressed by Confucius but clearly demonstrated in his life of moral courage and devotion to principles.

Ren（仁）, benevolence. The word ren in Chinese consists of two components- "person" and "two," referring to the way two persons should behave towards each other with mutual respect and heart. It implies a system based on empathy and mutual understanding. It is perhaps expressed in the saying, "Do not do to others what you would not like them to do to you（己所不欲，勿施於人）."

Junzi（君子）, gentleman. This term literally means "son of a ruler," but it is used to person who has a well-integrated personality. Such a man is expected to act as a moral guide to the rest of society. He cultivates himself morally, he participates in the correct performance of the rites, and he shows filial piety and loyalty where these are due, and the great exemplar is Confucius himself.

> **Notes**
> courtesy 禮貌；revive 復甦；etiquette 禮節；filial 孝順的；piety 虔誠；obedience 順從；equivalent 對等；demonstrate 說明；empathy 移情；cultivate 培養

漢武帝為什麼要「獨尊儒術」？
Why did Emperor Wudi make Confucianism the orthodox philosophy of the Han Dynasty?

The Han rulers founded a unified dynasty. They felt the need of a philosophy that could guide and strengthen their rule. In the previous short-lived Qin Dynasty, the first emperor who unified the country had made an attempt to unify thought. He had given orders that books be burnt, scholars buried alive, and that people be prohibited from the study of anything other than the laws then in force. However, the Qin Dynasty was toppled only fifteen years after he founded it and various schools of thought were again active. This made the Han rulers realize that they needed to unify thought along different lines. 70 years after the founding of the Han Dynasty, Emperor Wudi called on scholars to present suggestions for effective government. Dong Zhongshu (董仲舒, 179BC.-104BC.) presented three memorials to the emperor, suggesting that Confucianism be made the official orthodox philosophy, and that all other schools of thought be discredited.

The emperor decided to accept this suggestion, and this decision had a tremendous influence on the development of Chinese culture for it put Confucianism into a dominant position. From then on, in the civil service examination system of most dynasties of ancient China, it was compulsory for candidates to study Confucianism for imperial government positions.

> **Notes**
>
> orthodox 正統的；strengthen 加強；memorial 請願書；discredit 不被相信；candidate 候選人；compulsory 義務的

宋代理學是什麼？
What is the Neo-Confucianism in the Song Dynasty?

Neo-Confucianism is a term for a form of Confucianism that was primarily developed during the Song Dynasty (960- 1279). Zhong Dunyi (周敦頤), ChengYi (程頤) and other scholars initiated this Neo-Confucianism. The challenge of Indian Buddhist metaphysics and Daoist thoughts at the time required that attention be given to a philosophic framework which could explain the world and human nature. There was considerable debate between various schools of thought, but in the end Zhu Xi's (朱熹) comprehensive views prevailed, and he became the leader of a new orthodoxy, known in the West as Neo-Confucianism.

In the system of Zhu Xi, everything in the world is constituted by the interaction of two factors; li (理), or the form of an object, and qi (氣), or matter. Li was the origin of everything, and it governs the nature and human society. In the feudal ethical code, li consisted of "three cardinal guides and five constant virtues (三綱五常)." The three cardinal guides said, "The prince is the guide of his ministers; the father is the guide of his sons; the husband is the guide of his wife (君為臣綱，父為子綱，夫為妻綱)." The five constant virtues included humanity, rightness, propriety, wisdom, and trustworthiness (仁、義、禮、智、信). Zhu Xi advocated that people maintain the ethical code by abandoning selfish motives and following orders of the feudal rule; and he used those views to interpret Confucian Classics that were traditionally regarded by feudal rulers as orthodox.

Zhu Xi recognized, moreover, that the Confucian system of the time did not include a thoroughgoing metaphysical system. Therefore, he devised one. He believed in gewu (格物), the "investigation of things," which he understood in a particular sense. In his thought it meant something deeper than the English word implies; it implies something in the nature of personal commitment. Zhu Xi said that "the investigation of things" means that we should seek for "what is above shapes" by "what is within shapes (事事物物皆得其理，格物也)."

The ethical teachings by Zhu became accepted state philosophy from the Ming to the Qing Dynasty and came to be called Neo-Confucianism.

Notes

initiate 開始；metaphysics 形而上學；constitute 構成；interaction 互相影響；constant 不變的；propriety 禮儀；trustworthiness 可信賴；advocate 擁護；abandon 拋棄；motive 目的；investigation 調查

你能告訴我《論語》中的幾則名句嗎？

Could you tell me some proverbs from the Analects by Confucius?

學而時習之，不亦說乎。有朋自遠方來 ，不亦樂乎。

Isn't it a pleasure to study and practice what you have learned? Isn't it also great when friends visit from distant places?

吾日三省吾身，為人謀而不忠乎？與朋友交而不信乎？傳不習乎？

Each day I examine myself in three ways: in doing things for others, have I been disloyal? In my interactions with friends, have I been untrustworthy? Have not practiced what I have preached?

吾十有五而志於學，三十而立，四十而不惑，五十而知天命，六十而耳順，七十而從心所欲，不踰矩。

At fifteen my heart was set on learning; at thirty I stood firm; at forty I had no more doubts; at fifty I knew the mandate of heaven; at sixty my ear was obedient; at seventy I could follow my heart's desire without transgressing the norm.

溫故而知新，可以為師矣。

Reviewing what you have learned and learning a new, you are fit to be a teacher.

學而不思則罔，思而不學則殆。

To study and not think is a waste. To think and not study is dangerous.

見賢思齊焉；見不賢而內自省也。

When you see a good person, think of becoming like her/ him. When you see someone not so good, reflect on your own weak points.

默而識之，學而不厭，誨人不倦。

Keeping silent and thinking; studying without satiety, teaching others without weariness.

不憤不啟，不悱不發。舉一隅不以三隅反，則不復也。

If a student is not eager, I won't teach him; if he is not struggling with the truth, I won't reveal it to him. If I lift up one corner and he can't come back with the other three, I won't do it again.

三人行，必有我師焉。擇其善者而從之，其不善者而改之。

When three men are walking together, there is one who can be my teacher. I pick out people's good and follow it. When I see their bad points, I correct them in myself.

性相近也，習相遠也。

People are similar by nature, but through habituation become quite different from each other.

(Translated by Charles Muller)

Notes
proverb 名句；disloyal 不忠誠的；mandate 指令；transgress 違背；
satiety 滿足；weariness 疲倦；habituation 適應

第十六章
道教
Daoism

　　道教是中國唯一的土生土長的傳統宗教，是中國傳統文化的綜合體。要了解中國的傳統文化，就得了解道教。本篇介紹的是道教的形成、道教教義的基本組成部分以及中國道教的基本特點。

教是如何形成的？
How did Daoism take shape?

Daoism（道教）is a religion native to China. It took shape during the reign of Emperor Shun Di（順帝年間, 125-144) of the Eastern Han Dynasty. At that time, Zhang Daoling（張道陵）founded the Five-Picul-of-Rice Sect（五斗米教）, the early form of Daoism. Its followers worshiped Lao Zi（老子）as their great teacher and took Dao De Jing（《道德經》）as their accepted standard of thought. They believed that a man could obtain immortality through personal cultivation.

Zhang was born in Anhui Province and in his early years studied Confucianism. Later, however, he became dissatisfied with some of the Confucian principles because they failed to offer methods of immortality. So he began to study the way to immortality; and he soon mastered the process of producing dan（丹）, as a help to live forever. In his hometown, Zhang couldn't afford to buy the herbs that needed for the dan production; so he and his followers came to Sichuan Province and settled in Mt. Heming（鶴鳴山）in Dayi County（大邑縣）, where he could get enough herb material. While continuing his Daoist studies, he used Daoist methods to offer medical treatment to the local people and eventually gathered 10,000 followers to form the Five-Picul-of-Rice Sect. The five picul refers that each member of the sect must pay a certain amount of rice or firewood when he or she joins in the section. The sect was officially established in Sichuan, and Mt. Qingcheng（青城山）became the spot where Zhang preached his doctrines.

Towards the end of the Eastern Han Dynasty, a peasant rebel leader named Zhang Jiao（張角）established another Daoist sect called Tai-ping Dao（太平道, The Peace Sect). He also managed to gather 10,000 followers and he organized an uprising in the name of the sect which heavily weakened the feudal ruling class.

> **Notes**
>
> picul 擔；cultivation 培養；principle 原理；sect 派別；uprising 起義；weaken 減弱

道教教義的基本組成部分有哪些？
What are the essential parts of Daoism doctrine?

Daoist doctrine was rooted on age-old witchcraft, recipes for immortality and the concepts of Huang Di (the Yellow Emperor) and Lao Zi. It greatly influenced economy, culture and political thinking of feudal China for more than 1,700 years.

The age-old witchcraft goes back at least the 21st and 11th centuries B. C. People worshiped gods, ghosts, and numerous supernatural beings-heavenly, earthly and human. Heavenly beings include Blue, Yellow, White and Black Kings, as well as gods of the sun, the moon, stars, wind, rain, thunder, and lightening. Earthly spirits include local village gods, agricultural gods, river gods, as well as the gods of the five mountains-Taishan（泰山）, Hengshan（衡山）, Huashan（華山）, another Hengshan（恆山）in Shanxi Province, and Songshan（嵩山）. Human supernatural beings include ancestral, sages and personages of virtue, loyalty, filial piety, justice and chastity.

Beginning with the Spring and Autumn Period, many persons wanted to live forever. Some books from that time described how supernatural beings live eternally and propose methods by which human beings can do the same. One focused on increasing one's qi（氣）, which literally means "vitality." Itis thought that such method exercises to absorb qi from outside the body. Another method was gradually developed, called alchemy. Alchemists attempted to produce dan (丹) by refining cinnabar. People expected to achieve long life after ingesting dan, and Daoism included the recipes for immortality as part of its key doctrine.

Chinese people often refer to ourselves as the descendents of Huang Di, the Yellow Emperor. Ancients believed that he was a part-real and part-legendary being. In the early Western Han Dynasty, the ruling class believed in both the ways of Huang Di and Lao Zi for seeking peace and quiet; and they hoped this belief would dominate the whole country. At the beginning, Daoists accordingly worshiped both Huang Di and Lao Zi; but later they shifted the emphasis to focus only on Lao Zi who was generally admitted to be the founder of Daoism.

> ### Notes
> witchcraft 巫術；recipe 祕訣；supernatural 超自然的；personage 人物；chastity 貞潔；vitality 活力；alchemist 煉金術士；cinnabar 硃砂；ingest 嚥下

老子是誰？
Who is Lao Zi?

It is said that Lao Zi (老子) lived about the same time as Confucius. His proper name was Li Er (李耳); and he is also known as Elder Dan (老聃), Senior Lord (老君) or Daoist Lord Lao Zi (老子道君). However, few people know about his life. Legends say that he was born with grey hair in the later years of Spring and Autumn Period in Ku Prefecture (苦縣) of the State of Chu (楚國) on the present site of Luyi County (鹿邑), Henan Province.

Daoist legends say that he worked as an archivist in the Imperial Library of the Zhou court, and that Confucius intentionally or accidentally met him browsing through library scrolls. In the following months, Confucius discussed ritual and propriety with Lao Zi who later resigned from his post when he saw the state in decline. Little is known about him after this point. According to an old story, he rode a purple buffalo, travelled west into the State of Qin, and disappeared into the vast desert there. As he passed through the western-most gate, a guard said to him, "Since you are about to leave the world behind, could you write a book for my sake?" Lao Zi did so. He wrote a book in two parts, setting out the meaning of The Way and Virtue. The whole book has some 5,000 characters and it is called Dao De Jing.

> **Notes**
>
> prefecture 府；archivist 檔案管理員；intentionally 故意地；accidentally 偶然地；browse 瀏覽；scroll 卷軸

《道德經》是什麼書？
What is Dao De Jing?

Dao De Jing (道德經) is a philosophical prose that has had great influence on Chinese thought. It can be translated as "The Scripture of the Way and the Virtue", and it covers many areas of philosophy, from individual spirituality to techniques for governing society. Being often referred as the book of 5,000 characters, it has two parts-dao and de. Dao De Jing has been translated into European languages, and in English alone, there are over 30 versions.

The dao part traditionally has 37 chapters. Dao is usually translated into English as "the way ahead," and the dao is thought to be responsible for the creation and maintenance of the universe in being. The dao begets one; one begets two; two begets three; three begets the myriad creatures (道生一，一生二，二生三，三生萬物).

The de part comprises the other 44 chapters of the book. De has the approximate meaning of "righteousness" or "virtue" in the original English sense of inherent power. The de chapters discuss the virtue with relation to the nature or the universe and state that even the dao must follow nature.

> ### Notes
> beget 生；myriad 無數；righteousness 公正；spirituality 精神上的事情

什麼是「道」?
What is the dao?

The dao (道) is the central focus of Dao De Jing. It refers an unnameable, inherent order or force of the universe. The book begins by saying "The dao is that can be spoken of, is not the constant way; the name that can be named, is not the constant name (道可道，非常道。名可名，非常名)."

The dao is thought to be responsible for the creation and maintenance of the universe in being. One may say that it is misleading to say that the dao produced the universe. However, the book does not say that it produced the universe like a father produces a son. It produced the universe only in a figurative sense.

The dao is ineffable but then suggests some similes and gives a hint at its nature. It is humble like water, which flows downwards and always seeks the lowest place. It is like the yin-passive and yielding, not active or dominating. It is like empty space, but not an emptiness that has no value. The central Daoist philosophy is the nation that great inner peace and power come to persons who center their lives on the dao, the way of the universe.

Notes
unnameable 難以形容的；inherent 固有的；mislead 把……帶錯方向；misleading 使人誤解的；ineffable 難以形容的；passive 消極的；simile 直喻；yielding 聽從的；emptiness 空虛

什麼是「無為」？
What is wuwei？

Wuwei (無為) literally means "action through non-action" or "harmony with the flow of things." As has been said, the dao is like the yin or humble. Daoism stresses a person's harmonious place in the natural world and it advises people to abandon self-effort and ease themselves into the rhythm of the universe, life and death. Chapter 66 says, "River or sea can be lord of a hundred valleys because they excel in taking the lower position. Thus they can be lord of the hundred valleys. Accordingly, if one desires to rule over others, one must humble oneself in one's speeches, and if one desires to lead others, one must in one's whole person follow them (江海之所以能為百谷之王者，以其善下之，故能為百谷王。是以聖人欲上民，必以言下之；欲先民，必以身後之)." Such behavior is wuwei. A person of wuwei is like water in his movement, like a mirror in his stillness, like an echo in his responses...He never leads, but always follows. He achieves happiness by forgetting his own happiness and following the happiness of others. This does not mean that one should sit around and do nothing! It means rather that actions taken in accordance with the dao are easier and more productive than these that actively attempt to counter the dao.

> **Notes**
> humble 謙遜的；self-effort 自我努力；productive 富有成效的；
> counter 反擊

什麼是道家的「洞天福地」？
What are the Daoist Celestial Caverns and Blissful Lands?

Daoism teaches that all things in the universe have their own spirit (god). In ancient times, people thought that supernatural beings ascend to Heaven, or dwell in far-off beautiful places. During the Warring States Periods, those who sought immortality imagined that there are three divine mountains in the Bohai Sea (渤海)-Penglai, Fangzhang, and Yingzhou (蓬萊、方丈、瀛洲). Those mountains are the habitations of immortals and that the drugs of immortality can be found there. According to later Daoist teaching, the habitations of immortals came to include The Ten Continents and The Three Islands (十洲三島). The continents include Zu (祖洲), Ying (瀛洲), Yan (炎洲) and seven others. The islands are Kunlun (崑崙), Fangzhang (方丈) and Penglai (蓬萊).

The Ten Celestial Caverns (十大洞天) are residences of Daoist immortals on the famous mountains on this earth. They include Wangwu (王屋山洞), Weiyu (委羽山洞), Xicheng (西城山洞), Xixuan (西玄山洞) and six other caverns.

The Seventy-Two Blissful Lands (七十二福地) are also located on famous mountains on the earth, and all managed by perfect beings in accordance with the orders given by deities.

These include Mt. Jun (君山) in Dongting Lake (洞庭湖) and Mt. Damian (大面山) close to Chengdu, Sichuan Province.

Notes
celestial 神聖的；cavern 洞穴；blissful 極樂的；habitation 居住；
continent 陸地；immortal 不朽的

什麼是道家醫學觀？
What are the medical perspectives of Daoism?

Daoism values human life and stresses the saying "My life depends on my own effort; it is not dictated by Heaven (我命在我，不在天)." Daoist medicine aims at long life and immortality. According to a unique system that borrows from traditional medicine while maintaining particular Daoist characteristics and principle, the concepts of Daoist medicine stress on the Interaction of Heaven and Man (天人合一) and the Correspondence Between Heaven and Man (天人相通). Daoist medical thought teaches that the human body shares the same structure as that of the cosmos, so persons should nurture and preserve their lives in accordance with the law of nature. It recognizes the presence of a vital power and seeks to maintain healthy vitality and eliminate diseased vitality through a balance of the human body's physiological functions. Daoist medical practices encourage the cultivation of both bodily life and mental tranquility, which will benefit the body and contribute to longevity.

Concretely their practices include herbalism, acupuncture, and various decoctions as well as breathing exercise, abstaining from grains, inward focus in meditation and martial arts.

> **Notes**
>
> dictate 命令；cosmos 宇宙；preserve 保存；eliminate 消除；physiological 生理學的；mental 精神的；tranquility 平靜；herbalism 草藥醫術（學）；acu-puncture 針灸療法；decoction 煎熬的藥；abstain 避開

什麼是道家養生觀？
What is the underlying philosophy of Daoist health cultivation?

In a narrow sense, Daoist health cultivation aims at a harmonious state of body and mind that can achieve longevity. But in a broader sense, it depends on the Daoist view of life, theory of immortality, and techniques to achieve immortality. Based on the Daoist cosmology, the Dao is thought to be responsible for the creation of the universe and human beings, and human beings can achieve an ideal state of health when they abide by the law of the Dao and maintain harmonious integration with the nature.

According to the book called Collection on Life Cultivation (《養生集》), the key points for life cultivation include the achievement of mental tranquility, the preservation of vitality and body nourishment. According to another book called Scripture of Supreme Peace 《太平經》 , persons need to focus on mental tranquility, treasure vitality and worship the Deity.

Notes
abide by 遵守；preservation 保存；nourishment 滋養

第十七章
佛教
Buddhism

佛教作為世界公認的三大宗教之一，自兩漢之時傳入中國後，迅速地深入中國社會生活的各個領域，並與儒、道文化一起成為中國傳統文化的主流。本篇介紹的內容有佛教創始者、佛教基本教義、佛教能夠在中國扎根的原因、佛教的基本特點以及人們在寺廟裡常見的佛像的故事。

佛教的創始者是誰？
Who was the founder of Buddhism?

Buddhism was founded in India around the 16th centuryB. C. It is said that the founder was Sakyamuni (釋 迦 牟 尼). Sakya was the name of the clan to which his family belonged. Sakyamuni was born a prince. His kingdom covered an area that is today in southern Nepal in the Himalayan (喜馬拉雅山) foothills and the prince was brought up in luxury. But in his 20s, he became discontented with the world. Every day he encountered suffering-poverty in a beggar, pain in the cries of a woman in childbirth, sickness and death in the form of a corpse. Around the age of 30, in spite of his father's attempts to keep him within the palace, the prince made his break from the material world and plunged off in search of enlightenment, leaving behind his wife and young son.

Sakyamuni began studying Hindu philosophy and Yoga. Then he joined a band of ascetics and he entered upon a period of rigorous fasting. However, no matter how he held his breath until his head burst and starved his body until his ribs jutted out, he failed to achieve enlightenment himself. He came to feel that self-inflected suffering was not the way to the answer he sought. Finally, Sakyamuni followed the principle of the middle way in which he would live between the extremities of asceticism on one hand and indulgence on the other. As the story goes, he devoted the final phase of his search for enlightenment to meditation and mystic contemplation. One evening, as he sat beneath a fig tree, he slipped into deep meditation. His experience was rewarded for he achieved enlightenment and became Buddha. Afterwards Sakyamuni expressed his new insight in sermons, and his disciples were said soon to have gathered around him.

佛教的基本教義是什麼？
What are the basic teachings of Buddhism?

Sakyamuni founded an order of monks and for the next 45 years or so preached his ideas until his death around 480 B.C.. The basic teachings of Buddhism are summed up in The Four Noble Truths (四諦): life is suffering (苦); the cause of suffering is desire (集); the answer is to quench desire (滅); the way to this end is to follow The Eight-Fold Path (八正道). This path consists of right knowledge, right aspiration, right speech, right behavior, right livelihood, right effort, right mindfulness and right absorption. By following The Eight-Fold Path, Buddhist followers aim to attain Nirvana, a condition beyond the limits of the mind, feelings, thoughts, the will and ecstasy. Buddhist teaching includes the concept of reincarnation, the circle of rebirth and the law of cause and effort.

Monastic orders for men and women center their practice on The Three Precious Treasures (三寶): the Buddha (佛), the Dharma (法, Law or Way) and the Bonze (僧, the Monastic Order).

什麼是大乘佛教和小乘佛教？
What are Mahayana and Hinayana?

Buddhism was prevalent in India for about 1,800 years between the 6th century B. C. and 12th century A. D.. Buddhism early in its history came to take two directions: The High Seat (上座部) and The Masses (大眾部). The former continued the traditional teachings of Buddhism, and the latter stood for reforms. Between the 1st and 2nd centuries A. D., Indian Buddhism split again into major schools: Mahayana (大乘 , Greater Vehicle) and Hinayana (小乘 , Lesser Vehicle). Mahayana Buddhism holds that the fate of an individual is linked to the fate of all others. The Buddha doesn't float off into his own Nirvana, leaving other people behind. He not only shows people the way to their Nirvana, but also continues to exude spiritual help to those seeking Nirvana. On the other hand, Hinayana holds that the path to Nirvana is an individual pursuit. People who seek Nirvana must tread its path on their own.

> **Notes**
> prevalent 流行的；exude 滲出

佛教何時傳入中國？
When did Buddhism enter China?

Buddhism made its entry into China very slowly and it entered the south of China by sea and the north by land.

High-Seat Buddhism was even divided as the southward and northward dissemination sections. The southward section first entered Southeast Asia, and about 7th century it entered Yunnan, China, via Burma. Propagated in Bali language family, it gradually became the primary form of Chinese Buddhism. Up to the present time, this form is still prevalent as Hinayana or Theravada Buddhism (小乘, Lesser Vehicle) in regions inhabited by Tai nationality.

About the 2th century, when Mahayana Buddhism was in its middle stage in India, it entered Central China, inhabited by the Han nationality. There is a tradition that Han Emperor Ming Di (漢明帝), in response to a dream, sent to India for Buddhist images and scriptures. It is said that he had these scriptures translated into Chinese at Luoyang (洛陽). About 65 A. D., he invited two Indian monks to China, and he even established a monastery in the suburbs of Luoyang. At this stage, however, Buddhism in China was confined to a few believers at court.

About the 7th century, Buddhism entered Tibet from both central China and India. Since the 11th century, another prevalent form of Buddhism in India entered Tibet in a big way. Since that time, the evolution of Buddhism in China followed two major forms, one in the Chinese language family, and the other in the Tibetan language family.

Notes
dissemination 宣傳；inhabited 有居民的

佛教在唐代的發展如何？
How did Buddhism develop in Tang Dynasty?

During the Tang Dynasty (618-907), the state employed Confucian forms and learning, and Tang emperors often favored Daoism. The early Tang state could restrict the number of monks and regulate monasteries. However, monasteries gradually flourished; they fulfilled important roles, and the most outstanding monks had sufficient self-confidence to make their own formulation of doctrine and develop the teaching in new ways. For Buddhist art, it was an age of classic achievement.

There were eight Buddhist sects that appeared between 581 and 755 A.D. Of them, four enjoyed only temporarily or limited success: the Disciplinary Sect (律宗), the Dharma Image (法相宗), the Sect of the Three Stages (三論宗) and the Esoteric Sect (密宗). The growth of sects not only illustrated the inner vigor of Buddhist religion, but also it manifested the strength of Buddhist monasteries. In the countryside, Buddhist monasteries performed important economic functions operating mills and oil presses. The monasteries also held much land that cultivated with semi-servile labor. Much of their wealth was channeled into building and the arts.

Notes
monastery 僧院；flourish 昌盛；sufficient 足夠的；self-confidence 自信；formulation 規劃，構想；tem-porarily 臨時地；disciplinary 紀律的，懲戒的；esoteric 祕傳的，難理解的

普賢是誰？
Who is Puxian?

Puxian (普賢) is one of the numerous Bodhisattvas (菩薩) of Indian Buddhism. According to Beihua Scripture (《悲華經》), Puxian was the eighth son of Amitabha, the Holy King in charge of reincarnation. His son's name was Mintu (泯

圖). Long long ago, the Holy King came to the Buddha with all his sons. They each made a vow to the Buddha who took this into account as he offered them words of advice. When it was Mintu's turn, the Buddha praised him, saying, "You are a pious and charitable man. In the present Buddhist world, you have behaved in a quiet and dignified manner, and your moral conduct is beyond reproach. In the future world, you will be a moral guide to all living creatures, bringing their hearts into peace and serenity, and you will support and assist other Buddhas. Therefore, from today on, you will be called Puxian." The meaning suggests that his moral conduct is boundless and immeasurable. In short, his name of Puxian means "universal benevolence." A book called Huayanqingliang Record (《華嚴清涼疏》) says that Puxian has many images and transformations, which fall into three general categories. One is his "Fa Image (法 身)", which is often seen in monasteries. The second one is his "Bao Image (報身)", which reveal itself in the Buddhist Western Paradise.

The third is the "Suilei Image (隨類身)," the reincarnation of Puxian. This image can reincarnate at will into the body of any deceased person whose soul has been released from misery. Puxian takes bodily forms to show his own experience to others. In an image deeply loved by the broad masses of people, he enters the world on his six-tusk white elephant and appears on Mt. Emei in Sichuan Province. Therefore, Puxian followers everywhere seek to visit Mt. Emei to pay homage. The image of Puxian riding his six-tusk white elephant symbolizes the six supernatural powers, including those of the foot, the eye and others.

Puxian is considered to be one of Sakyamuni's close assistants. In some monasteries, the statues of Sakyamuni, Wenshu (文殊) and Puxian are placed in the Grand Buddha Hall.

Notes

numerous 許多的；vow 發誓要（做）；charitable 仁慈的；dig-
nified 有尊嚴的；reproach 責備；serenity 平靜；boundless 無窮的；
immeasurable 無邊無際的；be-nevolence 仁慈；transformation
轉變；homage 敬意

接引佛是誰？
Who is Jieyin Buddha?

Jieyin Buddha is also called Amitabha（阿彌陀佛）, or the Holy King in charge of reincarnation. Legend has it that Amitabha was an ancient Indian king who later followed Sakyamuni. Finally, he attained the state of Buddhahood through his perfect enlightenment. As the principal Buddha worshipped by Buddhist followers in Jingtu Sect, Amitabha takes charge of the Buddhist Western Paradise, and his work is to usher sentient beings into the paradise when they pass away. Towards the end of the Ming Dynasty, the Jingtu Sect reached the peak of its prosperity across China. It influenced large monasteries in Sichuan like the Wenshu Monastery（文殊院）and the Precious Light Monastery（寶光寺）, each of which established a hall for chanting the Buddhist Scriptures. The Jingtu Sect Hall is still in existence today. In the Jingtu Sect, there are more than ten Buddhas, with various Buddhist titles,including the Measureless Longevity Buddha, the Measureless Light Buddha, the Boundless Light Buddha and the Non-Obstacle Light Buddha, among others. They have extensive Buddhist power, a sublime position, and their own halls. There is a couplet which hangs outside a hall in Wannian Monastery（萬年寺）on Mt. Emei. It says, "May Buddhist hands come down; gently heal the hearts of human beings." This saying sums up the essence of the Jingtu Sect's belief: the salvation of all Buddhist believers.

彌勒佛是誰？
Who is Maitreya?

According to the Buddhist classics, Maitreya (彌勒佛) was born into a noble family in the Brahman caste in ancient India. He was the first to attain the state of Buddhahood through his perfect enlightenment, and afterwards he ascended to the Western Paradise. Maitreya will stay there for 56 billion years before he descends to the world to replace Sakyamuni and continue the spread of Buddhism. Therefore, Maitreya is considered as the successor to Sakyamuni, and his statue is usually placed in the first main hall of a monastery.

When Buddhism entered China, Maitreya took on Chinese characteristics and quickly became popular among the people. Popular folk legend depicts his image as a smiling Buddha with a large and exposed belly. This image is modeled on the appearance of Qi Ci (契此), a monk of the Liang State (梁朝) during the Five Dynasties. Qi Ci was from Fenghua (奉化) in Zhejiang Province, and his nickname was the Cloth-bag Monk. Legend has it that he carried a large cloth bag on his tin cane while traveling around. Into this bag he put all the alms given by people and redistributed them to other people in need. The masses of people deeply appreciated his kindness and honored him as the reincarnation of Maitreya. During the subsequent dynasties, the Maitreya statues seen in monasteries differ entirely in appearance from other Buddhist images, and was imbued with strong Chinese characteristics. A couplet inscribed outside the Maitreya Hall of Hongchun Monastery (洪椿坪) on Mt. Emei reveals the strong influence of Chinese culture and ethics. It says, "My face reveals my true nature; my belly shows my generosity and tolerance to others."

> ### Notes
> descend 下來；ascend 登高；caste 種姓；Bra-hman 婆羅門；expose 使接觸到；nickname 綽號；inscribe 題寫；generosity 寬宏大量；tolerance 寬容

觀音菩薩是誰？
Who is Guanyin?

According to the Buddhist classics, Guanyin (觀音菩薩) was the first son of the Holy King in charge of reincarnation. He has many followers and is considered the most well-known Bodhisattva in China. Guanyin has 33 various names and images, including an image with 1,000 hands, an image with 11 faces, and an image with 48 arms. Legend has it that when Buddhist followers are in trouble, Guanyin will come and help them if they recite his name single-mindedly. Therefore, Guanyin serves as the Bodhisattva of perfect compassion and kindness, helping the needy and relieving the distressed. His infinite Buddhist power is known in every household due to the popularity of the famous Chinese literary classic, Journey to the West. Guanyin is omnipotent and is said to have the power to bless women with male children in accord with customary Chinese saying "More Children, More

Joy." Consequently, he is extremely popular among the Chinese women. Since the Tang Dynasty, Guanyin became a female bodhisattva, the only female figure among numerous manifestations of Buddha. This is unique in Chinese Buddhism and reflects Chinese characteristics.

In monasteries in the region inhabited by the Han nationality, the figure of Guanyin usually sits in meditation holding a vial, with one leg crossed and the other leg hanging downwards. Large monasteries generally have a separate hall for Guanyin, but some monasteries place Mahasthamaprapta (大勢至) and Amitabha together with Guanyin in the same hall. The three are called "The Three Western Sages (西方三聖)."

In China, Buddhism and Daoism co-exist and interact in a harmonious way, and Daoism include some Buddhist images in the list of Daoist deities. Guanyin is, for example, worshiped in Daoist temples as Cihang Priest (慈航道人, Daoist Priest Dispensing Mercy).

Notes

single-mindedly 專心地；compassion 憐憫；relieve 減輕；distress 使悲痛；omnipotent 有無限權力的；cu-stomary 習慣上的

地藏菩薩是誰？
Who is Dizang?

According the Buddhist classics, during the period from the Nirvana of Sakyamuni to the advent of Maitreya, Dizang Bodhisattva (地藏菩薩) vows to save all beings from suffering in the Six Paths (Hell, Ghost, Animal, Man, Asura and Deva). He vows not to achieve Buddhahood until all the Hells are empty, and is thus therefore referred as the King of Hell.

In China, the image of Dizang has taken on Chinese characteristics. Chinese legend has it that he was born into a noble family in a state on the Korean peninsula, and his name was Jin Qiaojue（金喬覺）. After he became a monk, he made a trip to the Tang Empire, and during the Xuanzong Period（玄宗年間）of the Tang Dynasty between 712 and 756, he practiced Buddhism on Mt. Jiuhua in Anhui. He passed away while sitting cross-legged, and his whole body, still intact and not decayed, was buried under a pagoda. Gradually Mt. Jiuhua came to be revered as the key site for Dizang to deliver Buddhism. Usually, Dizang is depicted holding a tin cane in his right hand and ruyi pearls（如意寶珠）in his left. The former hand gesture indicates that he protects sentient beings and subdues evil, while the latter indicates that he will satisfy all the wishes of sentient beings.

Notes
peninsula 半島；revere 崇敬

文殊菩薩是誰？
Who is Wenshu?

According to the Buddhist classics, Wenshu（文殊菩薩）was the third son of the Holy King in charge of reincarnation. Legend has it that as Buddhists entered China, Wenshu appeared on Mt. Wutai. Therefore, people revere Mt. Wutai as the key site for Wenshu to deliver Buddhism, and monasteries there usually have his statue. Wenshu holds a sword that symbolizes his infinite Buddhist power and perfect wisdom. He rides a lion that also symbolizes his power and might. Wenshu and Puxian images are listed as close attendants to Sakyamuni image.

四大天王是誰？
Who are the Four Heavenly Kings?

The Four Heavenly Kings (四大天王) are depicted as the Four Warrior Attendants (Vajras). Their origin stems from an Indian Buddhism legend which says that there is a hill called Jiantuoluo (建陀羅) situated about half way up Mt. Xumi (須彌山) in the Buddhist Western Paradise. This hill has four peaks, and each Heavenly King protects one peak. They are thus called the Four Heavenly Kings. The Lord of the East is the King of the Gandharvas (持國天王 , Guardian of the Nation). He is dressed in white and holds a stringed musical instrument. The Lord of the South is the King of the Kumbhandas (增長天王 , Guardian of Sprouting Growth). He is dressed in blue and holds a sword. The Lord of the West is the King of the Nagas (廣目天王 , Guardian of Ugly Eyes or Deformed Eyes). He is dressed in red and has a dragon in his left hand. The Lord of the North (多聞天王 , Guardian of intelligence) is the best known. He is dressed in green and holds a trident in his right hand and a mongoose in his left. According to the Buddhist classics, the Four Heavenly Kings are able to drive out evil and monsters, protect Buddhas, and assure favorable conditions for the growth of crops each year. Therefore, their images are usually placed in the first main hall of a Buddhist monastery.

Notes

guardian 保護者；sprout 使生長；deformed 變形的；intelligence 智慧；favorable 稱讚的

你對十六羅漢、十八羅漢、五百羅漢的由來知道多少？

What can be said about the legendary origin of theSixteen Arhats, the Eighteen Arhats and the 500Arhats?

According to Buddhist classics, Sakyamuni's disciples are 16 Arhats. They were instructed by the Buddha not to ascend into the Buddhist Western Paradise, but to reside in the world, where human beings take care of them, and they, in return, bring benefits to human beings. This account is based on Fazhuji (《法住記》), a Buddhist scripture translated by Tang Xuan (唐玄) that lead to the great esteem of the 16 Arhats on the part of Buddhist followers of the Han nationality. Towards the end of the Tang Dynasty, the 16 Arhats in varied editions appeared.

The evolution from the 16 Arhats to the 18 Arhats began in painting. So far we know that the earliest painting of the 18 Arhats was painted by Zhang Xuan (張玄) of the Former Shu State (前蜀 , 907-925). Su Shi (蘇軾) composed 18 poems to eulogize this painting, but Su Shi did not name each Arhat. A Sichuan monk named Guan Xiu (貫休) painted another 18 Arhats, and Su Shi composed another 18 poems to eulogize his painting. This time Su Shi named each Arhat, and it indicates that the rise of the Eighteen Arhats was not in accordance with the original Buddhist classics. It was artists who added two more Arhat figures to the original 16. In later generations, Buddhist followers increased the number of Arhats by unsystematically picking out names from various scriptures to make up a total of 500 Arhats. Kao Taosu of the Ming Dynasty gave a complete list of their names on his Stone Name Tablets to the 500 Arhats in Qianming Courtyard.

> **Notes**
>
> reside 居住；evolution 發展；eulogize 頌揚；compose 組成；unsystematic 無系統的

什麼是大雄寶殿？
What is the Great Buddha Hall?

The Great Buddha Hall is the main hall of a monastery. It usually has a number of huge stone pillars that support the roof, and each pillar is carved with famous Buddhist couplets. On the top of the entrance hangs a board, which says Daxiong Baodian（大雄寶殿）. Daxiong means "Great Buddha" or "Great Hero"; baodian means "precious hall." The hall contains a central altar, on which Sakyamuni sits cross-legged on a lotus throne. His two closest disciples, Kasyap（迦葉）and Ananda（阿南）flank him. In Chinese Buddhist monasteries and temples, Sakyamuni may be depicted in different positions. Seating, he is in meditation, with his left hand on his left foot and his right hand pointing downward to the earth. This suggests that Sakyamuni sacrificed in this position before he founded the Buddhist religion. Standing, he points his left hand downward and raises his right arm upward. The raised left hand signs that he is able to satisfy the wishes of all sentient beings, the right hand that he is able to save them from sufferings. Lying on his side, he stretches out his legs, with his left hand placed on them, and his head supported with his right hand. Legend has it that Sakyamuni is talking to his disciples about final arrangements just before his death.

Notes

altar 祭壇；depict 雕出；throne 王位；su-ffering 受苦的；stretch 伸直

第十八章
民間信仰
Chinese Folk Belief

　　中國民間信仰的神靈並無普遍認同的體系，神靈的地位和神靈之間的關係因地而異，有很大的隨意性和靈活性，而且神靈有繁多的名目。本篇主要介紹民間信仰、廟宇的某些特點和中國歷史上一些影響很大的神靈。

中國民間信仰有哪些主要特點？
What is the main feature of Chinese folk belief?

Chinese folk belief refers to faith in both the supernatural and Chinese mythology about various gods and deities. It is generally considered to encompass two related but separate subjects. The first subject is associated with three domains: heaven, the realm of ghosts and the land of living. The second refers to deities, ghosts or human beings that can interact and sometimes transform themselves from one into another. Some of the mythical figures of folk religion have even been integrated into Chinese Buddhism and Daoism.

In Chinese folk belief the soul of a person is believed to either ascend to Heaven or go down to the realm of the ghosts when he or she dies. So while they are still alive, people should establish a good relationship with deities or ghosts by means of providing them with sacrificial offerings and burning paper money.

Chinese folk belief has lasted for thousands of years, so it retains traces of some primal religious belief systems, which include the veneration of the Sun, the Moon, the Earth, the Heaven, and various stars, as well as communication with animals.

Chinese folk belief also contains the custom of worshiping ancestors. People hold sacrificial services in memory of their ancestors, and as part of the ritual they usually burn paper money. It is believed that this type of the paper would be a financial support to their ancestors in the after-world.

> **Notes**
> supernatural 超自然的；mythology 神話；en-compass 包括；
> domain 範圍；interact 互動；transform 改變；mythical 神話；

什麼是民間廟宇？
What is a folk temple?

Folk temples (民間廟宇) flourished in the Ming and Qing Dynasties. These temples co-exist with Buddhist or Daoist temples or monasteries that have existed in China since ancient times. Due to the tide of modernization that started after the end of the Qing Dynasty in 1911, the number of folk temples has gradually decreased.

Chinese folk temples are generally small, and have different names and are located either in cities or in villages. Traditionally each temple has an image of the main deity together with some other deities that share the temple. Many of these deities represent good fortune or are responsible for the prosperity of the land.

One type of folk temples is called Tudi Deity Shrine (土地廟). The Tudi deity serves as a lower-level administrative spirit whose main responsibility is to ensure peace and security in his jurisdictional area, which is usually no more than a village in size, a bridge, a street, a temple, a public building, a private home, or a part of a field. Most of these buildings are simple and crude, and are only a few feet high, either located under trees or by the roadside.

Chenghuang Temple (城隍廟, city-ruling-deity temple) is another type of folk temple. It is devoted to Cheng Huang (城隍), one of the supernatural beings whose responsibility is believed to be that of defending the city and ensuring public security. The layout of the deities in a Chenghuang Temple usually consists of Cheng Huang, the grand deity being seated in the center of the temple's main hall. Some other deities flank Cheng Huang's image including Judges in Hades, Ox-Head and Horse Demons, Black-and-White Spirits, Bell-and-Drum Spirits (鐘鼓神), as well as the Ten Hell Kings (十殿閻羅) and the other images of the Nether World.

A communal temple (村廟) falls into the category of folk temples and enshrines the communal deities. Traditionally a communal temple is built with purple or violet walls, and blue and green tiles. The roof slopes down on two sides and the eaves overextend beyond the tall walls at the sides of a temple building. Due to various reasons, not many communal temples exist in North China. However, in the southern areas of Fujian, Guangdong and Taiwan, many traditional communal temples still remain as part of the life of the community. Along the coastal land, communal temples are usually located within residential areas; in the inland areas many temples are set on the edge of a village.

Notes

flourish 蓬勃發展；tide 趨勢；modernization 現代化；jurisdictional 管轄的；layout 布局，安排；a judge in Hades 判官；ox-head and horse demons 牛頭馬面；black-and-white spirits 黑白無常；Nether World 幽冥世界；enshrine 供奉；residential 住宅的

玉皇大帝
Jade Emperor

In Chinese folk culture, the Jade Emperor (玉皇大帝), the emperor of the supernatural pantheon, lives in the Jade and Pure Palace (玉清宮). In the Daoist supernatural circle, according to one version of Daoist mythology, the Jade Emperor is the executive ruler who ranks just below the one of the Three Pure Majesties (三清尊神).

Although the Emperor hasn't attained the state of the highest accomplishments in the Daoist supernatural circle, he has great authority, commanding all the deities in Heaven, the Earth, and the Land of the Living. In addition, he supervises auspiciousness and inauspiciousness: the prosperity and decline of all things in the universe.

It is said that on the 25th day of the twelfth month in the Chinese Lunar year, the Jade Emperor descends to the world for an inspection tour, giving rewards or penalties to deities and mortals in accordance with their annual deeds. On that day, people usually burn incense at home and provide food offerings to the Jade Emperor. Meanwhile, Zao Jun (灶君), the kitchen deity, makes his reports to the Emperor about each family'good and evil deeds.

The Jade Emperor's birthday is said to be the ninth day of the first lunar month. His birthday celebration is called the Jade Emperor Ritual (玉皇會). On this day, all the deities arrive at the ritual and join the grand celebration. In the folk and Daoist temples where the grand ritual is held, incense is burnt and food offerings are given.

<u>Notes</u>

pantheon 眾神；mythology 神話；executive 主管；majesty 陛
下，威嚴；attain 實現；accomplishment 成就；supervise 監督；
inauspiciousness 不吉祥；mortal 凡人

西王母
Queen Mother of the West

Xi Wangmu（西王母）is known as the Queen Mother of the West. She is considered the highest female goddess in fairy and folklore stories, as well as in the Daoist pantheon.

Most scholars assert that the earliest description of the Queen Mother was recorded somewhere between the third and second centuries B.C. in The Book of Mountains and Seas（《山海經》）. She was originally portrayed as a humanoid with tiger's teeth and the tail of a leopard. In later descriptions, she turned into a beautiful goddess of life and immortality.

The Queen Mother is immortal and has celestial powers. She takes charge of all the female celestial beings in and under Heaven. She is seated upon a spiritual western mountain range where her palace is believed to be a perfect and complete paradise. The Queen Mother is always surrounded by a female retinue of prominent goddesses and spiritual attendants. It is said that she holds a pantao（蟠桃）grand party in her palace, and many key celestial beings participate and taste pantao, the peaches of longevity in Chinese mythology.

Ever since the Ming Dynasty, the status of the Queen Mother has remained very high because of her popularity among many believers in folk circles. Many popular local shrines, as well as several Daoist temples, are dedicated to the Queen Mother as a symbol of longevity and eternal bliss.

> **Notes**
>
> folklore 民俗；humanoid 人形；leopard 豹；immortality 不朽；
> immortal 不朽的；celestial 神仙的；retinue 隨從；attendant 隨從；
> dedicate 奉獻；bliss 極樂，天賜的福

太歲
Grand Duke of Jupiter

The taisui (太歲) is literally translated as the Grand Duke of Jupiter. In Chinese folk belief, taisui is a ferocious deity, and people imagine that taisui might be an earthly deity whose formation corresponds with the revolution cycle of celestial Jupiter.

In the Chinese lunar calendar, the Ten Heavenly Stems (天干) and the Twelve Earthly Branches (地支) are used to formulate a sixty-year cycle. People believe that within the 60 years there will be 60 heavenly generals, each taking a turn for a period of one-year service that starts in lichun (立春, the beginning of spring) and ends in dahan (大寒, the great cold). Their responsibility is to take care of all matters and distribute fortune or misfortune into the world of mortals. A person's happiness, health, luck and fortune are all up to these generals who are called the jia-zi deities (甲子神) or the cycle deities. Although each jia-zi deity has his own specific name, people respectively give all the jia-zi deities a unified name: "the taisui deity" to identify the following characteristics.

One proverb says, "One can't break ground right above the head of a taisui deity (不得在太歲頭上動土)." This proverb is similar to the saying "One can't beard the lion in his den." People believe that each year's taisui deity governs taboo practices in ground-breaking and construction, moving from one residence to another, and marriage or burial ceremonies. Violating these may have adverse effects.

People also look upon the specific taisui deity who exercises authority over the whole year. Many Daoist temples or shrines contain a constellation hall (星宿殿) where the images of the 60 jia-zi deities are enshrined. When the new lunar year arrives, people often visit the constellation hall and worship these images by burning incense and providing food offerings. They hope that the taisui deity would bless them, give them a good health, and turn bad luck into good fortune.

Notes

duke 公爵，君主；Jupiter 木星；ferocious 凶猛的；correspond with 符合；revolution 旋轉；formulate 制定；den 獸穴；taboo 禁忌；ground-breaking 破土；adverse 不利的；constellation 星座；enshrine 供奉

福祿壽
Deities of Fortune (fu), Prosperity (lu), and Longevity (shou)

Fu (福), lu (祿) and shou (壽) are three deities who represent good fortune, prosperity, and longevity. Well-known in Chinese folk belief, they usually appear together as a trinity.

The fu deity is placed on the right of the lu. This deity, known for wealth and happiness, is holding in his arms a scroll, on which a Chinese character "fu

(福)" is written. The meaning of the fu character is all-embracing. It denotes people's bright hopes and goals in their common secular life.

The lu deity appears in traditional garments like an ancient Chinese scholar. He stands at the center, holding in his arms odd-shaped gold or silver ingots. In Chinese folk belief, the lu deity is an auspicious one who takes charge of prosperity, rank, and influence.

The shou deity is placed on the left of the lu. The deity also refers to the "South Pole Old Man Planet (南極老人)" in Chinese astronomy. The ancients believed that this planet possessed celestial powers that could not only affect the life-span of a state, but could also prolong a person's life. The shou deity appears as an old man with a long full white beard, a friendly smile, and an unusually protruding forehead. He is holding a walking stick or carrying a gourd filled with the Elixir of Life. In addition, he is usually accompanied by a bat, a tortoise, or a stag. All these creatures symbolize immortality.

> **Notes**
> trinity 三位一體；all-embracing 包括一切的；se-cular 世俗的；
> ingot 錠；take charge of 掌管；astronomy 天文學；life-span 壽
> 命；prolong 延長；protruding 突出的；elixir 仙丹；stag 雄鹿；
> symbolize 象徵

八仙
The Eight Immortals

The Eight Immortals (八仙) are Chinese deities. Their portraits are seen everywhere-on porcelain vases, teapots, teacups, fans, scrolls and embroidery.

Each immortal's power can be transferred to a tool of power（法器）that can give life or destroy evil.

Traditionally, "eight" is a lucky number, and therefore the "Eight Immortals" are associated with good fortune. In the Ming Dynasty, Wu Yuantai（吳元泰）wrote a book called The Origin of the Eight Immortals and their Trips to the East（《八仙出處東遊記》）. Hereafter, the legend of the Eight Immortals gradually spread across the country, and their images became popular among Chinese people. Below are some descriptions of each immortal.

➤ Li Tieguai or Iron-crutch Li（鐵拐李）is the most ancient of the Eight Immortals. He is depicted as a lame beggar, carrying a crutch. His spirit frequently leaves his body to wander the Earth and Heaven.

➤ Han Xiangzi（韓湘子）is a happy immortal. He is depicted holding a lotus flower, and sometimes with a sheng（笙, a flute) to accompany him. His lotus flower improves mental or physical health of people and animals.

➤ Lan Caihe（藍采和）is the least known of the Eight Immortals. Lan Caihe's age and gender are unknown. Lan is depicted often as a girl or boy, but sometimes as a woman or a man. She or he carries a flower basket. His or her behavior is out of norm and deemed strange by most people.

➤ Lü Dongbin（呂洞賓）is the most widely known of the Eight Immortals and hence considered by some to be the de facto leader. Dressed as a scholar, he often holds a sword that dispels evil.

➤ Cao Guojiu（曹國舅）was said to be the uncle of the Emperor of the Song Dynasty. He is shown in the official's court dress with a jade tablet which can purify the environment.

- He Xiangu（何仙姑）was born with six golden hairs on her head, and she spent her life as a hermit in the mountains. In a dream, she was instructed how to achieve immortality by the other Immortals.
- Zhong Liquan（鐘離權）is one of the most ancient of the Eight Immortals and the leader of the group. In Daoism, he is known as Original Master Truly-yang（正陽祖師）. His fan can revive the dead.
- Zhang Guolao（張果老）is the last of the Eight Immortals. Known as Master Comprehension-of-Profundity（通玄先生）, he claims to be several hundred years old.

> **Notes**
>
> be associated with 和……聯繫在一起；crutch 拐杖；lame 跛的；deem 認為，視為；de facto 事實上的；purify 淨化；hermit 隱士；revive 恢復；comprehension 理解；profundity 深奧，深刻

灶神
Kitchen Deity

There once was a fat mighty lord who loved to eat. His palace was full of all kinds of delicious food, and sometimes he went out to find new food.

One day he came to the house of a simple peasant woman. The mighty lord begged to taste her food so she gave him some sugar cakes, and soon he ate them all. He still was hungry and wanted more cakes, and he even threatened the woman to take her back to his palace to make cakes for him.

The woman became angry and slapped the mighty lord across the face. Her sharp blow was so strong that the mighty lord fell back and became embedded into the wall. He was completely stuck and could do nothing but watch other people eat food.

When the Jade Emperor heard this story, he appointed the mighty lord to be the Kitchen Deity (灶神). Since then, his altar has been set up somewhere near every family's kitchen stove. As the Kitchen Deity'his responsibility is to report to Heaven what the family has done the whole year. For this reason, each family carefully minds their conduct and behavior because they are afraid that a bad report would be given to the Jade Emperor.

Each year each family renews the Kitchen Deity's picture to make the Kitchen Deity happy. On the 23rd day of the 12th lunar month, people usually offer the deity some melon-shaped candies called "candy melons (糖 瓜)." This candy tastes sweet. The kitchen Deity's mouth will be so full with sugar that when he makes his report, everything will sound good. Others believe that the candy is so sticky that it will keep his mouth shut when he gives his report.

Notes

mighty 巨大的 ; threaten 威脅 ; slap 掌摑 ; appoint 任命 ; renew 更新 ; sticky 黏的

龍王
The Dragon King

In ancient China, the unicorn, phoenix, tortoise, and dragon were regarded as the Four Spiritual Animals (四靈) that symbolized auspicious signs. The image of the dragon has the head of an ox, the horn of a deer, the eyes of a shrimp, the claws of a hawk, the body of a snake, and the tail of a lion. Besides, scales and shells cover the whole body. The dragon can walk on land, swim in water, and fly among the clouds.

In ancient times Chinese emperors claimed that they were the incarnation of the dragon, symbolizing power and dignity. The common people under their jurisdiction should respect emperors as the incarnation of virtue and strength.

In Chinese mythology, there are four grand Dragon Kings that rule the Four Seas (四方之海) and manipulate the clouds and rain. In addition, there are many little Dragon Kings that reside in other waters, taking charge of local weather for crops. In ancient times, people built up shrines or temples dedicated to either grand or little Dragon Kings. Whenever floods or droughts occurred, local people believed that the Dragon King was in a rage, punishing all local living creatures. People would go to the Dragon King temple where they prayed in front of the dragon image, burning incense and providing food offerings, and wishing that the Dragon King would expel floods or droughts and bring good weather for harvests.

Notes
unicorn 麒麟；hawk 鷹；incarnation 化身；ju-risdiction 管轄；
reside 居住；in a rage 一怒之下；expel 驅逐

閻王
Yan Wang in the Nether World

In Chinese folk belief, the Jade Emperor (玉皇大帝) acts as the executive ruler of all supernatural beings, so Heaven and the Nether World are both under his jurisdiction. However, the Emperor is so deeply involved with the Heavenly Palace affairs that Yan Wang (閻王 , King Yama) serves as the executive ruler of the Nether World.

Yan Wang is the shortened Chinese transliteration of Yama Rājā in Sanskrit. The information about Yan Wang was first recorded in an early stratum of Vedic mythology and in Vedic tradition.

After Buddhism entered China, many changes were made in Buddhism to fit Chinese culture and adapt to Chinese ways of thinking and practice. The belief in Yan Wang became more prevalent after the Six Dynasties (六朝). The Buddhist concept of Naraka (the Sanskrit word for the underworld) was combined with the aboriginal Chinese Nether World. The result brought about the saying of "Ten Kings in the Underworld (地府十王)." In the Tang Dynasty such a saying widely spread amid common people in the country, and people gave the ten kings a unified name:Yan Wang.

Traditionally, Yan Wang is enshrined in a hall inside the Chenghuang Temple. Very few temples are used only for the placement of the images of Yan Wang and evil ghosts, except for Mount Pingdu (平都山) which became well-known in the Ming and Qing Dynasties for its ghosts, due to the stories from novels like The Journey to the West (《西遊記》) and The Strange Tales of Liaozhai (《聊齋》), which heightened the ghastly and evil atmosphere of Mount Pingdu.

Notes

be involved with 涉及；transliteration 音譯；Sanskrit 梵文；stratum 地層，社會階層；Vedic 吠陀的；prevalent 普遍的；aboriginal 原產的，原始的；unified 統一的；heighten 提高

第十九章
日常禮儀
Daily ceremony

　　中國傳統文化深刻地影響著中國社會關係的各個層面，包括
家庭、社區、學校等。本篇簡要介紹至今仍影響著中國社會各個
層面的社會文化習俗。

如何稱呼中國人？
How are Chinese people addressed?

In China, the family name is followed by the given name. In the Western practice, it is just reverse. The Chinese sometimes reverse the order of their two names to confirm with the Western practice, and this may confuse Westerners who know that family names in China are traditionally placed first.

The Chinese themselves generally address each other by the family name and an appropriate title, or by both the family and full given name together, with the family name first. The reason is that it helps distinguish all the Zhangs, Wangs, and Lis from one another.

It is also customary to address Chinese by their given name, using the title Miss, Mrs. , or Mr. until persons become good friends and know one another's nickname. There are a large range of official titles and formal address forms in daily use, especially occupation-linked titles such as doctor, professor, and mayor. Younger members address older members according to their formal role within families such as older brother, cousin, sister-in-law and so forth.

Notes
reverse 相反的；confirm 證實；appropriate 適當的；occupation 職業

如何稱呼中國婦女？
How are Chinese women addressed?

A woman in China does not take her husband's name after her marriage but keeps that of her father. The word, nüshi (女士), translated as "Ms." is a formal title for an adult woman, married or unmarried. The Chinese seldom use nüshi among themselves, but welcome its use by foreigners. You may address any young woman who is not likely to be married as xiaojie (小姐), translated as "Miss," but this form of address is socially delicate in the case of women in their late twenties and early thirties because it is widely believed that by that age a woman should be married. If you do not know whether a woman of this age is married, address her as nüshi.

「老」和「小」的含義是什麼？
What is the meaning of lao and xiao?

Older persons who have no work-related title are commonly called lao (老); younger persons with no identifiable name or job title may be addressed as xiao (小). Xiao may be translated as "young" or "junior," lao as "old" or "senior." Which term is used depends on the relation between the ages of the speaker and the person spoken to. The general rule is this: an older person calls a younger person with whom he and she is familiar Xiao So-and-so; a younger person calls an older person Lao So-and-so. Xiao or lao may be used with persons of either sex, although lao tends to be used more frequently with males.

Notes
identifiable 可認明的；familiar 熟悉的

中文有沒有特別的問候語？
What are typical Chinese greetings?

The most common form of greeting is ni hao（你好）, usually translated as "Good day" but literally meaning "You are well." The same greeting phrased as a question（"How are you?"）is "ni hao ma"（你好嗎？）. The response is usually nihao. You may use it on any occasion regardless of the time of day or the social status of the person you are greeting.

A most common greeting is "ni qu nar"（你去哪,"Where are you going?"）. Although its typical use occurs when passing another person on the street or in a building, it is not really a question because exact information is not being requested. It is similar to the greeting "How are you?" used in English speaking countries. You need give no precise information about your destination. You may say vaguely, "I'm going there," or gesture slightly with the head or hand in the direction in which you are moving.

Another common form of greeting is "chi le ma"（吃了嗎,"Have you eaten?"）. This greeting normally occurs around mealtimes, but it, too, is not a question as for information. It sounds like an invitation to join the other person for the coming meal. The way to response is to say either "wo chi le"（我吃了,"I have eaten."）or "kuai yao le"（快要了,"I am going to eat soon."）depending on one's situation.

Notes
inquiry 詢問；destination 目的

傳統的問候姿勢是什麼樣子？
What gesture is used as a traditional Chinese greeting?

The handshake is now a common form of greeting among Chinese, but young Chinese tend simply to nod as a greeting. To some extent, this reflects the ever-increasing paces of modern life.

The traditional greeting is to cup one's own hands (left over right), chest high, and raise them slightly as a salute. In earlier times when greeting a person of superior social standing, it was customary to raise the hands as high as the forehead and to execute a low bow. This tradition has a history of more than 2,000 years, but nowadays it is seldom used except in the Spring Festival or on other special occasions.

> **Notes**
> evolution 進展；ever-increasing 越來越多的；su-perior 上級的

中國人一般用什麼話題開始交談？
What are opening conversational topics in China?

Opening topics tend to be personal. Between strangers, a typical opening question might be "ni zai na gongzuo"（你在哪工作，"Where do you work?"）. Between persons known to each other, initial questions are likely to be about the other person's family life, especially about his or her children, but some Chinese feel uneasy about going into detail about a husband or wife.

Another good conversation starter is to ask where the other person was born and then talk about each other's hometown. There are many possibilities in this case. One can follow up by asking about the town's location, the dialect, the cuisine, regional customs, etc. These topics are safe in the sense that they are unlikely to lead to any kind of cross-cultural misunderstanding.

At present, the topic of weather is popular because it is completely impersonal. One may begin a conversation by mentioning some items in the daily news, discussing a sporting or entertainment event, or commenting on a recent event.

> **Notes**
> subtle 難捉摸的；cross-cultural 跨文化的；mis-understanding 誤解；
> impersonal 非個人的

中國人和西方人在日常告別時有什麼不同習慣？
What is the difference in daily farewells between Chinese and western people?

In some western countries, a visitor may state that he or she must depart soon, but will not leave immediately. One may continues a conversation or shared activity for several minutes or perhaps even as much as an hour. However, when a Chinese thinks it is time to leave, he or she announces that fact and immediately prepares to depart.

The western visitor who intends to depart may explain that something in his or her own personal situation compels the departure. Someone may say, for example, "I've got to study for my chemistry test tomorrow, so I'd better be going." When a Chinese offers a reason for leaving, it is unlikely to be related to his or her personal situation. What one usually says is often related to the other person's needs, such as, "I won't take up any more of your time" or "I'm sorry that I've wasted so much of your valuable time."

As a western leaver is actually leaving, the host accompanies him or her to the door and may even step outside to offer a farewell wave as the visitor goes away. However, a Chinese host commonly accompanies a guest out of the door and for some distance, while continuing to talk. The distance that the host accompanies a guest is a sign of the respect shown by the host.

中國人如何回應讚美？
How do Chinese respond to a compliment?

Chinese is unlikely to respond to a compliment with thanks or any other acknowledgement of its validity. One rather responds with a certain mood of self-depreciation. For instance, if a foreigner says to his or her interpreter, "Your English is very good," a typical reply is bu hao, bu hao (不好，不好) or na li na li (哪裡，哪裡), meaning "Oh, no! My English is poor."

Chinese expressions of modesty can be seen everywhere.

When one is invited to a Chinese home for dinner, one finds the table over-flowing with six to eight dishes, beautifully presented. But host or hostess is likely to say, "We hope you won't mind joining our simple meal. We are not good at cooking, so we have only prepared a few dishes this evening." Chinese habitually say things to suggest that their creations, family members or themselves are of small value. This may lead you to conclude that you should offer no compliments to Chinese acquaintances. But that is not correct. Chinese like to receive compliments just like anyone else; they merely respond to them differently.

Notes

unlikely 不太可能的；acknowledgement 致謝；interpreter 譯員；
modesty 謙遜；overflow 使漲滿；compliment 讚美的話

你可以告訴我一些中國人表現謙虛的其他方式嗎？
What are other behavioral features of Chinese modesty?

Traditional Chinese values require a person who wishes to make a favorable impression to avoid being self-assertive. Consequently it is wise to be modest about own personal ability and experience. When Chinese meet for the first time in a social situation, they tell each other their names and identify their work units, but they seldom reveal their titles or positions in their work units. It is unusual for a Chinese to list his or her title or similar information below the signature. Now, Chinese increasingly use business cards that include such information. Cards are exchanged at many social gatherings.

Being a good listener is considered good manners. Young Chinese listen to their elders and speak little, thus showing modesty and good manners. In the same way, subordinates show respect to their supervisors.

During conversations, Chinese can keep silence for a much longer time than Westerners, and juniors wait for their seniors to finish speaking. Discomfort occurs if a junior speaks out of turn.

When a large number of Chinese prepare themselves for a group photograph, all understand that the front row, especially the center-front, is the place of honor. Even senior persons try to be away from the front row in attempt to display proper modesty. After some good-natured scuffling and earnest appeals from juniors, the situation resolves itself properly.

> **Notes**
>
> signature 簽名；supervisor 管理人；scuffle 扭打；self-assertive 自作主張的

什麼是「關係」？
What is guanxi?

The word guanxi (關係) has no precise English equivalent. It is literally translated as "relationship" or "connection," and technically, it stands for any type of relationship. In the Chinese business world, however, it is also understood as the network of relationships among various parties that cooperate together and support one another. The Chinese business mentality is very much "You scratch my back, I'll scratch yours."

Developing and nurturing guanxi requires time and resources. Chinese and Western cultures conduct business differently, even if, on the surface, transactions seem the same. Chinese prefer to work with persons they know and trust. This relationship extends between companies and also between individuals at an ongoing personal level. With manners, diligence, courtesy and goodwill, one constructs his or her own web of supporting relationships.

Guanxi can take on many forms. It does not have to be based on money. It is completely legal in their culture and not regarded as bribery in any way. Trustworthiness of both a company as a whole and individual is an important component, and following through on business promises is an essential indication.

Notes

technically 技術上；scratch 搔；transaction 辦理；bribery 行賄；
courtesy 禮貌

為什麼「面子」對中國人來說非常重要？
Why does face have a great importance for Chinese?

Sociologists know that the concept of face is a universal concern of human beings, but it has particular social significance for Chinese. There is a Chinese proverb that says, "A person needs face as a tree needs bark." There are several reasons. Over the centuries, many people in China have seldom moved away from the location of their birth. They spend their entire life in the company of the same friends, neighbors and relatives. Face-saving behaviors are necessary to maintain harmony, avoid conflicts and protect the integrity of the group.

Confucius emphasized that human beings exist in interactive relationships with others. According to his thought, a senior party is assumed to have authority with respect to his or her juniors; the junior party, in turn, was bound to be respectful and obedient toward his or her seniors. These obligations are expressed in the Chinese virtue known as li（禮）, which means "right conduct in maintaining one's place in the hierarchical order" and is currently used by the average Chinese to mean manners. One important way to be acceptable is to respect and accept each person's need to maintain his or her face. Loss of face is not a matter of personal embarrassment; it also threatens to disrupt the integrity of the group and destroy long-established relationships.

什麼是「緣分」？
What is yuanfen?

Yuanfen（緣分）is a Buddhist-related concept that refers to the predeter-
mined principle that dictates a person's positive relationships and encounters such
as the affinity among friends or lovers. It is always used in conjunction with two
persons, and it can be defined broadly as the binding force that links two persons
together in any relationship. Some believe that the driving force behind yuanfen
are the actions done in previous reincarnation to emphasize a meant-to-be rela-
tionship.One may exclaim, "It is yuanfen that has brought us together!" When
one encounters another repeatedly in various situations that seem beyond coinci-
dence, one can refer to yuanfen. On the contrary, when two persons know each
other but never get a chance to meet face-to-face, it can be said that their yuanfen
is too weak. Often yuanfen is said to be the equivalent of "fate" or "destiny." However, these words do not have the element of the past playing a role in
deciding the outcome of the future.

「客氣」的重要性是什麼？
What is the importance of keqi?

Ke means "guest" and qi means "behavior," but when these characters are used together to form keqi (客氣), they mean a lot more than "guest" and "behavior." As used to describe behavior, keqi means politeness, courtesy, modesty, humility, understanding, well-mannered behavior and so on. All of these definitions are natural in the Chinese cultural context. Being humble refers not only to person of humility, it also means downplaying the status of one's family, friends, employer, etc. The importance of keqi also indicates how sensitive Chinese are to any sign of arrogance or haughtiness. Chinese are expected to demonstrate keqi in all of their actions and especially toward foreign guests. As social conditions continue to change, the force of keqi is diminishing, but it is still discernible in the behavior of all Chinese, including overseas Chinese.

Notes
context 上下文；downplay 貶低；haughtiness 傲慢；diminish 減少

什麼是「禮」？
What is the Chinese li?

China is well-known as an "ancient civilized country (文明古國)" or "nation of etiquette (禮儀之邦)." Throughout China's long history the relationships between people in all classes were based on carefully prescribed forms of the Chinese li (禮) that covered virtually every aspect of conduct. Although the li has no precise English equivalent, it is understood as "a strict code of conduct," "propriety," "rituals" or "etiquett e."

The origin of the li can trace back to remote antiquity. At that time people were inter-dependent for survival, and the li, to begin with, was a conduct performed without much significance. Gradually people accepted the "order of human relations (人倫秩序)," which might be considered the primitive li. As time went by, the primitive li rose to the height of human relations and ethical values.

At a later time Huang Di (黃帝), Yao (堯), Shun (舜), Yu (禹), and other sages founded specific proprieties for the purpose of restricting avarice and ending disorder. Meanwhile, they strictly observed the established proprieties. Their observation set an good example for their people to follow.

As early as 3,000 years ago, the Duke of the Zhou created rituals and music. Later, Confucius and other sages greatly contributed to the final foundation of the Confucius system that was a training and ongoing experience in such cultural arts as music, calligraphy and poetry, as part of a moral education.

After the Western Han Dynasty, The Etiquette and Rites (《儀禮》), The Rites of the Zhou Dynasty (《周禮》) and Record of Rites (《禮記》) were successively listed as text-books and required readings for scholars in ancient times. These classics detailed knowledge of hundreds of correct forms of etiquette. Training in this highly prescribed way of living was so pervasive that people were judged first, last, and sometimes always on how closely they followed these rules of behavior. The li came to be equated not only with learning in general, but with culture and morality. Accordingly, the li in the traditional "six arts (六藝)" was considered as the first art. Behind the li, came music (樂), archery (射), driving a chariot (御), learning (書) and mathematics (數).

The book of the Analects of Confucius says, "look not at what is contrary to li; listen not to what is contrary to li; speak not what is contrary to li; make no movement which is contrary to li (非禮勿視、非禮勿聽、非禮勿言、非禮勿動)."

The following is a basic summary that is helpful to understand the Chinese li:

➤ a. Originally, li meant "to sacrifice," for divine beings or supernatural power. Later, it extended to mean an attitude of reverence.

➤ b. The li is a series of conducts through which an inner reverence and devotion are genuinely expressed.

➤ c. The li is a rite or a ceremony to be performed to show respects or admiration to people of esteem.

➤ d. The li is an article with which to express congratulations or compliments.

Notes

prescribe 規定；virtually 實際上；propriety 禮儀；etiquette 禮節；inter-dependent 相互依存的；survival 生存；ethical 道德的；avarice 貪婪；observation 觀察；ongoing 正在進行的；pervasive 普遍的；chariot 戰車；contrary to 與……相反；reverence 崇敬；genuinely 真誠地

什麼是「磕頭」?
What is ketou?

Ketou (磕頭) is the act of deep respect shown by kneeling and bowing so low as to touch the head to the ground. Ke means "bump" or "knock" and tou means "head." Traditionally, the formal Chinese ketou included three kneelings and nine prostrations.

Traditional Chinese etiquette contained situations in which ketou was performed. According to imperial Chinese protocol, ketou was performed before the emperor. During the Spring Festival, younger family members would ketou to members of each generation above them. At a wedding ceremony, the bride and bridegroom had to ketou to everyone from the eldest down to their parents in order. During ancestor worship services and the Bright and Clear Festival, ketou was also often performed. People lit incense, and the eldest male led the ancestor worship. People then did ketou or bowed. Afterwards, they gave food and wine to the ancestors, and burnt paper money. In Buddhist or Daoist mona-steries, ketou is often performed before Buddhist or Daoist statues.

> **Notes**
> prostration 倒下；平伏；incense 香

什麼是「請安」？
What are the features of Qing An Etiquette?

Qing An means "wishing somebody good health." It is said that this etiquette started as a military salute in the Ming Dynasty. At that time, as a soldier or an officer of lower ranks met with an officer of higher ranks, he would show respect by bending one of his knees. This behavior was called "One-Knee-Bent Etiquette (屈一膝)."

In the Qing Dynasty this tradition continued. The Qing Eight Banner-men followed the etiquette in Eight Banner families and some Han-nationality families of Qing government officials. Within the family, the junior members to the elders, children to parents, wife to husband, servants to the family host or hostess usually performed this etiquette. By this time, this etiquette was called "qing an," which meant "wishing somebody good health." The following is the movement of the one-knee-bent etiquette.

Stand naturally upright. Step forward with the left leg and then bend the left knee with the left hand placed on the left knee. Meanwhile, kneel down with the right knee, with the right hand hanging downward. Eyes look straight ahead; shoulders are relaxed; don't bend one's back.

Notes
bend 彎曲；behavior 行為；banner-men 旗人；kneel down 下跪

中國人接受禮物有什麼習俗？
How do the Chinese traditionally accept a gift?

The traditional Chinese practice in gift-exchange is quite different from that of Westerners. Chinese are taught as children that in order to show modesty and avoid any suggestion of personal greed, they should decline twice or three times when offered a gift. Usually when a gift is offered, there is then a seesaw battle in which the gift is offered and refused, offered and refused but finally accepted with appropriate expression of appreciation. The gift is supposed not to be opened on the spot; it is tucked away in a pocket or left on a table until the giver has departed. Only then is the parcel opened. One interpretation of this practice is that the receiver is preserving the face of the giver by avoiding any possibility of evaluating the gift in the presence of the giver and others. Such behavior is simply the Chinese manner.

在公共場所有什麼禮儀？
What is the etiquette for public places?

Chinese get used to being pushed and buffeted when they use public transportation or go shopping in public stores. They accept this as normal behavior without expecting apologies. At the same time, the Chinese have been conditioned for centuries to ignore "outsiders," meaning anyone not a member of their family, work unit, or circle of friends. They thus behave more or less as if others do not exist.

你知道孔融讓梨的故事嗎？
What is the story of Kong Rong who let his elder brother take larger pears?

Kong Rong was a well-known man of letters in the late years of the Eastern Han Dynasty. According to historical records, he always abided by the courteous manners.

When he was quite young, Kong usually ate pears together with his elder brothers. Each time when they started eating pears, Kong would pick up the smallest pear and let his brothers take larger ones.

One day his father saw it and said to Kong, "Why do you pick up a small pear, and not a large one?"

Kong replied, "I am the youngest in the whole family, and I should eat a small pear, so I'd like my elder brothers to take large ones."

Kong Rong's courteous manner made his father very happy, and his story thus spread far and wide through the following dynasties.

Notes
a man of letters 文學家；abide by 遵守；courteous 禮貌的

你知道程門立雪的故事嗎？

What is the story of Yang Shi and You Zuo, who stand at Cheng Yi's entrance gate in a snowy day?

In the Song Dynasty, Yang Shi（楊時）and You Zuo（游酢）studied under Cheng Hao（程顥）, a well-learnt scholar of that time. After Cheng Hao passed way, Yang and You went to Luoyang and continued their studies with Cheng Yi（程頤）, Cheng Hao's brother.

One day Yang and You made a trip to visit Cheng Yi. When they arrived at Cheng Yi's household, they found Cheng Yi sitting in a meditative pose with his eyes closed. So, the two visitors stood quietly by Cheng Yi's side, waiting for the gentleman to finish his meditation.

It was winter, and it began snowing. Yang and You patiently waited until Cheng opened his eyes. "Oh," said Cheng Yi when he saw them in his room. "You are still standing here!" By then, the snow outside Cheng's house was one-third meters in depth.

Notes

pass way 過世；meditative 沉思的；meditation 沉思，冥想

第十九章　日常禮儀　Daily ceremony

第二十章
婚姻禮俗
Marriage Etiquette and Customs

中國人稱婚姻為「終身大事」，可以說婚姻在平民百姓生活中的重要性是排在第一位的。民間的婚姻儀式在千百年的時間裡發展出了豐富的禮儀和禮俗，也呈現出多樣的民間習俗。本篇介紹的是近世民間傳統結婚的一些特點和相關禮俗。

什麼是舊時婚姻的「六禮」？
What were the six-rituals of Chinese marriage in ancient times?

Chinese marriage is usually referred to as a "Great Event in Life-time (終身大事)." In ancient times, the marriage procedure usually consisted of the following "six rituals."

➤ When an unmarried boy's family finds a prospective daughter-in-law, they will invite a "middle man" to approach the prospective daughter-in-law's family, present gifts, and propose the possible marriage between the two families. If the proposal is declined, the gift is rejected.

➤ If the girl's family accepts the proposal, the boy's family will write a letter to the girl's family asking her date of birth.

➤ When her family replies, the boy's family will pray to their ancestors to ask if the couple will be auspicious. If the prediction does not feel right, the marriage will be called off.

➤ If the couple appears auspicious, the boy's family will arrange the "middle man" to deliver the marriage documents and wedding gifts to the prospective daughter-in-law's home.

➤ Once the boy's family finalizes the wedding day, they will confirm the day with the girl ' s family by sending a formal letter and more gifts. If the girl's family refuses the gifts, another date must be found.

➤ On the wedding day, the groom departs with a troop of escorts and musicians who play cheerful music all the way to the bride's home. The bride's father meets the parade outside the home. He would take the groom to the ancestral temple where they pray to their ancestors. At the same time, the wedding sedan chair is placed outside the home until the bride arrives. The groom bows his head low to invite the bride to take the chair, and then they both travel together for the wedding ceremony in the groom's home.

It is said that these six-rituals were performed in the period between the Han Dynasty and the Tang Dynasty. In the Song Dynasty, the rituals were simplified into "four-rituals" or "three rituals." In the Ming Dynasty many families of officials abided by the "six-rituals," but non-official families still followed the "-three-ritual" procedure.

Notes

procedure 程序；prospective 未來的；reject 拒絕；auspicious 吉祥的；call off 取消；parade 結隊，行列；non-official 非官方的

自古以來對結婚年齡有什麼規定嗎？
What was legal age to marry in olden times?

In Chinese history the prescribed age of marriage varied. During the Zhou Dynasty, a man should be married by the age of 30, and a woman by 20. At that time, people thought that a man's bones and muscles would be strong enough to withstand the burden of fatherhood at the age of 30; a woman would be full-grown and ready to be a mother when she reached the age of 20.

As the dynasties went by, the prescribed age for marriage gradually lowered. During the Spring and Autumn Period, Qi Huangong (齊桓公), king of the Qi State decreed a man should be married by the age of 30 and a woman by 15; towards the end of the Spring and Autumn Period, King Gou Jian of the Yue State

(越王勾踐) said that parents would be penalized if their son did not get married by the age of 20 and their daughter by 17.

During the Han Dynasty, unmarried women of 15 years or older had to pay 5 times more taxes than required, thus forcing them to marry at an even earlier age.

In the Western Jin State (西晉), local officials would select a groom for the woman who had not been married off by the age of 17. In the Northern Zhou State (北周), a man was required to marry by 15 and a woman by 13.

In the early Tang Dynasty, the Tang rulers adopted a rehabilitative policy in order to relieve people out of the severe social conflicts. Part of the policy stated that a man should get married by the age of 20 and a woman by 15. In the middle period of the Tang Dynasty, the latest age for marriage changed to 16 for a man and 13 for a woman. The local government would interfere if any man or woman failed to get married by the prescribed age.

From the Song Dynasty to the Qing Dynasty, the latest age for a man was about 16 years old and for a woman about 14.

A new Marriage Law, which went into effect in 1950, stipulates that although later marriage should be encouraged, the minimum age for marriage is currently 22 for men and 20 for women.

Notes
withstand 承受；fatherhood 父親的身分，父性；full-grown 發育完全的；penalize 懲罰；rehabilitative 使復原的；conflict 衝突；interfere 干擾；stipulate 規定；minimum 最低限度

在包辦婚姻中媒人要做些什麼？

How did a matchmaker act in "the arranged marriage"?

A matchmaker is also called "the old man under the moonlight (月下老人)." This saying originates from an ancient legend. As it says, there was a scholar whose name was Wei Gu (韋固). One night Wei Gu passed by a town where he came across an old man who sat at the roadside and read a book under the moonlight. The old man had a large bag with him. For curiosity the scholar came to the old man and said, "what are you reading?" "It is a marriage registration book," replied the old man. The scholar said again, "what's inside the large bag?" "Well," said the old man, "the bag contains pieces of red threads. I use the threads to tie the feet of an unmarried man and woman. Once the feet of the man and the woman are tied with my red thread, they are destined to get married with each other even though they are thousands of miles apart."

In bygone days the sexes were segregated, and a maiden was not supposed to see a male stranger under any circumstances. The higher the family standing was, the stricter the segregation. Such being the case, marriages had to be arranged. In looking for a prospective wife or husband for their son or daughter, the parents had to consider a number of factors, and they would invite a professional matchmaker to act for possible mates for young boys and girls and perform in the following old-fashioned wedding procedure.

When an unmarried boy's family found a prospective daughter-in-law, a matchmaker would approach the prospective daughter-in-law's family in the most casual manner; it had to be casual to avoid embarrassment. The matchmaker visited the daughter-in-law's family with gifts. She proposed the possible marriage between the two families. If the offer was not unacceptable, the girl's details would be written on red paper and given to the matchmaker, who would return to the boy's family. Afterwards the matchmaker frequently commuted between the two families, delivering letters, marriage documents or gifts, interpreting the horoscopes and confirming an auspicious date for a wedding.

On the wedding day the matchmaker would accompany the bridegroom to the bride's home to pick up the bride. In addition, she would work as an assistant in the wedding ceremony. After the ceremony, the boy's family would give her some gifts and money wrapped in red paper as a token of thanks. The amount of money was largely dependent on the family's financial situation.

Notes

matchmaker 媒人；curiosity 好奇心；registration 登記；bygone 過去的；segregate 隔離；maiden 少女；standing 地位；old-fashioned 老式的；embarrassment 尷尬；unacceptable 不可接受的；commute 通勤來往

什麼是「相親」？
What is xiangqin?

Xiangqin（相親）refers to a blind date where the couple involved has not met each other before. In ancient times, the xiangqin date seldom occurred due to the fact that a marriage was completely arranged by parents'order or on the matchmaker's word. A prospective bride was not expected to be exposed to her prospective bridegroom under any circumstances prior to their wedding night. However, some prospective bridegroom's parents wanted to see what the prospective bride looked like as early as possible. So, on many occasions they concealed their identity and silently stood near her residence in the hope that they could steal a glance at their son's prospective bride. A silent glance, they believed, might not give trouble or pain to the prospective bride's family, and their mutual marriage between the two families would continue as usual.

In early modern times, the xiangqin date gradually became popular. The following were two commonly-accepted ways for the xiangqin date process.

a.Parents or aunts would take their son to visit the prospective bride's family. It aimed to let their son have a chance of meeting the prospective bride. Accompanied by her parents, the prospective bride came out, presenting tea or lighting a cigarette to the visitors. The group of visitors might include some close relatives whose comment on the prospective bride would be of some value to a mutual marriage promise between the two families. During this period the prospective mates remained separated and only stole a few glances at one another. After this xiangqin date, it would be the matchmaker's duty to communicate between the two families for the confirmation of the mutual marriage promise.

b.A matchmaker would accompany a prospective bridegroom for his xiangqin date in his prospective bride's home. Right before his departure, his parents would specifically instruct their son how to address his prospective bride's family, how to offer cigarettes to the prospective bride's father and how to make a wine toast to her family. Accompanied by the matchmaker, the man arrived at his prospective bride's home. He was warmly hosted, and his prospective bride came out for a greeting. She made her appearance just for a short time and then hid herself elsewhere. Meanwhile, the bride's parents took advantage of the date to confirm if they were satisfied with their daughter』s prospective bridegroom.

On the xiangqin date, if the bridegroom's family felt satisfied with the prospective marriage, the family would give to the potential bride a small red-color packet, which contained some cash. The packet was called "a gift at the first meeting."

Notes

be exposed to 暴露；prior to 在……之前；con-ceal 隱瞞；submit 提交；commonly-accepted 普遍接受的；confirmation 確認；address 講話；potential 潛在的

傳統的訂婚有哪些特點？
What is the feature of a traditional marriage engagement?

After a xiangqin date, both the two families became involved in the preparation for the marriage engagement. A traditional engagement required a marriage contract, which was formally written on high-quality paper, bent in six folds and printed with happy designs on its surface.

A matchmaker acted as the contract deliverer, making round trips at least two times between the two families. On her first trip, the matchmaker received the marriage contract from the prospective bridegroom's family and carried it to the prospective bride's family. The main content of the contract was a proposal of marriage; upon its arrival, the prospective bride's family would reply with a written acceptance. On her second trip the matchmaker delivered an updated contract to the prospective bride's family. This time the contract was called "lijian（禮束, etiquette card),"which appeared in form with dragon designs on its surface.

In return, the prospective bride's family would present a formal acceptance letter, which had phoenix patterns on its surface.

On the contract-delivery date friends and relatives would visit the prospective bridegroom's family, and the bridegroom's parents entertained them with an "Engagement Dinner (定親飯)." The dinner attendants would include the bridegroom and the matchmaker who would depart for the bride's family with the contract after the dinner.

On the matchmaker's second trip to the prospective bride's family, there would be some more people to go with the matchmaker. These people's responsibility was to carry gift boxes in hands or on shoulders. When they arrived at the prospective bride's home, the visitors attended another banquet hosted by the prospective bride's family. After the banquet, the matchmaker brought the acceptance letter back to the prospective bridegroom's family.

In some areas visitors who participated in the Engagement Dinner held by the prospective bridegroom's family would present gifts to the hosts. Visitors who participated in the Engagement Dinner held by the prospective bride's family would receive gifts from the prospective bridegroom's family. More importantly, the prospective bridegroom's family would present expensive gifts to the prospective bride's grandparents and parents, as well as the prospective bride. The gifts for the prospective bride might include jewels and materials for clothing.

Notes
contract 合約；fold 折疊；deliverer 遞送人；acceptance 接受；
entertain 熱情款待；engagement 訂婚

什麼是生辰八字？
What are the Eight Characters of a Horoscope?

The Eight Characters of a Horoscope is a Chinese conceptual term in Chinese astrology. It describes the four components creating a person's destiny or fate. These four components are the year, month, day, and time (hour) when he or she was born. In Chinese each of these components is expressed by two characters, which are a combination of the Heavenly Stems (天干) and Earthly Branches (地支), yielding a total of eight characters. The Eight Characters are also known as the 4 Pillars of Destiny or Pillars of Destiny (四柱命) because these 4 pillars make up a chart or a configuration of eight characters, which helps a fortuneteller determine a person's qualities, relationships, potential for good career, and health risks.

In ancient China, when parents looked for a prospective wife or husband for their son or daughter, they had to consider a number of factors. One of the factors was to see if the prospective couple would be auspicious based on their four-pillar-birth-chart in conjunction with the Chinese Almanac (黃曆). If the prediction did not feel right, the marriage would be called off.

> Notes
>
> conceptual 概念上的；astrology 占星術；com-ponent 組成部分；
> destiny 命運；earthly branches 地支；pillar 支柱；configuration
> 表面配置；形態；conjunction 連接；almanac 年鑒；黃曆

第二十一章
中國民間傳統節日
Traditional Chinese Festivals

中國是一個多民族的國家，有許多別具一格、絢麗多彩的節日。人們在不同的地方用不同的方式慶祝自己的節日，民間傳統節日已成為民族風俗習慣的重要組成部分。本篇介紹部分傳統節日的特點和風俗習慣。

什麼是陽曆和陰曆？
What are the solar calendar and the lunar calendar?

Since ancient times, Chinese people have adopted over a hundred kinds of calendars. The most widely observed are the yang li and the yin li. The former is the solar or Gregorian calendar that is now in use in various countries, including China. In English, yin li means "the lunar or agricultural calendar." It has been used in China since the Xia Dynasty for about three or four thousand years. Yin li actually contains a mixture of solar and lunar elements. The length of time of the rotation of the moon is counted as a month. There are 12 months in a year of 354 days, 13 months in a leap year of 384 days. In ancient China, the year was divided into 24 solar periods (24 節氣), each of which is marked by three climatic signs. Those periods are directly related to farming and have been observed for several thousand years. Currently Chinese use the lunar calendar for the scheduling of holidays such as Chinese New Year (the Spring Festival), the Mid-Autumn Festival, and for divination, including choosing the most auspicious date for a wedding or the grand opening of an important building.

> ### Notes
> solar 太陽的；Gregorian calendar 公曆；rotation 循環；a leap year 閏年

什麼是春節？
What is the Spring Festival?

The Spring Festival, the Lunar New Year, is the most important traditional national festival in China. It is called nian (年) or xinnian (新年 , New Year) in

Chinese. As originally written, the Chinese character nian means "harvest." The Spring Festival always falls sometime before or after lichun (立春 , the beginning of Spring).

The celebration of the Spring Festival is more or less similar across the country. People set off firecrackers, which enliven the festival and bring great joy to people, especially to children. Chunlian (春聯) are spring couplets posted on gates during the Spring Festival. They contain auspicious words such as, "The Best of Things and the Treasures of Heaven"; "Days of Peace, Year In, Year Out"; "A Spring of Good Fortune, This Year, and Every Year." In addition, New Year pictures are a unique part of the New Year celebrations. Today, farmers and citizens in small towns still keep the customs of posting these on their doors or on the walls inside their rooms.

During the Spring Festival, the Chinese people eat a lot of good food. In North China, the most popular food is jiaozi (餃子), or dumplings. In South China, for breakfast on New Year's Day, round rice glutinous dumplings are served to signify family reunion.

On the eve of the Spring Festival, it is a folk custom to stay up late or all night, praying for peace in the coming year. That night every house is brightly lit in the hope that anything that might bring people bad fortune will disappear under the dazzling light. New year is ushered in at midnight, 12 o'clock sharp. On that day, everybody, men and women, old and young, puts on new clothes. When the younger generation extend their New Year greetings to their seniors, the latter give them money wrapped in red paper that is called yasuiqian (壓歲錢 , money to keep for the year). On the second day, after breakfast, there are exchanges of visits between friends and relatives who bring each other New Year cakes, oranges, tangerines, and crunchy candies as gifts. All in all, everyday from New Year's Eve to the fifteenth day of the first month, there are various entertainments. Lion dances and drum and gong contests are grand events in the New Year celebrations, especially in the countryside. Wedding ceremonies also abound in cities and villages throughout the land at this time.

Notes

originally 起初；enliven 使活躍；auspicious 吉利的；dazzling 耀眼的；seniors 年長的；tangerine 橘子；crunchy 易碎的

放鞭炮的由來是什麼？
What is the origin of setting off firecrackers?

Setting off firecrackers is a practice handed down from the remote past. It is related with burning bamboo stems. Bamboo stems have joints and are hollow inside. When they are burnt, the air inside expands after being heated, and the stems themselves burst open and make a loud cracking sound. Later on, people placed gunpowder in the bamboo stems and thus invented firecrackers. Still later, paper rolls replaced bamboo stems. By the close of the Qing Dynasty, there had been already special workshops in China making all kinds of firecrackers.

At first, people set off firecrackers for the purpose of keeping away evil spirits and seeking happiness. Legend has it that there was a strange savage beast whose body looked like a human being and who hid itself in remote mountains.

Toward the end of every year, it would come out to kill people and animals.

However, the beast was afraid of light and noise. Whenever it heard the noise of firecrackers, the beast was so scared that it ran away. Therefore, at the beginning and end of every year, people set off firecrackers in order not to be disturbed by the beast.

Recently local regulations have been issued to forbid setting off firecrackers in cities, for they can cause fire accidents and hurt people. Despite these regulations, however, many citizens go out into the countryside to light firecrackers for the New Year celebration.

> **Notes**
> stem 莖；hollow 空的；cracking 爆裂的；sa-vage 凶猛的

春聯的由來是什麼？
What is the origin of spring couplets?

Chunlian（春聯）are couplets posted on gates during the Spring Festival. These originated from the "peach-wood charms" in the ancient times, which were meant to send off the old and usher in the new. These charms were tiny rectangular plates and made of peach-wood. In the Song Dynasty, paper came to be used instead of wood plates for writing spring couplets, and in the Ming Dynasty, encouraged by Emperor Taizu（太祖）, spring couplets came to be greatly vogue. On one New Year day after he made Nanjing as his capital, Taizu issued an imperial decree requiring all officials, scholars and common people to paste a pair of couplets on their gates. As he traveled around, he was pleased to see these colorful spring couplets.

The time-honored practice of pasting spring couplets is still being followed to these days. However, the current couplets are quite different from those of the past as far as their meaning is concerned. They now either describe the flourishing national progress or wonderful sights of the land. They also give expression to people's wishes for a still better future.

> **Notes**
>
> peach-wood charms 桃符；vogue 流行；decree 命令；time-honored 確立已久的

為什麼人們常常倒貼「福」字？
Why is a Chinese character "fu" often pasted upside down on a door or a wall?

During the Spring Festival, each household pastes a big or small Chinese character "fu（福）" on its entrance door or on walls inside houses as part of the Spring Festival celebration.

The character means "happiness" or "fortune." Throughout the course of the Chinese history, people have kept the custom of pasting the character during the Spring Festival, yearning for good fortune and a bright future.

How did the custom come into being? Legend has it that when Jiang Ziya （姜子牙）granted titles to deities, his wife came and asked him to offer her a title. Jiang said to her, "You are a spendthrift. All the families suffer from misfortune and become poor after you visit them, so I am going to offer you the title of the Poverty Deity." On hearing of this, his wife said, "Where am I going to stay as the Poverty Deity?" Jiang answered, "You are welcome to stay anywhere except places where 'fortune' exists." Jiang's words passed far and wide among common people, and they quickly pasted the Chinese character "fu (福)" in the hope that the Poverty Deity might not descend to their houses. This practice passed on from generation to generation until it became a custom for the festival celebration.

Sometimes the "fu" character is pasted upside down. Why? The word "reverse" or "upside down" means "dao (倒)" in Chinese. This "dao" and another "dao (到 , arrive)" are pronounced exactly the same although the former one has a radical on the left, and the latter has none. People use the same pronunciation simply to demonstrate that "the happiness or good fortune has arrived."

There is a folktale that explains the origin of why the character is put upside down. Once during the Spring Festival, Zhu Yuanzhang (朱元璋), the first emperor of the Ming Dynasty arrived in a small town. He took off his emperor's dress, decided to put on common clothes, and then left the guesthouse. As he toured the town, he saw a group of people staring at a drawing of a bare-footed woman who carried a huge watermelon in her arms. The caricature made fun of big-feet women. At that time, many women had bound-feet as the style was considered lovely and alluring. Incidentally the empress happened to have big feet, so this drawing irritated the emperor. He returned to the guesthouse and ordered his palace men to find out who was involved in the mischief. His men then pasted the character "fu" on the doors of houses to indicate these families that were not involved in the mischief. Next morning the palace men would arrest the people whose houses'doors did not have any character.

Upon hearing of it, the kind-hearted empress immediately ordered all the people in the town to paste the "fu" character on the doors of their houses. She even emphasized that this task had to be done before daybreak. One illiterate local person pasted the character upside down by accident. The next morning the emperor and empress went out into the street and found out that each household had the character on their doors. However, the overturned character caught their eyes. The emperor stopped to view it for a moment. He became angry again and ordered his palace men to arrest the man and his whole family and put them into jail.

The empress immediately interrupted. She said, "This family pasted the character upside down on purpose because they were told that you would pass by their house today. The overturned character actually means 'arrival of fortune.' " The empress'explanation convinced the emperor to set the man and his family free. From then on people began to follow this custom.

> **Notes**
> yearn 渴望；grant 授予；spendthrift 揮霍無度；descend 下降；
> upside down 顛倒；radical 部首；bare-footed 赤腳的；caricature
> 漫畫；alluring 誘人的；irritate 刺激；mischief 惡作劇；overturn
> 顛倒

元宵節的起源是什麼？
What is the origin of the Lantern Festival?

The Fifteenth day of the first lunar month is an important traditional festival in China. Members of a family get together to mark the occasion. This festival dated back to the Warring States Period, when people observed the custom of watching lanterns under moonlight. At first, they did this on the day for offering sacrifices to the Sun God, who was known as the Lord of the East. It is said that people began to mark the Lantern Festival in the Han Dynasty. According to ancient Chinese history, after the death of Liu Ying (劉盈 , Han Emperor Hui), the Queen Lü (呂后) monopolized the power of the state, and placed Lü's family persons in key governmental positions. However, after her death, Zhou Bo (周勃), Chen Ping (陳平) and others then jointly got rid of Queen Lü's powers and made Liu Heng (劉恆) the new emperor of the Han Dynasty. Because Zhou Bo and Chen Ping drove the Lü's relatives and officials out of power on the fifteenth day of the first month, the emperor would leave his palace in civilian dress that night every year to celebrate the festival with the people on the streets. In ancient times, the word ye (夜 , night) and xiao (宵 , evening) were synonyms, and the first month of a year was called the yuan (元 , primary) month. Therefore, Emperor Wen (漢文帝) named the fifteenth day of the first month the Lantern Festival.

> **Notes**
> the Warring States Periods 戰國；monopolize 壟斷；get rid of 擺脫；
> civilian 平民；synonym 同義字

什麼是清明節？
What is the Qingming Festival?

The Qingming Festival (清明節) has been one of the most popular festivals in China for thousands of years. On the day, people go and pay respects to ancestors at their tombs. The festival takes place in early spring, when all life begins to renew. It is also a good time for outings.

The festival originates in the Spring and Autumn Period. At that time, Duke Wen of the State of Jin (晉文公) was forced to live in exile for 19 years, but later he became king of the state with the help of Duke Mu of the State of Qin (秦穆公). Duke Wen rewarded those who followed him in his exile according to their merits. One of these, Jie Zitui (介子推), decided not to accept wealth and a high position. He preferred to live a secluded life with his mother on Mountain Mianshan (綿山). The duke personally went to look for Jie Zitui there, but even after several days, he couldn't find him. He knew that Jie Zitui loved his mother deeply and would come out with his mother if he set the mountain on fire. This he did, and for three days and nights, the fire kept burning, until it finally reduced the whole area to ashes. Unfortunately, however, Jie and his mother were found burnt to death. It turned out that he would rather die than accept a reward. The duke was very sad. He had Jie and his mother buried on the mountain, and he gave an order that every year on the anniversary of Jie's death, all the citizens of his state should put out their kitchen fire and eat cold food prepared beforehand. Later, this became a day on which people customarily swept and cleaned the tombs of their ancestors and mourned the dead. This custom continues until to-day.

Notes

forbear 忍耐；renew 使更新；outings 遠足；exile 流放

端午節的起源是什麼？
What is the origin of the Dragon Boat Festival?

The Dragon Boat Festival or Duanwu Festival(端午節) commemorates Qu Yuan (屈原), a patriotic poet from the State of Chu during the Warring States

Period. There Qu Yuan proposed a series of progressive reforms, including domestic political reforms and a legal system set-up, but forces of corruption, represented by Jin Shang (靳尚) who opposed Qu Yuan, led the king not to trust him. Qu Yuan had to leave the capital and began a wandering life. With patriotic fervor, Qu Yuan produced many odes to display his concern for the fate of his state and people. In 278 B. C., when the Qin troops stormed the capital, and the downfall of Chu was expected at any moment, he took a rock in his arms and drowned himself in the Miluo River (汨羅江) near the present-day Changsha. He chose not to live and see that his state to be vanquished by the enemy. When the news of his death came, the local people rushed to the scene and rowed boats along the river in an attempt to find his remains, but they were never recovered. The people of Chu mourned his death, and every year afterwards they threw bamboo tubes filled with rice into the river as a sacrifice to him. This is supposed to be the origin of the custom of rowing dragon boats and eating zong-zi (粽子) on the Dragon Boat Festival.

> **Notes**
> commemorate 紀念；progressive 進步的；co-rruption 墮落；
> wandering 徘徊的；patriotic 愛國的；fervor 熱情；vanquish 征服

粽子的起源是什麼？
What is the origin of zong-zi?

Zong-zi (粽子) is glutinous rice wrapped in reed leaves. One story tells about why rice is wrapped this way. During the Eastern Han Dynasty, there lived in Changsha a man named Ou Hui (歐回), who one day chanced to meet a man who called himself the Minister in Charge of the Affairs of Three Aristocratic Families (閭大夫). This man told Ou Hui, "It is very good of you to offer me gifts of rice, but most of them are stolen and devoured by the river dragon. In the future, please wrap them up in chinaberry leaves and tie them up with color threads. The leaves and threads will scare away the dragon, and he will never touch them again." People did as they were told, and this is why zong-zi is made the way as it is.

Notes
reed 蘆葦；chinaberry 楝樹

什麼是中秋節？
What is the Mid-Autumn Festival?

Every year on the 15th day of the eighth lunar month is held the Mid-Autumn Festival (中秋節). According to the ancient calendar, the eighth lunar month is in the middle of autumn, and the 15th day of the month is in the middle of the month. On that night, the moon is supposed to be brighter and fuller than in any other month and the moonlight is the most beautiful. In China, a full moon is symbolic of family reunion, so the day is also known as "The Day of Reunion."

Notes
moonlight 月光；reunion 團聚

月餅是什麼時候出現的？
What is the origin of moon cakes?

During the Mid-Autumn Festival, people eat moon cakes (月餅) that are also called "reunion cake" because they are round in shape. People began making moon cakes in the Tang Dynasty, but they became popular in the Song Dynasty, when they were available everywhere as an offering to the moon. Some people ate them after a sacrificial ceremony while others kept them until the New Year Eve. In the Ming Dynasty, it was a custom for people to exchange moon cakes as a way to express the happiness of a family reunion. In the Qing Dynasty, moon cakes came to be stuffed with walnut paste, similar to these we have now.

> **Notes**
> sacrificial 獻祭的；walnut 胡桃

重陽節有什麼習俗？
What are the customs for the Double Ninth Festival?

The ninth day of the ninth lunar month is the Double Ninth Festival (重陽節). It occurs in the middle of autumn and peasants use the day to celebrate the harvest with varied activities:

➤ Viewing chrysanthemums on the day is a delight. Chrysanthemums are flowers that smell sweet and blossom in spite of cold, frosty weather. At flower shows, thousands of chrysanthemums are on display. People appreciate them, poets write odes about them and artists paint them.

➤ Drinking chrysanthemum wine is another custom. It is said that the wine is good for one's eyes and helps bring blood pressure down.

➤ People also climb mountains or go boating.

Notes

chrysanthemum 菊花；ode 頌歌

什麼是七夕節？
What is the Qixi Festival (the Double Seventh Night Festival)?

The seventh lunar month in China falls in hot summer. In the evening of that day, people would look up at the starry sky and tell fairy tales. One of these tales says that at this very night every year, a Cowherd and a Weaving Maid will walk across a bridge spanned by magpies over the Heavenly River (the Milky River). It is said that the Weaving Maid is the seventh daughter of the Queen Mother. She works at her shuttle in Heaven, while the Cowherd herds cows in the human world. Once the Weaving Maid came down from Heaven and by chance met the Cowherd. They two fell in love, got married and settled down in the country-side. When the Queen Mother found this out, she brought her daughter back to Heaven, separating the pair with expanse of the Milky River. However, the true love between the Cowherd and Weaving Maid moved a kind-hearted phoenix who called on all the magpies in the universe to form a bridge across the river for the couple to cross and reunite on the evening of the seventh day of the seventh month. This story represents the wishes of people for a happier life.

Notes

starry 布滿星星的；cowherd 牧牛者；magpie 喜鵲；shuttle 梭子

和老外聊中國：

外國人不懂的中華文化，用他們能懂的英語來解釋！

編　　著：楊天慶

發 行 人：黃振庭

出 版 者：崧燁文化事業有限公司

發 行 者：崧燁文化事業有限公司

E-mail：sonbookservice@gmail.com

粉 絲 頁：https://www.facebook.com/
　　　　　sonbookss/

網　　址：https://sonbook.net/

地　　址：台北市中正區重慶南路一段六十一號八
　　　　　樓 815 室

Rm. 815, 8F., No.61, Sec. 1, Chongqing S. Rd.,
Zhongzheng Dist., Taipei City 100, Taiwan

電　　話：(02)2370-3310

傳　　真：(02)2388-1990

印　　刷：京峯彩色印刷有限公司（京峰數位）

律師顧問：廣華律師事務所 張珮琦律師

定　　價：450 元

發行日期：2023 年 03 月第一版

◎本書以 POD 印製

國家圖書館出版品預行編目資料

和老外聊中國：外國人不懂的中華
文化，用他們能懂的英語來解釋！
/ 楊天慶編著 . -- 第一版 . -- 臺北市
：崧燁文化事業有限公司 , 2023.03
面；　公分
POD 版
ISBN 978-626-357-127-3(平裝)
1.CST: 英語 2.CST: 讀本 3.CST: 中
國文化
805.18　112000315

電子書購買

臉書